ARABIC
FOR
BEGINNERS

ARABIC
FOR
BEGINNERS

a novel

ARIELA FREEDMAN

Cover design by Debbie Geltner
Book design by WildElement.ca
Author photograph by Jeremy Wexler

Library and Archives Canada Cataloguing in Publication

Freedman, Ariela, 1974-, author
    Arabic for beginners / Ariela Freedman.

Issued in print and electronic formats.
ISBN 978-1-988130-33-0 (paperback).—ISBN 978-1-988130-34-7 (EPUB).—
ISBN 978-1-988130-35-4 (MOBI).—ISBN 978-1-988130-36-1 (PDF)
    I. Title.
PS8611.R4227A73 2017   C813'.6   C2016-907028-X
                                 C2016-907029-8

Printed and bound in Canada.

The publisher gratefully acknowledges the support of the Government of Canada through the Canada Council for the Arts and the Canada Book Fund, and of the Government of Quebec through the Société de développement des entreprises culturelles.

Linda Leith Publishing
Montreal
www.lindaleith.com

For Lev and Ben

PART 1

1.

She said her name was Jenna. A few weeks later she told me that wasn't really her name. Jannah, Jannah was her name. Jannah, meaning "paradise." Jenna was easier, she said, more familiar to English speakers, simpler to say. Jenna required no explanation. In America she was Jen or Jenna or Jenny, in Shuafat she was Jannah or sometimes Yanna. I could call her either one, Jenna, Jannah, it didn't make a difference. I tried shifting the first vowel back in my throat, but I felt awkward, so she was always Jenna to me.

She stood in the middle of the crowded room, unmoved by the crying children, the floor littered with toys, the random unfiltered chaos of the first day at daycare. She held a baby on her hip, and a little girl who had inherited the same uncanny pale green eyes clung to her knees. The baby kept slipping a hand into the scooped neck of her dress, and she kept impersonally fishing it out. She wore taupe heels and a cream dress patterned with roses, as if she'd dressed for a garden party. I had pushed a stroller all the way up the hill of Hebron Street and was shining with sweat, conscious of my bare arms, my flat sandals, the hippie swing of my red skirt. Jenna looked cool and serene. As she raised her hand to straighten her hair, diamonds glittered on her fingers and in her earlobes. She was pretty, of course, but pretty isn't word enough for what she was. When I think of her now, I see her standing there, stillness at the centre of the room, everything around her in motion.

I had signed Sam up for "The Peace Preschool" in Jerusalem from the depths of a snowy winter in Montreal, corresponding with a director who signed all her emails, "Salaam, Peace and Shalom." *At the Peace Preschool,* the website said, *we all laugh in the same language!*

On the first day, I was late. The room was full, and nobody said hello. Some of the parents sat at the small children's tables, and all of the spaces were taken. There was nowhere else to sit. They had segregated themselves by language. I heard Hebrew to the left, and the breathier, sibilant sound of Arabic in the right-hand corner of the room.

A teacher navigated the maze of children with a clipboard, registering names. The children wandered the room looking shell-shocked. One or two were crying in anticipation of their abandonment. The parents were gladly oblivious, catching up with one another at the tiny picnic tables, their adult knees slantwise because they wouldn't fit underneath. They looked relieved to have the long summer over. The teachers seemed distracted, tracking new arrivals, gathering registration information, stamping out the small disputes over favoured toys and tumbled block towers, finding the criers in the general cacophony.

Bins of plastic toys were arranged around the room, organized by type and by size. "Animals!" "Blocks!" "Balls!" The toys were spread out on low white shelves so the children could reach them by themselves. On the wall were colourful alphabet charts in Arabic and Hebrew. Tall Ottoman windows had been left ajar, and gauzy white curtains filtered the light and breathed in and out with the wind. It was a pleasant room, only there were too many of us.

My son picked up a plastic tyrannosaurus from a bin of dinosaurs, and stood still, looking lost. The teacher was suddenly in front of me, thrusting the clipboard at my chest in a gesture that felt aggressive though it was really just Israeli, with that entirely different topography of personal space, and I was empty-handed and unprepared.

And then the woman in the lovely dress saved me. "I'm Jenna," she said. "You can borrow my pen."

"Thank you," I said.

I smiled at her. I felt suddenly, excessively grateful. Jenna's voice was husky, a smoker's voice, and her accent was a strange mix of Brooklyn and something else, some elusive other flavour. That was one of the first things I noticed about her.

"Where are you from?" I said.

As soon as I had asked her, I wanted to take it back. My cheeks flushed, and I looked towards the children. But Jenna didn't seem to mind.

"I'm from here. From here, but I grew up in Louisiana."

"Louisiana? I would have guessed New York."

"Well, my mother's from Brooklyn. I sound like her, I guess."

I wrote my name down on the clipboard. I didn't have a cellphone, didn't know my passport number. The teacher tssked loudly with her tongue, and said in Hebrew, strict as a border guard, "Where's the rest of your information?" I half expected her to turn me away.

"I'll have it for you next time," I said.

She looked at me with heavy eyelids, her expression exasperated and resigned. I would get used to that gaze of weariness from Israelis, the one that said, "We are disappointed in you, collectively and as individuals, though we expected no better." I could see clumps of mascara clotting her lashes and holding them together. Her eyes were lined in the kind of glittery pale blue pencil I used when I was fifteen and just starting to experiment with makeup, the kind that had once caused my father to remark, when I came downstairs from my long sojourn in front of the bathroom mirror, that I looked as if I had asphyxiated myself.

"Don't forget," she warned. She moved heavily over to the next parent. I turned back to Jenna.

"I'm Hannah," I said. "This is Sam. He's three."

"That's Zac, he's nearly four," Jenna said, and Zac scowled at her.

Zac had a long brown face, huge solemn eyes, and no front teeth.

"Come on, Zac," she said, looking down at the somber

little boy and pointing a delicate shoe at the plastic bin of dinosaurs. "Play! You love dinosaurs."

Zac looked up at us soulfully, then reached over and grabbed the tyrannosaurus from Sam's hands. Sam's face began to crumple. Quickly Jenna leaned down, snatched the tyrannosaurus, and handed it back to Sam. Her boy started wailing, and Jenna reached into her purse, pulled out a pacifier, and inserted it into his mouth. He quieted down but kept looking at my son.

"My son," Jenna said, "he can't wait for anything. And this is my daughter, Aisha." She gestured down at the girl, her tiny double, in a frilly plaid dress, who had finally let go of Jenna's knees to dump a box of Lego onto the ground.

"And this is Noor. She looks like a boy, but she's a girl. It's because she's got no hair. I got her ears pierced, but people still think she's a boy."

Noor grinned at me toothlessly, snuck her hand back down her mother's dress. Her fat brown earlobes were dotted with gold studs. She had round eyes and dimpled plump cheeks. Her hair was short and curled tight to her skull, held back with an unnecessary pink hairband.

Sam put the tyrannosaurus down on the ground, just for an instant, and Zac swooped it up, sucking hard on his pacifier, looking at Sam all the while. Sam started to scream, and suddenly we both were on our knees, negotiating, holding back arms and legs, talking to our children and over each other. "It's all right, he put it down," "Had it first," "Sam, you can share the dinosaur. Share the dinosaur! You had a turn already and at home we have

...'" "He had it first. He had it first. Give it back. Give. It. Back."

Jenna took Zac's wrist, yanked him to standing. I picked Sam up onto my hip. They stared at each other in mutual distrust. I smiled at Jenna.

She had dark hair that curled down to her shoulders. She looked like a girl playing dress-up—even her heels seemed a little big for her, as if she'd borrowed them. Jenna had three children already. I tried to count backwards from Zac, who was a little older than Sam. Was she twenty-three? Twenty-four?

Noor started crying, and the sound of her crying triggered the other children so that the room filled with the dissonance of wails and screams. Jenna took charge, introducing me to the teachers, Sarah and Jameelah, and to some of the children. Sarah's hair was intensely maroon, and Jameelah's head was covered tightly with a black headscarf. They smiled sweetly at Sam. Sarah asked me how many children I had.

"Two," I said, and she said, "Only two? That's not even a family!"

I heard more English than I had expected. I collected introductions, promptly forgot names. There was an American boy with a blonde crew cut. Near him, a dark, scrawny monkey of a child with big eyes and a flat head. Only one girl, with long straight black hair down her back, who immediately became the centre of attention. And the mothers, who now clustered together in the hall near the doorway. They all seemed to know one another;

their children had been sharing a classroom since they were two years old.

Jenna introduced me to the other mothers, announced that she was dying for a cigarette, opened the emergency door off the hallway, and leaned out to smoke, Noor still on her hip. Noor followed the cigarette with her eyes, on its way in and out of Jenna's mouth. Zac came out into the hallway, and Jameelah fetched him back into the room; he did this again and again, and Jenna, exasperated, drew a baby bottle of what looked like apple juice out of her purse and handed it to him. Sucking it down, he retreated back into the classroom. The crying and bright hubbub had subsided. I peeked inside and saw Sam quietly playing in a corner. His mouth moved as he talked to himself, playing the parts of both the figurines clutched in his fists. He lifted his arm and crashed one figure into the other; as he separated them he rebuked himself sternly. I leaned back out before he spotted me. He was fine, just fine.

On this first day, the children only stayed long enough to meet their teachers. The preschool occupied a small section of the grand, neo-Byzantine building; a larger portion housed a hotel, and I took Sam for a celebratory ice cream on the terrace. There was a round stone fountain, green with moss. Birds kept landing on the tables, and the staff kept shooing them away. It was almost too hot to be outside, and most of the guests—pink-faced tourists and diplomats—stayed inside behind the glass doors. Sam got upset when his ice cream melted into pink and white puddles in the bowl before he could finish it.

He fell asleep in the stroller as I pushed him home, his mouth smeared with ice cream, his head lolling against his shoulder, rolling with every bump in the sidewalk.

I thought about Jenna all the way home. I shouldn't have asked her where she came from. The way she said "from *here*," as if staking a claim, made it clear that she was Palestinian, and it struck me, with a sense of shock, that in all the time I'd spent in Israel I'd never really had a conversation with a Palestinian woman before. As soon as I had that thought I put it away, as if my mind had opened a drawer and slammed it shut.

When I got to our apartment, I realized I had never returned her pen. On the walk home it had exploded in the heat, and the ink now formed a dark stain on the seam of my bag.

2.

My parents moved to Israel when I was a year old. They were in their early twenties. In the photos my mother is beautiful and my father is thin. They belonged to a youth group whose motto was *"am Yisrael b'eretz Yisrael al pi torat Yisrael"*— "the nation of Israel in the land of Israel living by the laws of Israel." Back then, the group still clung to its socialist roots, and groups of young men and women made *aliya*, moving "up" together to *kibbutzim*, in order to embody the ideals of *torah v'avodah*, "bible and labour." They called them the *olim*: "those who rise." My father had just finished his dissertation, and took his new PhD, his new wife, and his new child on the plane. The flight was free: the Jewish Agency paid the tickets for the *olim*, the new immigrants. Needless to say, they were one-way.

My parents were worried about me crying on the flight so they decided to drug me so I would sleep. The doctor gave them something to put in my bottle, and by the time we boarded the plane I was unconscious. But the plane was delayed for hours. I slept and slept as my nervous parents shifted in their seats. It wasn't until the plane rose into the air that the noise of the engine woke me up and I started to wail.

I'm not sure why my father, an asthmatic, allergic Brooklyn Jew with a doctorate in philosophy and a love of science fiction and Heinz ketchup, believed that he could meet his destiny in a small communal agricultural settlement, a *kibbutz* in the middle of the desert. I think he had vague ideas of working on the *kibbutz* and teaching at a nearby university, like Marx's dream of the peasant who fishes in the morning and reads philosophy in the afternoon. My father ended up sorting carrots. He was allergic to everything, as if the land itself was trying to expel him, or he was trying to expel it with his streaming eyes and his explosive sneezes. My mother was made of tougher stuff, but his misery was her own.

The Israelis who founded the *kibbutz* were distrustful of these latecomers, with their soft hands and elementary grammatical errors. The *kibbutz* was moderate in its collectivism. For example, the children were allowed to sleep at home rather than in the *bayt yeladim*, the "children's house" where they spent their days as their parents worked in the fields. But even the group dining and the constant social contact were too much for my father, who was like Freud in loving only the people who deserved it. My father liked to tell me that anti-Semitism meant hating Jews for the *wrong* reasons.

During the day I played in the children's house while my mother worked nearby. The structures were all small and minimalist; the public buildings were rectangles and the family houses were squares, so that a child with a crayon and a ruler could have drawn the entire settlement. All day long, the sand sifted in through the doorways. No matter how many times you swept the floor, the sediment settled once again under your feet. I don't remember much, but I remember the grit under my bare toes. The desert was trying to bury the houses. Day by day the *kibbutzniks* carved out their space again, pushing back the wild with a broom. To wash the floor, you emptied a bucket of warm, soapy water and then mopped towards a sunken hole in the corner of the room. The vistas were barren and flat, and the sky was as blue and unblinking as God's own eye. When the wind blew, all the windows shook. Irrigated patches of green shocked the arid land—these were the fields where carrots and potatoes were grown. My dreamy, near-sighted father learned to drive a tractor, to navigate the fields in rows.

All the children my age were boys, so I tried to pee standing up, in the open row of toilets in the children's bathroom. Hebrew was my first language; I dreamed in Hebrew, woke up crying in the night, yelling "*Chava hirbitza li! Chava hirbitza li!*" "Chava hit me, Chava hit me!" I toddled down roads that led only to more desert, my shadow shrunk to nothing in the midday sun.

My mother was soon pregnant again. Work the land, settle the land, populate the land. My sister, our family's only *sabra*, was born in Israel. When my mother's water broke, she frantically mopped it up before leaving for the hospital, worried about the Israelis and their judgment of her housekeeping. My sister's skin is darker than that of the rest of us, as if the Mediterranean sun is imprinted on her more deeply. All her life, her Israeli citizenship has been a mild inconvenience, requiring extra paper-work, occasional interrogation at the airport, and even the threat, when she was eighteen, that she just might be drafted on her way into or out of the country.

I can't really imagine the conversations, the debates, the tears, the fights, that led my parents to pack up the few things that belonged to them and carry me and my sister out of the *kibbutz*, onto a plane, and back to a tenement building in Brooklyn. I think of them as figures resem-bling those pictures of Adam and Eve leaving the garden: bent, sorrowful, looking backwards. They had imagined no other future for themselves, and now they had to start again, poorer and a little bit older and infinitely more de-feated. It isn't really the kind of thing you recover from, although, all told, they built a good life back in the land of their fathers. By which I mean, of course, America. My father taught ethics to the NYPD—it sounds like the beginning of a joke—and sent out applications for jobs all over the continent.

It didn't occur to me that I could type the name of the *kibbutz* into the Internet and the vanished place would just materialize in front of me. I thought of it as the lost terri-tory of my early childhood. Even when I visited Israel, I never bothered to look for it. It seemed as futile as look-ing for Shangri-la or Never-Never Land—it existed only in my imagination. It doesn't look anything like my old photographs, or like the memories that piggybacked on the pictures. It is still an agricultural *kibbutz* run according to the principles of collectivism, one of the very few that remain. There is a new dining hall with a large glass door, the roof furled like a sail. They also have a guesthouse to supplement the income earned from the cows, the chickens, and the fields. All of the *kibbutzim* have turned to tourism, so that the old socialist boat can float a little longer on the sea of shekels brought in by visitors. The tourists sleep in air-conditioned guesthouses and eat in the communal dining hall, but they have their meals supplemented with additional treats—soda, cake—that are only for paying guests. The photographs show gardens and lawns, though I remember the place as mostly desert. The old *kibbutzniks* would have never countenanced the waste of water for a flat, non-utilitarian stretch of grass, or for the flagrant turquoise oasis of a pool.

The guesthouse has been suffering because it borders on Gaza. The sound of the mortars is disruptive to weekend getaways; the rockets mar the peacefulness of the rural setting. In those old photographs, when I am walking away towards the vanishing point of the desert—what seems to be nothing but open, empty space—I am, in fact, walking towards a border. There were lines all around us, but they were invisible; the perimeter of the *kibbutz* was always, always patrolled. I just never saw it.

3.

Before we planned our year in Israel, I had imagined a frictionless journey—visas flying into our hands, tickets purchased and paid for, a new life waiting for us, fresh and gleaming as a newborn child. Of course, the move was nothing like that. Neither is birth, come to think of it. There were decisions to be made, schools to be found, a renter for our house, a system for our bills, a process so odious and troublesome that it's a wonder anyone ever goes anywhere. Though once we got there, we could have stayed forever and ever and ever, as the fairytales say. Sometimes I thought we would.

One reason I agreed to spend the year in Israel was because the winter in Montreal, the one before we left, had been so cold. We had moved because Simon got a job at McGill, and I missed our old life in New York, the structure of graduate school, the proximity of friends and colleagues. I spent an unconscionable amount of time fantasizing about warm places while I was supposed to be working on my dissertation, which I had started right around the time Gabriel was born. As it had done for years, the goddamn dissertation felt farther away from completion, as if I were making the opposite of progress. Sometimes, after dropping the children off in the morning, cleaning up the detritus of our hurried breakfast, and making a desultory pass over the general slovenliness of our apartment, I felt so tired that I went back to bed, and then, before I knew it, it was time to pick the children up again. Each day was colder than the next, and it seemed as though winter might never end.

Simon often worked late at the university, and I was frequently home alone with the children. Home alone—what an odd way to say it when the truth is I was never alone. Aloneness was the thing that I missed and craved. I loved the boys, but small things constantly undid me. For instance, getting the boys outside was especially difficult that year because Sam had decided that he hated coats and winter boots and would stand at the door in his T-shirt and sneakers, waiting to be let out like an eager and foolish puppy, though it was freezing outside, and I had explained to him a hundred times that in winter he needed to wear a coat.

So when Simon said he was thinking of applying for a visiting position at Hebrew University, I said, "Oh yes, let's go," without thinking about anything except escaping winter, which smelled like wet boots and felt like hunched shoulders and sounded like my children whining forever about their winter clothes and about one another.

The morning I booked our tickets, Simon was supposed to drive the children to school. He went outside to unbury the car, and when he came back inside he realized he didn't have his keys.

"Did you put my keys in some crazy place for some strange reason?" he said, his voice sharp with accusation, and I said, "I absolutely did not."

The children were already dressed for the outdoors, sweltering and sausaged in their snowpants and coats and scarves. It was that point in the morning when every moment is precious and perilous, like the scene in a film when the timer is set and the bomb is about to explode, except that we didn't know how long we had. Sooner or later one or both of the children would start crying or undressing, and then the whole day would fall apart.

"What did you do with your keys last night?' I said, my voice too bright, and Simon, "Well, look, if I knew that I'd have my keys, right?"

I looked at the children, red-faced and overheating by the door, and ran upstairs. I looked on the dresser and under the bed, on the desk and in the pocket of his pants, and could not find them. I ran downstairs, out of breath, and I said, "You better just take the metro, I can't find them, I'll take the kids, are you sure you can't remember what you did with them?"

Simon said, "I have no idea, maybe I threw them in the fucking snow." He gave me a furious glance. As he slammed the door Sam threw his hat on the floor and Gabriel started crying.

It was a stupid and senseless fight, but as I drove the children to school and the daycare—every light red, every driver impatient, the children subdued and silent in the back seat because we had both been yelling—I was furious. When I came home I looked again. I still could not find the keys, and as I looked, in my mind they grew bigger and bigger until they were the size of the whole house, the size of our entire marriage. I spent an hour looking for Simon's keys before giving up and going outside to buy groceries. The fridge was as bare as the house was cluttered. On my way out the door a glint of black and silver caught my eyes, half buried in the snow.

By the time Simon came home I had calmed down. When he walked in the door I said, "You will not believe where I found your keys."

"Huh," he said. "They must have fallen out of my pocket."

He had a high, clever forehead, and his hairline had recently begun to recede, which made him seem more vulnerable. Behind his glasses, I couldn't read his eyes.

"You're welcome," I said, and waited for more, but he walked upstairs to his office and shut the door, which meant he was either working or playing computer games somewhere the children and I could not reach him.

We were in the middle of our thirties, and it was shipwreck weather for marriages. Some of our friends had recently announced that they were separating, others were expecting new babies, and the women we knew with neither husbands nor babies were starting to panic. I had coffee with my friend Andrea that week, and she said, "You just need to have another baby, that's all." She was pregnant with her third, and she was radiating the smug bravado of the second trimester. "Another baby, or an affair," she amended. "It's your choice."

"I don't think I can have another baby," I said. "I think it would kill me," and then I felt immediately guilty as Andrea's hands went to her stomach and her eyes went wide. I'd never told her about the pit I'd fallen into when the children were born, the nights I went to bed crying and woke up with my face still wet. She didn't need to know, especially not now. I pressed my lips together.

The night before he lost his keys, Simon had reached for me in bed, but instead of touching my hip or breast he put his hand on my stomach.

"Do you ever miss it?" he said.

"What?" I said. My body had tensed up.

"Having a baby in there," he said. "Do you remember when I used to lie next to your stomach and I could see the baby moving, like a wave?"

"I remember," I said. My throat was tight.

"I used to touch you there," he said, pressing his thumb into my back, "and he would kick. Was it Sam or Gabe? I didn't think I'd ever forget, but it's all blurry now."

I curled away from him, and closed my eyes. But I didn't fall asleep for a long time, and I could feel him awake beside me. His breath was restless and strained. Since then something strange had happened. I didn't know how to describe it except to say that we suddenly seemed to find it impossible to make eye contact. When I looked at him it was as if his eyes slid right around my face to the wall beyond me. Thirty-four years old and in the middle of my fucking life.

4.

In Israel, school and work began on Sundays, which made the week feel interminable. Simon was busy trying to establish himself in the Political Science department at the University. He left early and came back late at night. In September, it was still dreadfully hot. I felt the weight of my body, my slow thighs, the pitiless heaviness of the day. By the time I dropped Gabriel and Sam off in the morning, I was drenched and wrung out.

We were accustoming ourselves to this landscape that was not ours—bougainvillea, morning glory, dark and hairy eucalyptus, something that smelled like jasmine but was not jasmine. I was still not used to rounding a corner and seeing the walls of the Old City, the smoky hills in the distance, or the stark bowl of the valley.

But a pattern began to develop: Simon and I soon knew the names of our children's teachers, the phone number of a doctor, the closest place to buy milk, the best place to buy vegetables. We knew the neighbour-hood, the corner cages where they collected bottles for recycling, the overpriced little stores where we bought ice cream, the best bakery for croissants and the best bakery for cake and the best bakery for bread. We had a library card. However, in the heat of the day it was still a dream life, a haze we walked through until the cool of evening brought some clarity.

We did not know exactly what we were doing. That was becoming clear. We told each other it would take time. We would settle the children in, and then surely we would feel settled ourselves.

The year before, Sam had been in daycare with a little boy named Cayden. Cayden was the youngest child in the group; he didn't talk and didn't walk and didn't really play, but spent the day cycling between the laps of the daycare workers. He was a moppet of a child, with a pale and pointed face smaller than his wild mess of curly hair. On the way home one day, Sam had said, in a genuinely puzzled voice, "What is Cayden *for*?"

That's what we were like; we weren't certain what we were *for*. It wasn't that we had ever been *for* work or habit or routine, all of the things that structured our lives back home, but somehow those things muted the question, or we didn't have time to ask it. Now, our new freedom had an aimless hollow drift.

During our first week in Jerusalem, Gabriel learned to read to himself. He had known the letters for a long time, and already knew how to read out loud. He'd even read entire books, although he grappled with each word carefully, as if the word was a lifejacket and he was drowning. Suddenly he could swim. He woke in the morning before we were up, lay out on the black leather couch in his cotton pajama bottoms and his naked, skinny torso. And then, like it was a trick he had performed a thousand times, he vanished into his book.

The adventure was inside Gabe now; when we spoke to him while he was reading, it was as if the book were the real world and we were faint and spectral. We had to call his name several times before we could get his attention.

Sam watched him read silently and said, "Look at me! I can count inside my head! Watch!" And then he screwed his face into an expression of hilarious ferocity.

"How will I do well if I don't understand anything?" Gabriel asked me on his first day of school.

"You're already doing well," I said. "You'll always do well if you try your best." But my heart was in my throat. I knew that he was right to be concerned, and the truth was, I was just as frightened.

Gabe went to a public school down the road. In his first week, the Prime Minister came to speak to the children. The roads around the school were blocked off, and the corners were congested with men in dark grey uniforms carrying Uzis and exuding aggression. Parents were not allowed in the school that day, and it was strange to see my son's small back walk straight through that gauntlet. That afternoon, when I picked him up, he told me that the Prime Minister seemed nice. Nice, and very old.

The next day, the soldiers were gone, and the only guards were the children who did crosswalk duty each day with curious poles that seemed like sabers, which they swept down to block traffic so that their classmates could cross the street. They used their poles and they used their hands, fingers and thumbs pinched together in the ubiquitous gesture that turned your hand into a claw, which at once signified patience—yours—and impatience—theirs. The tsking sound they made with their tongues against the roofs of their mouths was one of the first truly Israeli expressions my children mastered. This raising and lowering of poles, the tsking and tocking of tongues, was a choreographed ballet against the morning stream of traffic, with cars and children's bodies struggling for priority.

Gabriel sat in a cramped classroom from nine to three and understood nothing. His schoolbag was half his size, and it broke my heart when he walked into the school in the morning, turtled under its weight. Sometimes at night he was too homesick to sleep, and I lay beside him, cradling his thin brown hand, trying to be enough of a home. It was exciting and painful to watch my boys approach other children with their stilted Hebrew; they were so brave.

At home we read Harry Potter every night. Sam had me draw a lightning bolt on his forehead in eyeliner, and spent hours in his Batman cape and underpants, dueling with a stick he had picked up in the courtyard. Gabriel was reading about Greek mythology, and one morning at the kitchen table he looked up at me, and spoke tentatively.

"I think," he said, "I've just thought of something that no other Jewish boy has ever thought about."

"What is it?" I asked, and he looked abashed.

"I don't think I should tell you," he said. "I think I should try to forget it."

"You can tell me," I said. "It's alright."

"Well, do you know the stories about Zeus and about Athena," he said, "how they are all mythology?"

"Yes," I said.

He had been reading a lot of D'Aulaire, and we'd been talking about Hera and Zeus, Hades and Persephone.

"Well, what if the Jewish stories are like that? What if that's also just mythology?"

"What if it is?" I said. "Would that matter? What would that change?"

He looked at his hands, then looked back at me.

"But there are the miracles," he said. "The miracles prove it must have really happened."

Reassured, he went back to his breakfast cereal.

Sam was still transparent; he was what he was throughout his whole body, joyful or angry or sad, and sometimes it seemed like we were still the same person. But Gabriel was changing fast, though the change was all inside him. He was becoming more complicated and more internal and more himself, and the person he would be was still a stranger. He started to write stories and they had the structure of the stories he read in books: suspense and then conflict and then resolution. "Rocket knew that something was wrong," one of them began. But then he would get frustrated that the words did not emerge on the page as smooth and as polished as they were in his head, and our house was full of the crumpled beginnings of his

24

imaginings.

I knew how that felt. I kept beginning chapters of my dissertation and then abandoning them. When people asked me what I was writing about, my mouth filled with cotton. I tried out different answers, practicing them in front of the mirror. "I'm writing about trauma in contemporary Canadian literature," I'd say, trying to project confidence. But the one time I tried my blurb on an Israeli, she looked strangely at me and said, "What trauma?" My shoulders began to hurt a lot, as if someone had put their heavy hand on the yoke of my neck.

The electrical towers on the street had bright yellow signs that showed a cartoon figure falling, electrocuted, off the pole. They said "Danger of Death!" in English, Hebrew, and Arabic. Everything felt dangerous.

We lived a few blocks away from the promenade that overlooked the Old City. A wide stone road and wall bordered the view, and as one descended into the valley, the paths grew narrower and were lined with olive trees, rosemary bushes, and broad stretches of grass. Sometimes the promenade was crowded with tourists, all taking the very same photograph: themselves, smiling and juxtaposed against the landscape, so that you could have just photoshopped them in. We saw an ultra-orthodox family on a bicycle built for twelve, knees whirling, *peyos* flapping in unison.

After dark the promenade was oddly deserted. I took Sam for a walk there one evening, but at night it felt almost haunted. The grass glowed green under the lights, and above the lights the sky was black. There was nobody else on the path. I put my back into pushing the stroller up the hill and towards the road and then I could hear it, the fast trot behind me, coming closer. I half-turned as three horses rode past me, near enough for me to feel their warm breath. A boy twisted around on one of the horses and rode up to me, pulling up right before the stroller and shouting something I didn't understand. My son was asleep; I stood there, rigid and unmoving. I couldn't see the boy's face. He rode away to catch up with his friends, and I took care not to walk on the promenade in the dark anymore. Three horses, three riders; the experience had felt like a dream. A few weeks later, a couple was stabbed on a nearby path.

Still, the city was safer than it had been in years. Even taking the bus wasn't frightening anymore. It had been a couple of years since a bus blew up in the city. Everyone still had the memory of the attacks in their bodies: you could still feel eyes sliding around the bus, looking for abandoned packages, sudden movements, suspicious faces. If you forgot your backpack, you might still return to find a bomb squad blowing it up. That was normal, as customary as the sunset and the traffic jam.

Though a boy had driven his new BMW into a wall through crowd of soldiers near Jaffa Gate. Jenna knew the family.

"It's not a terrorist attack," she said. "He just got that car. Why wouldn't he use an old car if he wanted to destroy it? There is no way he would have driven that car into a wall—he loved it."

His family said that he'd been driven to despair after being turned down by the cousin that he wanted to marry. They were afraid, surely, of being punished for his actions. But the boy couldn't tell anyone the reason he'd driven into the wall. An off-duty officer with a quick pistol shot him dead within seconds of his driving into the square.

The President was being investigated for rape. The Prime Minister, for corruption. And new national elections were coming too. I read the paper in the mornings with a mixture of fascination and horror. "I can't believe you are still reading the newspapers," our friends said. It was a rookie mistake, they maintained; we would learn, as they all had.

5

I frequently returned to Israel in my youth. But I hadn't been back since my first year of university. Since then, I had travelled to India, Morocco, Turkey, all over Europe. At first, I hadn't thought of this as deliberate avoidance; it was just time to explore other places, that was all. Staying away from Israel, I had gone all over the world.

When I was fifteen, I spent the summer in Israel with a group of teenagers. We travelled for five weeks, each day or two moving to a different location, sleeping on the bus, crossing the country back and forth. Our counselors yelled themselves hoarse, partly from enthusiasm and partly because otherwise it was difficult to be heard, since we were so loud and undisciplined. We climbed up the snake path at Masada, prayed at the Western Wall, swam in the Sea of Galilee, canoed down the Jordan River. There were hundreds, maybe thousands of kids like us in the country that summer on organized tours, swarming like locusts, consuming all the pizza and falafel and ice cream and tacky souvenirs that the Holy Land had to offer. We travelled in groups all the time, slept four or six to a room, crammed around campfires and picnic tables, as if the very thought of solitude was threatening. We sang songs together in one voice; we all wore blue and white on *Shabbat* in imitation of the flag. We bought versions of the same Magen David necklaces to wear around our necks, as if it weren't already clear enough who we were.

That week we were over the Green Line in the West Bank though we called it Judea and Samarea, by the biblical names of the places and ancient cities. I was taken aback by the barbed wire fence that surrounded the settlement. At the checkpoint we drove through, the guard—barely older than we were—had a heavy gun strapped across his hip.

Of course, we had grown used to the sight of guns; we had our own "*noseh neshek*" on the bus with us, a young soldier whose assignment was our safety and who was referred to by the name of his weapon. The boys on the trip were fascinated with his gun, and kept asking to hold it, though he always said no. The bolder girls flirted with him, especially a girl from Baltimore who had bleached hair and heavily lined eyes like Madonna and who surprised us all one morning by convulsing on the floor of the bus, the permed fleece of her hair all over her face, her mascara smeared, so she looked like she had given herself two black eyes.

The *kibbutz* was in a beautiful spot, the Judean hills like the gentle humps of vast animals against the horizon. There was a wall of bougainvillea outside the dining hall, and people rode their bikes up and down the green paths as if they were in a hippie version of paradise. They put us in bunks that resembled our camp cabins back home, and we hurried to claim our beds, the hierarchy firmly established so that without speaking we all knew where we lay. Sunset was a performance that night, concentrated and flashy. Dinner in the dining hall—*challah*, chicken soup and chicken, salad and *kugels*—was a variation on a theme so familiar we knew all its chords, unlike the Israeli breakfasts that had staggered us all with their cold tomatoes and cucumbers, hard-boiled eggs, and disappointing lack of North American cereals.

Shabbat slowed us down. We usually arrived at our next destination on a Friday morning, to give us enough time to get ready for Friday night and Saturday. There were extensive preparations to be made, hair to be washed and blow-dried, make-up bags as heavy and glittering as sacks of treasure, photos to be taken before we lit the candles, our arms draped around each other's shoulders, our mouths set in rigid grins. There was never enough hot water for the showers, were never enough mirrors as we shouldered each other out of the way to make sure that we were beautiful.

For the girls with boyfriends, *Shabbat* was the time to hook up. They vanished after dinner, vanished Saturday afternoons, or sometimes, if they were long established, paired up with other couples as if practicing for future suburban barbecues.

The unpaired among us mostly slept. We slept so little, all week long, and were constantly on the move—the epileptic fit on the bus was triggered by lack of sleep and inconstant diet. I've never again experienced a sleep as heavy as the naps I took those *Shabbat* afternoons, which could last until five or six, when somebody woke us up for supper.

I was fascinated and repelled by the couples who seemed to be rehearsing for their adult lives. Most of them would be married young, within the next four or five years. As it turned out, so would I, though at the time I would have never believed it—I was convinced, in those days, that I would always be alone.

That *Shabbat* I took a walk instead of sleeping. A group of us was going for a walk outside of the settlement, accompanied by some of the teenagers from the *kibbutz*. And the local teens fascinated me; they seemed harder than we were, and more experienced. Two of the local boys took guns with them, and I was surprised, less at the guns than at the transgression of *Shabbat*: two *averahs,* "transgressions," *eruv* and *muktza*, "carrying outside of a specific domain" and "using something that should have no purpose on the Sabbath." "Preserving your life trumps both of those," they said, and the other boys, our boys, looked in envy at the handguns they had tucked into the backs of their pants.

From the *kibbutz* the surrounding hillsides had looked empty; white rocks jutting out of the curved earth like vertebrae, silvery green groves of olive trees, their trunks gnarled and full of character. But as we left the gated *kibbutz* and walked on a winding road down the hillside, it became apparent that other people lived here, too. They sat on their front steps in groups, drinking coffee, playing backgammon, and looking at us from under lowered eyelids. Most of them were old men. We had taken a dog with us from the *kibbutz*, a rowdy, friendly retriever. The dog barked loudly and seemed less friendly as we walked by these houses, wheeling up and down the paths. The men gathered their robes and looked scared and angry. One of the boys, whistling, took his gun out of his waistband and clicked the safety on and off a few times. In the quiet of the hills, the sounds echoed. The group was loud and high-spirited; I straggled behind. The boys walked in the middle of the street, and a car driving behind them was forced to slow to a crawl until it reached a turn in the road. I wanted to ask them why they were clicking the safety, why they were walking in the middle of the road and acting so generally obnoxious, but I didn't have the right words in Hebrew and anyway, they were now far ahead of me and I had to run, sweaty and panting, back to the gate of the *kibbutz*.

Everyone knows the code. You don't tell on your friends, and even if they aren't your friends, you are supposed to preserve the silent solidarity of your generation. Telling a grown-up is weak. Beyond weak, it's pathetic; it means you've forfeited your place among the adolescent community.

Of course I told on them right away, and as it always did, it got beyond me. I meant to just tell my counsellor about the incident, but he went straight to some of the senior members of the *kibbutz*, and they came to see me, their faces serious but also pitying.

"And you are telling us that our boys did it on purpose?"

"You understand that this is a serious accusation."

"You don't know what it's like living here. And besides, they never would have behaved that way—I know those boys, they are good boys."

"And why did you go with them?"

They reassured me that nothing like that had ever happened, that the misunderstanding was all mine, and besides, it wouldn't happen again. And then I had to face my peers.

"Hannah, why did you have to *tell*?" one girl said, speaking for them all, her voice thick with disapproval. For a few days, before something else happened to displace my shame—a boy smuggled liquor into his hotel room and broke a lamp—no one would talk to me, but I heard hard whispers everywhere I went.

I was mortified. I was indiscreet, had overreacted, had told the wrong person, shouldn't have told at all, was marked by my priggishness as surely as if my virginity was stamped onto my forehead. I cried myself to sleep like a baby, compounding my shame; I tried to imagine scenarios in which I hadn't told, in which I hadn't gone on the walk at all, had stayed prone and unconscious. I can close my eyes and see them still: the low bungalows, the small groups of men on the doorsteps, the late summer haze, and a group of teenagers walking down the middle of the street as if they owned the road, owned the village, owned the sun and owned the air and owned the men who stared at them with equal parts fear and resentment.

6.

I ended up spending a lot of time with a group of mothers from the daycare. We had a window of about four hours a day in which we could make our own choices, undetermined by the demands of three-year-olds. We went out for coffee after depositing the children in their classrooms. We went to the park at one o'clock when classes let out, and then had play dates at one another's houses, more for us than for our children, who played politely beside each other rather than playing together. We were all trapped in that bell jar of early parenthood, madly in love with tiny creatures that bored us to death. We diverted each other, the women who were free all day long but never really free at all.

The preschool was advertised as Jewish and Muslim, with classes in Hebrew and in Arabic. It would take me some time to learn that many years earlier, half of the classes had switched to a unilingual Hebrew curriculum. They couldn't afford to run the school solely on the income of the bilingual classrooms; there wasn't enough interest. And there was strange slippage in the language around the school. "Jews and Arabs," the director would say in interviews, flashing her lipsticked smile, or, "Jews and Muslims." But the school was located in the YMCA, a fulcrum for the Christian community in Jerusalem. Many of the students were Christian, the Palestinians and Israelis and expats alike. Somehow nobody ever mentioned them. The Hebrew classes were filled with Israeli Jews, but the bilingual classes had become strikingly international. In Sam's class the children spoke Hebrew, Arabic, Japanese, German, Turkish, and Swedish, but mostly English, to my disappointment and relief.

Only a few parents—and those mostly Jews—sent their children to the YMCA because the school reflected their politics. Then there were the internationals, the UN and embassy affiliates, and the sabbaticants like me, who found in the daycare an idealized image of a country they were only passing through. And for some of the Arab-Israeli and Palestinian parents, the daycare was an entry into Israeli society, a way to ensure their children were fluent in Hebrew and could pass easily between the Arab and Jewish parts of the city.

I asked Jenna why she sent her children to the daycare, and she said, "Well, I want them to speak Hebrew. Without an accent. And this is a very good daycare, they get music, they go swimming. Education is important to us, to Aden and me. Aden wants them to go to one of those British schools when they grow up, Oxford or Yale."

"Yale isn't in Britain," I said.

She looked at me blankly and said, "It is."

Jenna's mother was Puerto-Rican, but her father was Palestinian. They both lived in the United States, and her father hadn't been able to return in a dozen years. She was unpopular in her extended family, she said, because her father had left his Palestinian first wife for her Puerto-Rican mother.

"They didn't like it that he left her. My mother converted, but they didn't care."

Her parents only stayed married for a few years, long enough to have her and her sister. She went to Catholic school in Baton Rouge—"Because my parents didn't want me going to school with boys. Their mistake. You would not believe what *sluts* they are in Catholic school." She was sent to boarding school in Jordan, then she moved to Israel and studied to become an esthetician. Jenna was halfway through learning to cut hair and wax eyebrows when someone turned her in for being in the country illegally. She spent the night in jail and was put on a plane back to America the next day.

She was convinced the informer was from her family, this extended, amorphous mass to which she constantly referred. Whatever she was or was becoming, she wanted it to be in contrast to this family that she always referred to in the aggregate. She hated them, but she couldn't shake them: she was bound to their judgments, their gossip, the many fingers that prodded and shaped her life. She was only able to come back to Jerusalem after marrying Aden, who was her second cousin. Now, for the first time, she had legal status in Jerusalem. She carried her passport all the time, flipped it open to show me her visa.

"Look," she said, "I can even work!"

She had not worked since she'd gotten married.

Her husband Aden was tall and aloof. He wore sunglasses all the time so I never saw his eyes. I was starting to work on learning Arabic, but when I tried to speak to him in Arabic, he answered me in Hebrew. He was some kind of a middleman: he worked with Palestinian contractors and developers, Israeli lawyers and architects. Jenna was constantly going to the bank to deposit thick wads of cash for him.

"That's the great thing about Israel," she said to me. "No taxes!"

At first I didn't understand what she meant, and when I finally figured it out, I felt like a fool. If you paid your taxes you were a *freier*, a "sucker." The Yiddish word had entered into everyday use; it didn't matter if you were Israeli or Palestinian, nobody wanted to be a *freier*.

We were standing outside the daycare, waiting for the children to spill out of their classroom. Jenna introduced me to Yumiko and Katie. Yumiko was Japanese. She was tall and slender, looked at least a decade younger than her age, and seemed unhappy. She told me that she had studied translation in America, where she met her husband, Andrew.

"I am not American," she said definitively, "I absolutely do not feel American. I do not want my daughter to be American."

Her daughter Ana was the only little girl in Sam's group. She had long black hair to her waist, her mother's almond eyes, her father's dimpled chin, and she ran the wild class of boys like a queen commanding a rowdy group of courtiers.

Yumiko knew Katie from translation school, and it was a tremendous coincidence that they'd both ended up as embassy wives in Jerusalem. Back then Yumiko was learning English. Katie was studying Arabic.

Yumiko said, "I remember this short, angry girl, always in a big rush, and always wearing a—what do you call those things—a *keffiyeh* around her neck."

Katie laughed. She was petite, blonde, ponytailed, and always in a uniform of khakis, collared shirts, pert sweaters. "Those were my political days."

The consulate women were having a spa party that day, somewhere up on French Hill. Neither Katie nor Yumiko was going. "I once made the mistake of going to a Tupperware party for the consulate women," Katie said, "and I spent the whole time standing against the wall and drinking fruit punch. God, I got so drunk," she said nostalgically, "never again." Katie dragged an imaginary razor up the inner vein of her arm as she described it.

Katie was an unusual presence at the embassy because she had grown up in the Middle East. Her father, a congregational minister, had worked in Saudi Arabia, and then in Yemen. The oil companies had a secret agreement with the government: they were allowed to provide clergymen for each of the denominations represented among their employees, as long as they didn't proselytize and kept a low profile.

"Jews, too?" I said, and Katie said, "Well, no, obviously."

"What was it like in Saudi?" I said, and Katie said, "It

was strange. The expats there are crazy. There's something wrong with all of them or they wouldn't be there. Either they can't function back home, so they've fled, or they've been driven crazy by the money, or they're drunks or addicts. Or all three. I had to wear an *abaya* during the day and I was driven around in a chauffeured, shuttered car. I wasn't allowed to even drive, but at night we all drank in expat bars and went skinny-dipping in pools inside the compound."

After Katie left Yemen she taught English in Bethlehem for two years, before the second Intifada. "All those kids I taught, they're all gone now. Moved to America, or Greece, or Jordan. Anyone who was educated, anyone who had a real choice, left. That's what scares me the most. Of this generation, all the leaders, all the smart kids, and all the kids with potential—they're gone and they're not coming back. And who remains?"

As a consulate wife Katie wasn't allowed to travel to Bethlehem, and her old friends couldn't get visas to visit her. She could only speak to them on the phone, as if she were still in Washington. She could have driven to Bethlehem in fifteen minutes.

"Who would know if you went?" I asked, and she said, "Spies are everywhere. I mean, my husband could lose his job."

"Age tames us all," she said. "It's time—the kids must be out. We'd better check on them."

Katie and Yumiko told me that the spouses of diplomats were not allowed into the West Bank. They weren't supposed to go to the market: also, on buses, to city fairs, into certain parts of town. They couldn't go to public events—they were banned from all crowded spaces— they couldn't walk around at night, they couldn't go to political demonstrations or express opinions that might hurt the reputation of the embassy. They couldn't work. They *could* park anywhere they wanted to, and they did, using the immunity of their diplomatic stickers to roll their giant SUVs into handicapped spots and onto side- walks, having awkwardly navigated the old donkey roads of Jerusalem. They had fundraisers and social events, worked out at the gym, filled the hours in between by watching their children. The domestic bookends of the day were dropping off the children and putting them to bed. Everything else was variations on a theme: what to buy for supper, when to work out, where to have cof- fee while the children were in school, where to go in the early afternoon when class finished.

Husbands appeared occasionally for performances or events, or to pick up their children, once in a blue moon. They wore open-necked button-down shirts, pressed khakis, an aura of business-like competence. Their wives spoke of them with pity and disdain. Sure, they knew a lot about embassy policy in the Middle East, and their new boss was Hillary Clinton. But they were remark- ably obtuse about the simplest things, did not remember which day their child had swimming lessons (Wednesday, Wednesday all year long), would not pick up their socks, and, like Simon, could never find their keys.

There was a conspiracy of wives who silently ironed

shirts and washed underpants and pressed keys into their husbands' hands as they rushed out the door to meet the foreign minister by nine o'clock. The wives shared the secret among themselves: it was important that the world saw their husbands as men of industry and men of power, important too that they alone knew how quickly it would all collapse without their own tireless behind-the-scenes engineering, their weary, resentful housewifery. They spoke with affectionate superiority of the women they had once been, the way you might speak of a younger sister who travelled the world, fell recklessly in love, believed in radical change, had not yet been disciplined by her life.

When I came home and told Simon about the women from the daycare, he seemed indifferent. "It doesn't sound like you have much in common with them," he said. He was full of news about the infighting in his department, the colleagues who hadn't spoken to one another for years, and the ones who spoke only to exchange barely veiled insults.

"You know," he told me, "I said something at a meeting, and my colleague said, 'I completely disagree with everything you just said.' Everything! Can you imagine that!"

I shook my head. His shirt was rumpled and he had dark sweat stains under his arms. He was starting to look like one of those academic men who wanted to project that they were more mind than body. As the years passed, the university seemed more and more of a petty place to me, a game played where nothing was at stake. I couldn't bring myself to care. "I should iron that shirt," I said, knowing that I would not.

7.

I was feeling more than disciplined by my life. I was feeling beaten. I had never expected to be derailed by having children. Simon and I had started our degrees at the same time; he was already on sabbatical, and I was floundering. Of the two of us, I had been the more promising.

We had waited a long time before having children, or at least, it had seemed a long time in a community where baby announcements followed wedding announcements with only just enough time in between to ensure the appearance of decency. I am certain that people believed something was wrong, and that when they didn't ask about our plans to have children it was out of their strained, fastidious attempts to protect us. We had met young, had married young, and the path of least resistance would have been to join those instant families, three or four years out of high school, baby-faced parents promenading their new strollers and responsibilities. No. Not us. We said we would find ourselves first, and would have some time for only each other. If only we'd known it wouldn't matter in the end, all of those years of establishing our coupledom, once the children arrived and made our romance just the prelude for their arrival.

Two months after Gabriel was born, I was so desperate for solitude that I started to take long walks in the evening, after he'd gone to bed and before he woke up for his first feeding. It was my only opportunity to be alone since the baby was so needy and the nights so interrupted. I would walk for an hour, quickly, as if I were being followed, through the alleys and streets of my neighbourhood, looking into the lit windows of the houses. Because the streets were dark, if the curtains were open I could see right into the living rooms of strangers. I could see the colour of the paint, I could look at the art on the walls, I could even see the television programs on the new flat screens that dominated the rooms, though the sound was muted. I imagined other lives in other houses as I walked the tight circle that always brought me home.

The nightly walk became a kind of compulsion. It was as though I were driven outdoors as soon as the sun went down, and when I couldn't go, I'd be uneasy and restless all the next day. Almost none of my friends in the city had children, and the tribe of new mothers was frightening to me. I did have one friend with a new baby, and when we called each other, we were like prisoners whispering through a crack in the wall between their cells.

Simon and I talked about the old days with wonder, as though they'd happened to other people: "Can you imagine," we would say, "we used to stay in bed until noon on a Sunday, we used to wander out in the evening without a destination?" As if staying in bed for three or four extra hours was the unlikeliest, the most exotic thing in the world. Only other new parents understood that degree of incredulous nostalgia for something so ordinary. Our friends without children thought our new limitations were pathetic—"Can't the baby amuse himself for a while in the morning while you sleep in?" they would say, in their awe-inspiring obliviousness, not realizing that it would be like asking a tornado to rest for just a little while, or a tidal wave to stand still. Friends with older children assured us that this overwhelming period of early parenthood lasted only a little while, forgetting that while we were inside of it, it felt like it would last forever.

But it was right that the children should become the centre of our lives. Parents who stayed too flagrantly in love with each other always had children who seemed a little famished, outside the grand feast of the parental romance. Those children surely could never feel truly loved. Our children, on the other hand, had slid right into the spotlight, bawling and squinting, from the moment of their arrival in the delivery room; it was our marriage that had been left in shadow. I had never forgotten the words of a character in a film who described having children as running a small daycare with someone you used to date. But at least we were equally besotted with our children, and besides, there was this new kind of love, the love for a person who is essential for your child's care and happiness. Simon was definitely not my boyfriend anymore, or my new husband, but he was the father of my children, and that was the least transient category of them all.

At least, that was what I told myself.

Routine is the prison and the refuge of raising small children; we obsessed about it, tried endlessly to implement it, and then felt constrained by its demands. Sometimes it felt like we spoke to one another only to make or correct household arrangements; who would drop off or pick up or buy milk or fill out the form or make plans or remember every single thing. I think of those now as the scarcity years; not enough time or money or sleep, especially sleep. I think a low-grade anger, like a low-grade fever, ran under the skin of the relationship.

All the women I knew in Israel hated their husbands. Aden was having affairs. Andrew was just clueless. Roger had just come back from Iraq and was angry all the time. There was this women's chorus, this consensus of complaints, this combination of pity and disdain for men who could not, after all, be expected to behave better.

"And you, Hannah," Jenna said, "you shouldn't think Simon is so great either." It felt like she had punched me in the gut.

Truth be told, I was worried about Simon. Since we had arrived, he was restless in his skin, moody, quick to take offence, quick to disappear. The first day he went to work he came back in a foul mood. It was a rainy day, and when he walked in it was as if the bad weather came with him. He threw his jacket on the bookcase, and it slipped off onto the floor; he left his bag in the middle of the hallway. Without saying hello, he walked into the bathroom and closed the door, and he stayed in there for a long time. That coat on the floor was a slap.

The boys had worn me down that day. I was tired from walking them to and from school in the rain and keeping them inside all afternoon. But these were my days: I woke up early and put out breakfast. I cleaned breakfast up and walked them to school. I shopped for groceries and picked them up. I made a snack and wiped down the counter. I picked up their shoes and did the dishes. I put the television on and started supper. I picked up their toys, I picked up their shoes, I wiped down the toilet. I did it again and again. I couldn't figure it out, how this had become my life. I wasn't even good at it; the house was sloppy, our meals were dull. Only the children were happy, and how long could they stay happy, with a mother like me?

Simon remained full of complaints about the university. They hadn't set him up with an office, his colleagues were cold, his students indifferent. How quickly he became withdrawn and I became shrewish; the response was so automatic it seemed almost a chemical reaction. After all this time it shocked me that we could become strangers to each other, but it was, after all, the easiest thing in the world.

We had been so young and promising, and now we were getting to an age at which nobody called you promising. We'd buried our heads in the sandbox of raising the children, and now that we were able to take a breath, to reach back up and look around, we found we had arrived, astonishingly, at the middle of our lives. There was no reason for it to astonish us; all that had happened was we had settled down into the bedrock of cliché, which, because we were people who hated clichés, we imagined would never apply to us. But there we were, and both a little stranded, facing a horizon of diminished possibilities and fighting the temptation to blame each other.

But I wasn't about to talk about it, not with them. It was as if their betrayal made me more loyal, their loquacity made me more tight-lipped. I didn't want him to become just another piece in this conversation we were having about men. No.

The families we met outside the daycare also seemed unhappy. One friend couldn't help but make a face when her husband spoke. It was entirely unconscious and flickered across her features like a wind, this deep grimace of discontent. He did the same thing when she was speaking. And then there was an array of sounds, sighs, audible breaths, skeptical mews, so that speaking to them was almost intolerable, because the nearly silent theatre under the conversation we were having was so distracting and in its way so very loud.

And many of the children we met ran wild, hit, bit, talked back. Their parents were all American and had moved to Israel as adults; they were naturalized, to some degree, but they would never be natives. Their children had already surpassed them, already disdained them, their stupid grammatical mistakes, their poor pronunciation, their intolerable helplessness. Some of these children were already deciphering contracts for their parents, filling out forms, dealing with the plumber on the phone. When you were an immigrant you had to abdicate the mastery that was the birthright of the native-born; you had to be willing to appear a little ridiculous to your children, who were born swimming in this culture not your own. And perhaps the discord that ran under the surface of everything had gotten under the skin of these families, too.

There was one family, with three beautiful children. We often had dinner with them on Friday nights. They were meticulous cooks and set a beautiful table and spoke softly and carefully to one another and to their children. As we walked home we said, "How lovely they are to each other! How well behaved their children are! How restful to spend time with a peaceful family!"

Eventually, we learned that she had told him to move out and was filing for divorce. It hadn't been peace after all—everyone had just been holding their breath.

I had a pregnancy scare, a brief one, or less a scare than the brief flicker of paranoia that always came over me when I thought I was overdue. I was standing with Yumiko in the park across the street from the daycare, and our children were climbing a sculpture made out of pink stone with warm, involuted curves that looked like a cross between an ear and a vulva. Snapdragons bloomed in bright clashing rows, standing like soldiers, and massive cacti grew along the path. Someone had scratched a heart into the long, spiny leaves of a giant aloe and had added up two sets of initials to equal love. The heart and letters were ridged in white, scar tissue against the deep green.

"I am a little worried," I said to Yumiko.

I was terrified. I still hadn't recovered from the infancy of the boys, when the sleepless nights and constant need undid me. For a little while, I stopped sleeping entirely, lying tensed in bed and waiting for the next hungry cry.

Yumiko's dark glasses covered half of her narrow face. She'd recently cut her hair, and it lay like a smooth black wing against her cheek.

"That would be impossible with me and Andrew," she said.

"Impossible? You're awfully confident."

"Impossible," she repeated, and if she looked at me in disdain because I was so slow I couldn't tell because of the dark glasses masking her face. "I think it's been a year, almost. His last birthday. And I had to get drunk. Now, if he's horny, he knows what to do." Her long, pale, elegant fingers mimed an obscene gesture so quickly that I almost wasn't sure it had actually occurred.

The afternoons were open with a heavy freedom. Jenna, Yumiko, Katie, once she stopped working for the consulate midway through the year. And me.

8.

When I last visited Jerusalem, I was still a teenager. Now everything shocked me: the separate buses, the way the city divided along invisible lines. North was a sea of black and white, wrists and ankles covered, eyes down, women at the back of the bus. East felt like an entirely different country—all of the signs were in Arabic, the sidewalks disappeared, buildings were crammed too close to one another, and piles of garbage bordered the streets. And West Jerusalem was glistening stones and fancy cafes, a Gucci on the rich new promenade into the Old City. People from the three Jerusalems crossed there, on the street corners and at the bus stops, but they didn't look at each other. It was as if only their own people were solid flesh: they looked through everyone else, as if the other Jerusalems didn't exist.

Getting used to the people was no less jarring. Israelis were an odd mix of hospitable and hostile. Any interaction could jump in emotional temperature in an instant; at any moment you might be either slapped or embraced. The country ran a constant fever. Traffic was a war zone,

50

and in the grocery store people cut in line with naked aggression. When a car backfired, everyone jumped, and nobody smiled at anyone else while walking down the street. But they liked to talk, liked to tell you exactly what you were doing wrong.

An Israeli reality show had staged an encounter in a grocery store. An actress, dressed as a Muslim, walked in and asked for a cappuccino, and another actor behind the counter refused to serve her. One after another, Israeli passersby intervened with great passion and eloquence. Several friends posted the clip on Facebook; to them it was evidence of an absence of racism in the culture. But to me it was further proof that Israelis would take every possible opportunity to contradict you, to grandstand, to prove you wrong, to tell you how you ought to have behaved. It was a culture of busybodies and grandmothers, and the warmer and more intrusive the people around me became, the more I shrunk into myself, cold and reserved, though in America I thought of myself as warm, open, artless.

One day, I took Sam to the park. People called it "The Grove" because it was sheltered in a circle of eucalyptus trees. A man on a bench struck up a conversation. He had a kind smile; he sat with his arm around his daughter, and as he spoke he played with her long brown hair. He had come from Morocco, he said, "Which is how I know, *for an absolute fact*, that the Arabs want to push us all into the sea."

He placed his palms up benevolently, letting go of his

daughter's braid. He said, "What choice do we have but to expel them?"

The swings at the park hung in a circle, so each child swung towards the others' feet. The late afternoon sun caught and tore on the upper branches of the eucalyptus trees. My boys took turns surfing down the green slide, their arms outstretched for balance, holding open handfuls of light. The man sent his daughter to buy a popsicle, turned back towards me, but I couldn't think of anything to say.

This kind of encounter was not uncommon. Strangers were so very eager to tell you whom to hate. A taxi driver honked at a man in a long black coat and luxuriant *peyos* slowly crossing the street.

He said, "They're a cancer on the country."

He wore the crocheted dark blue *kippa* of the modern orthodox Zionist. It covered most of the bald spot on the back of his head, but a ring of scalp showed around it. I didn't know how the *kippa* stayed attached; it wasn't the kind of thing you could ask, really.

"A cancer?" I said, and he said, "Trust me."

He told me his son had been killed during the Lebanon war. Soon after the death, he was driving his cab on Remembrance Day. When the memorial siren sounded, he stopped the car, as was customary, and sat in silence, thinking of his son and of the dead. His customer, a Chasidic man, leaned forward impatiently in the back seat and cuffed him on the shoulder. "*Nu*," he said, "let's go! What am I paying you for?"

"Trust me," the cabbie said again, grimly.

People were always telling me to trust them, but nobody trusted anyone else.

But despite this current of hostility, we were also often overwhelmed with kindness. We had more dinner invitations than we could accept. People called the house, offered casseroles, cookies, favours. A stranger at the bus stop clucked her tongue at my open coat and gave me a shawl out of her bag. Old women wiped my sons' noses, commented on their bare hands, their dirty shirts, their summer sandals, told me to have more children, to buy better shoes, to make sure they wear a hat, to always carry a tissue.

Hebrew in the street still sounded like birdsong to me, faraway and incomprehensible, but the gears were starting to shift back in my mind so sometimes I was actually listening, not just translating. Still, I did not feel at home. I missed autumn leaves, the smell of woodsmoke, brick houses, and cold cheeks. I kept having bad dreams.

I tried to talk to Simon about the dreams, but I couldn't, because they would have become ammunition in his new campaign to bring us home. "It was a mistake to come here," he kept saying grimly, and each time he said it, I felt the walls close in around us. He came home from work looking stooped, his body a tall thin question mark. He'd launch into news about his day as I stood there with my hands full of nothing. "I'm disappointed with my colleagues," he'd say. "It's all nepotism here, everybody is somebody's nephew or cousin, there is no real chance for collaboration." Or, "I can't see why they want me at their departmental meetings, it's an utter waste of my time, if they were interested in my feedback that would be one thing, but they talk right over me."

So I turned into a tap-dancing, finger-snapping parody of positivity, which was my default role when faced with sadness. "Look at how beautiful these morning glories are!" I would say, or, "Can you believe, it's snowing and freezing back home and look at these gorgeous blue skies!" I couldn't help myself, couldn't help putting on the exaggerated clownish mask, the grotesquely happy face. Under the bluster, it was as if I was really whispering, "Couldn't you just try to be happy?" Besides, I would have given almost anything to change places with him, to go to the university in the morning, to have colleagues and conversations with adults about something, anything other than children.

There were city elections that fall, and the city was papered with posters, rolling by on the sides of city buses, covering the old stone walls, littering the streets. Three main candidates were running for mayor: One was an ultra-orthodox rabbi whose publicity posters drew him as a smiling, bearded cartoon—a Jewish Santa Claus, more than one journalist had commented. There was a Russian billionaire with thick and clotted Hebrew, wanted in France for smuggling arms to the civil war in Angola. He looked so sinister on the posters on the sides of bus shelters that my sons had taken to calling him "the super villain." Then there was a slick, millionaire businessman, three-quarter profile in his posters and steely-eyed, wearing a conservative black suit and a blue tie.

Everyone was terrified that the Santa Claus *rebbe*—his name was Porush—would win, and that he would turn the city into an ultra-orthodox fortress. He had been caught on tape saying, "In ten years, all of the cities of Israel will be ours."

"We are losing our *city*," a friend said hysterically; she was canvassing at night for a fringe candidate, and she was convinced he would do well because everyone she knew was voting for him. But that was only our friends.

The Jerusalem Arabs usually boycotted the election, and the Russian billionaire was the only candidate who bothered meeting with them; for most voters, this only increased his apparent villainy.

Nir Barkat was the clear front-runner. We were invited to a film premiere one Saturday night, and on the way to the theatre, we kept passing posters of his sleek and smarmy face.

Simon said, "God, I'm sick of him. I don't need to ever see his face again." No sooner had we walked into the theatre than Simon nudged me and said, "Look." There was Barkat, in the flesh, looking smooth and handsome, barely more dimensional than his posters, with a military straightness to his back.

We kept rubbernecking until the introductions to the movie started. A dowager minced down the aisle, dressed in a fluted and architectural white coat, like the rabbit in Alice in Wonderland. The seats were reserved with the names of the luminaries of Israeli politics, past and present.

Many of them sat empty.

Natan Sharansky was there, his lips like two greying pieces of meat. I remembered the Cold War rallies back in the eighties, when Sharansky was imprisoned. How many times had I stood outside in the cold and chanted with a small crowd: "*Da, Da, Aliya, Nyet, Nyet Soviet!*" In solitary confinement, Sharansky played chess against himself in his head. He dreamed of a place he'd never seen. Now here he was, fat and prosperous, glad-handing down the aisles, kissing women on the cheek. He introduced the film and made a show of adjusting the mike "for short people."

But his introduction was interrupted; a plump woman was walking down the aisle, flexing her rosebud mouth in an approximation of an apologetic smile, fluttering wide painted eyes under a stiff carapace of hair. She walked like a pigeon, all bustle and chest and backside, and everyone turned away from Sharansky and watched her.

It must have been a bitter pill to swallow, after surviving prison and solitary confinement, to lose his audience to a former flight attendant with a reputation for abusing the help, and who had happened to marry a man who was once Prime Minister. When her housekeeper had complained about being mistreated, the Prime Minister's wife had said, "But I am the mother of the nation! You should feel honoured to work for the Netanyahu family."

Sharansky recovered quickly. "Sara," he boomed, his voice much larger than his body, "how good that you could make it." She flapped her hand at him like a bird with a broken wing.

9.

Though we'd gone halfway around the world, it seemed like everyone we met was North American. Our neighbours Deborah and David were from Boston. They invited us to their house for the holiday of *Sukkot*. We entered the house through a small courtyard, climbed uneven steps, and stepped into a great room with cathedral ceilings and heavy wood beams that seemed more Swiss than Israeli. Set for twenty, the table groaned.

The fabric walls of their *sukka* were covered with a stylized mural of the Old City of Jerusalem. It took a minute to figure out what was missing; the domes and steeples of the mosques and churches were gone. "How nice to see Jerusalem without the mosques and churches. Just our own," one of the guests said, and everyone laughed.

"Those are Ottoman walls. Jews didn't build those walls," I said, and he said, "You don't have to take it so seriously."

But this was a common fantasy; Jerusalem pictured without the ubiquitous golden cap of the Dome of the Rock, or the slate fish scales of the Church of the Holy

Sepulchre. I'd seen the pattern in kitschy paintings sold in the alleys of the Old City, printed in silhouette on ceramic platters and household blessings and other tacky Judaica for sale by the basketful all over Jerusalem so that Jewish households in Pittsburgh or Chicago could take this little piece of Jerusalem back with them. Our city, not theirs. Even the way that locals referred to the golden dome as the "*kippa*"—even that claimed it. One day Gabriel came back from school saying, "Israel is the centre of the world and Jerusalem is the centre of Israel and the Western Wall is the centre of Jerusalem." I was reminded of those gorgeous old medieval maps, the world as a woman and Jerusalem at its navel. But I also sat down with him and with a globe. I pointed to the small lopsided carrot of the country and said, "Does this look like the centre?"

At the *Sukkot* dinner party, my children played with toys from the baskets kept in the living room, while a cornucopia of dishes appeared from the kitchen: broiled eggplant with a sauce of tahini and sun-dried tomatoes, lasagna because the children would eat it, spreads from the best place in the *souk*, fish because Deborah was promised it was fresh, a salad of fennel and apples to stimulate the appetite, Jerusalem artichokes because she hadn't made them for a long time, a mushroom pie that she just was trying out, asparagus since it was in season, squash because it was hard to get. I knew two of the faces around the table—an old acquaintance from ten years back and her handsome, feckless husband. The children whispered tense negotiations over toy figurines and Lego structures.

The bottle of wine we had brought sat on a side table, crowded by four or five other better bottles.

I was sitting next to a rabbi named Zev. He told me that his synagogue had done a special program for children that week. "We visited a children's hospital ward in East Jerusalem," he said. "We dressed up as clowns, you know, to communicate with them. Lots of those kids can't even speak Hebrew."

"What about communicating with them in Arabic?" I said. "Instead of dressing up like clowns. Aren't the kids supposed to learn Arabic in school here?"

He looked down at his plate, and made a show of cutting his eggplant. Shelley piped in from across the table. "I wouldn't bother with them," she said. "They don't appreciate it. Trust me."

I knew Shelley from New York. She was the daughter of a judge. She had steadily become more observant, and now drew her hair under a tight beret that left her face looking feline and pointed. She was talking about the last time she had given birth, though it was hard to hear her across the table. "You don't know what they're like," she said. "There was an Arab woman in the room with me at the hospital. The Arab doctors had completely screwed up her delivery, and she'd had to be transferred to Ein Kerem. She kept complaining because she'd been held up at the checkpoint, she said she almost died. But really, it's her own people that almost killed her. I told her, if you guys didn't smuggle bombs in ambulances you wouldn't be held up. It's your own fault. It's that simple, really." Her eyes shone in the light of the holiday candles. Her baby lay asleep in her stroller behind her, sweetly plump, oblivious.

"She almost died?" I said. "And they wouldn't let her through?"

"Look, we treat them, in our hospitals. They would never do that for us. I'd rather she be held up at the checkpoint, and my children be free to play in the streets of Jerusalem. They have no right to complain. If they suffer, it's their own fault."

"But she had just given birth."

"I feel no sympathy for them," Shelley said. "They don't deserve our sympathy."

"You don't understand what it's like here," Zev chimed in. "They dance in the streets when we die, you have to remember that. Remember the Gulf War? Dancing on the roofs when the rockets came. They're savages."

"They," I said, "who is they? How can you say that every single Palestinian is responsible ...?" I broke off, feeling flushed and furious. The room was hot and someone kept refilling my glass of wine.

Zev said, with an air of concession, "Yes, it's too bad that the good ones have to suffer because of the actions of their countrymen."

Shelley said, "When I lived in the West Bank during the last Intifada, if my car had broken down, I would have had to get out and hide until the soldiers came, or they would have lynched me. My children and me. Every time I drove that road I was frightened."

At the head of the table our benevolent, gnomic host

smiled sweetly. "It's the Arab mentality," he said, "to kill. What is it? I mean it must be something in their religion."

On the table, old dishes were whisked away and new dishes continued to appear: three kinds of ice cream, two kinds of cake, a massive platter of fruit, and five kinds of cheese on a sacrificial wooden cutting board. In the distance someone was singing.

"Dessert!" Deborah said, sounding the closing chime on the conversation. "Look at all this cheese. I can't trust you at the market anymore, David," and then to us, fondly, "he must have spent two hundred shekels on cheese."

"Guilty as charged," David said, and the table dissolved into requests for lemon sorbet or coffee ice cream, to pass the cake and pour the wine, and people asking, "What kind of cheese is this one? It's delicious!" Amidst the choreography of exchanged platters and reaching hands, I noticed Deborah looking at me, quick and worried, trying to protect everyone at once.

I got up to go to the washroom. I sat there for a long time, looking at the wall, trying to calm down. I had forgotten so much about this country. When I came out, Simon was hovering near the door.

"Are you all right?" he said in a low voice. "You need to remember that it's complicated, very complicated here. People are frightened. They mean well."

He put his arm on my shoulder and I could feel my throat constrict, because it had been a long time since I'd felt like he was looking after me. I leaned into the softness of his neck. He smelled like home.

"It's alright," I said, "I think I'm going to be fine."

There was a dispute around the toy basket; I slipped back down to the floor next to my boys, lost myself in Lego battles until it was time to go.

10.

After that dinner, I decided I needed to do—to do, god, I didn't know what. Anything. My old friend Elah from graduate school had moved to Israel to work on her dissertation, but had gradually been drawn into activism. She always seemed busy with meetings and demonstrations though it was unclear exactly what she did. She had been asking me to come to Bi'ilin so I could see for myself, and though I'd been in Israel for two months, I hadn't yet managed to join her.

Elah attended a protest in Bi'ilin every Friday. The security wall had separated the Palestinian farmers of Bi'ilin from their olive groves; the Supreme Court had ruled in their favour a few years earlier and ordered for the wall to be moved. But the wall was still in place, grey and implacable, and every Friday a motley group of protestors walked towards it until the soldiers stopped them. The group of demonstrators was pretty diverse; local Palestinians, Israeli Arabs, and Jews on the left, as well as journalists, tourists, and activists who rotated through protests as if they were visiting museums or national parks.

People were routinely arrested; the year before, a man had been killed when he was hit by a rubber bullet at close range. I had a friend who had served his *miluim*, his annual month of reserve duty, at that stretch of the wall. "It's choreographed," he shrugged. "Everyone knows exactly what will happen." It reminded me of Kafka's parable, "Leopards in the Temple," in which the leopards break into the temple and drink the wine of sacrament until that, too, becomes a part of the ritual.

A man named Micah drove us to Bi'ilin. He was grey haired and slim hipped, with pale eyes, and he said he'd been an activist for forty years. I wore a T-shirt and a knee-length skirt—in the car, it had hiked up to my thigh. Elah's friend Shira, also in the back seat, looked at my legs disapprovingly.

"Didn't you tell her how to dress, Elah?"

I pulled the skirt down.

"She's fine," Elah called back from the front seat. "You'll see when she gets out of the car. It isn't short."

"It looks short to me," Shira said.

Shira was in her thirties, buxom, cat-eyed, with pillowy, pouting lips. She wore wide cotton trousers, and a scarf over her hair. "It's for you that I'm worried," she said. "Because the first time I went, I dressed like that, and the women of the village, they pulled me aside and told me it was not appropriate. They don't have any of these freedoms, you know—we shouldn't be flaunting it in front of them. It's difficult enough for them already."

"Don't give her a hard time," Elah said, "she's fine.

Anyway, I have a scarf."

"It's for your sake," Shira repeated, "because I felt so awful about it." I looked out the window.

Elah had been traveling to Hebron on the weekends. The Jewish settlers in Hebron were known to be among the most extreme; they assaulted farmers who were working their own land, goat herders with their flocks, shepherds on the hills. Elah was part of a group that tried to stand witness, but her presence didn't always protect them, and she had been spat on, called names, even hit. "It makes me understand the Bible better, actually," she said. "The sheep, the pastoral landscape, the stranger. It makes me feel very Jewish." She had been called a heretic and a traitor, but mostly they just called her a slut.

In fifteen minutes, we had passed into the West Bank and back out of it—through part of the patchwork that makes up Israeli territory around Jerusalem. We'd passed two checkpoints without slowing down, and then a settlement, clean tall apartment buildings and new roads and two women in long skirts and headscarves waiting at a bus stop. Now we were in the hills, winding up a country road. A biblical landscape: olive trees, rocky hills.

"I never come from this direction," Micah said, frowning and reversing. "I think this is right." The town was pretty, with low white houses and flowering gardens. A skeleton of a house was rising, or rising again, near the road where we entered the town; some boys were balanced on the scaffolding, and looked like they should be playing with blocks, not buildings. "Good for them,"

Micah said, as he honked and waved.

"Rebuilding already?" Elah said. "How long ago did that house get knocked down?"

"A couple of weeks, I think," Micah said, pulling up in front of a little store.

Elah went in to buy a soda and I wandered over to the crowd. There was a group of German tourists, perhaps thirty of them. A few tanned, dreadlocked men with serious cameras and video equipment were laughing and smoking. Kids from the town wore white T-shirts and bad denim, and milled around old-school punks with green hair and safety-pinned ears and noses.

Before we left Jerusalem, Elah had emailed me, "I promise you will not get arrested." She had brought me a scarf, for the tear gas. She'd said, "In the worst-case scenario, they will use skunk. It smells terrible but it will not hurt you. It's meant to shame you, actually. You must not panic when the gas comes. That is the worst thing you can do. You need to cover your mouth and breathe slowly, otherwise you will not be able to breathe at all and you might feel quite sick." We walked slowly, near the back of the line.

"Don't you want a picture of yourself in the olive grove, before things start going crazy?" Elah asked. "This peaceful, pastoral landscape?" She waved her hand. Instead I took a picture of her smoking. We passed the Germans. They were part of a church group, and were actually wearing *lederhosen*. They stayed on the top of the hill, so that they wouldn't get too caught up in any fallout from the protest. The average age in the group looked to be about seventy—they were elderly activists with bad teeth and sunburns and cardboard signs—and even though it probably wasn't fair I didn't trust their motives at all. If you were German, and you lived through that war, then you didn't get to say anything about a Jewish state.

Beside me was a man from Boston. His name was Jeffrey and he looked like he was in his mid-thirties. He said that he was in Israel to write a book about the conflict. I asked him how long he'd been in Israel. "Three weeks," he said. I asked him if he knew Hebrew. "A little," he said. "Arabic?" "No." "And how much longer will you stay?" He scowled at me, sensing that my questions were no longer just polite. "I'm halfway through my trip," he said. "What qualifies you to write about the conflict?" I said. He looked at me angrily and trudged ahead. He had an odd, rolling walk and was sweating profusely. A young Palestinian man hovered at his elbow.

The path rose up a hill, and once we were past the crest we could see the grey stretch of security wall. It was just a dull ribbon on the landscape. Then we heard a popping sound, like fireworks. People were running before I realized what was happening. Against the clear blue sky the rockets rose like an air show before the grey-blue plumes drifted into the crowd.

A boy running past me was wearing a gas mask, people were coughing and running, and then I couldn't see anymore. The taste was acrid in my throat, like something I'd vomited out, and the gas burned my skin and especially my eyes. I ran slowly. "Internationals," I heard a voice behind me calling, "Internationals ...come help! Come help us! They are arresting people."

I did not come back. I kept running, faster now, in the other direction. The German tourists had stayed at the top of the hill, banners unfurled; they looked alarmed as we ran past them, eyes streaming. I had lost track of Elah and tried to look for her as I ran.

At the village, I sat on a low wall in the shade. In the distance I could still hear the faint popping sounds, and see the mist of smoke. Elah finally appeared over the top of the hill, her eyes red.

"Good," she said when she saw me. "Now let's find Shira."

Her cellphone rang and she listened, eyes wide. "It's Shira. She says Micah's been arrested. Wait, I can't hear her." She plugged her other ear with a finger. "She's still down there, in front."

Small knots of people had started to gather around us, looking for ways home. I wondered how anyone had ever protested before cellphones. The protestors now had a Facebook page; they tweeted updates and warnings; they found each other by texting.

Elah's phone rang and she said, "It's Micah." She spoke to him for a minute, and then put the phone down. "He's in the police van. They let him call. He sounded mildly amused, to tell you the truth. He wants someone to pick up the car. My fleece!"

"What?"

"My fleece is in that car! I really like that sweatshirt. I hope nothing happens to it."

The phone rang again. "We're getting a lift. With Ori."

Ori was a man in his eighties, in ill-fitting pink pants, big sunglasses, and a large, floppy red cap. He was a member of Anarchists Against the Wall; he had been an activist, he said, since he was 14, before the establishment of the state. There were two other activists in the car, both women, one young, one old. The younger one had purple hair, a stretched-out black tank top, camouflage pants; the older one had whiskers on her chin and cheeks, and was small and a little hunched. We kept pulling over as Ori made phone calls, trying to figure out who'd been detained, arranging the logistics of stranded cars and passengers.

"I am too old to drive and talk," he announced, pulling over for the fifth time.

"Is he the leader of the group?" I asked the woman sitting beside me, gesturing towards the driver's seat. She looked at me like I was an idiot. "Well, we're anarchists."

Ori pulled over before the checkpoint—the soldiers knew him and were more likely to stop the car if he was driving. He pulled his absurd hat over his head as if it made him less conspicuous and the woman in front drove, pulling her T-shirt inside out so it hid the anarchist slogan. After the checkpoint he drove us the rest of the way into the city, explaining the system of psychotherapy he'd helped pioneer, which involved, as far as I could understand, giving full expression to your emotions as they emerged so that they weren't suppressed into symptoms.

"If you want to cry," he said, "you just cry. If you want to weep, you weep. You feel what you feel. I teach people to do that."

The smell of the gas was stuck in my nose, and in the back of my throat like a dead thing. Still, I was free.

It was strange to drive over the hill and be back in Jerusalem in time to pick Sam up from school, to meet the other mothers outside the daycare. Which was the real Israel? The protesters running from a cloud of tear gas with the sounds of shooting in the background, or these women smoking cigarettes where their children could not see them and waiting for the school day to end?

I mentioned Bi'ilin to Jenna and she said, "God, I wouldn't do that."

"Why not?" I said.

Jenna said, "Well, you're a mother. You have responsibilities. Anyway, those people just do it because it makes them feel special—they're not accomplishing anything." She looked at the camera hanging from my shoulder and said, "Did you get some good pictures?"

That night as I lay in bed next to Simon, who was not asleep, I could not forget that when I heard the people down the hill calling in English for help, I had run faster than I knew I could run, straight in the other direction, away from the voices that were calling for me.

PART 2

11.

Bi'ilin had left a strange taste in my mouth. Not just the gas, but the whole scene—the surface drama and the indelible sadness underneath. I kept thinking of what Jenna had said about my responsibilities, only I wasn't sure where my responsibilities lay. The more time I spent in the country, the more confused I felt. Everything disoriented me. Different trees, different flowers, different smells in the air, the opalescent glimmer of Jerusalem stone on all of the buildings. I was unused to the stark beauty of the city, with its white houses and a sky too bright to look at directly. One morning the *khamsin* blew in from the desert and covered the city in a yellow fog, so that the hills vanished in the thick mist. Drifts of sand built up on the windshields of cars, and I reached over and rubbed the grains between my fingers, thinking of the snow I had left behind.

We still did touristy things, like taking the boys to the market on a Friday afternoon. The last time I was in Israel, they had not yet built the promenade into the Old City, lined with fancy cafes, upscale shops, and American and European chain stores. Even now, some of the buildings were still being renovated and the stones were numbered in red so that they could be repaired and then put back into place. The arcade was a brand new temple where you could worship the gods of Louis Vuitton and American Apparel. But ever had it been thus; when Christ overturned the tables of the moneylenders, that must have been right where they sat.

Even in this shiny and neutral space there was an edge of hostility. As we were walking through Mamilla to Jaffa Gate a man came up to me. He was tubby and sweaty, unshaven and insistent, slogans shouting loudly on his ill-fitting T-shirt and his hat. He wore a fanny pack around his hips, under the sloppy swag of his belly, and he held a roll of stickers in his hand.

"Here!" he said in a tone of false jollity. "Have a sticker! I'll put it on your hats!"

"No thank you," I said, walking faster, but he followed us.

"I'll put it on your children's hats!" he said. "It's just a sticker. It's free! What's the matter? What's your problem? You don't want it even though it's free!" His voice squeaked, as if he'd never heard something so absurd. "Take it. Just take it!"

I was pulling the children now, looking straight ahead. A few people looked at us but nobody stopped. The man lumbered after us like a tank, his face red and his breathing heavy. "What's wrong with that man?" Gabriel said, and I said, "He's crazy. Don't pay any attention to him." I said it loudly, so that the man would hear me.

Simon had gone ahead to buy some juice; I hoped he would be back quickly. I didn't feel exactly unsafe, just harassed and uncertain.

As we reached the steps to the Old City, the man stopped. "Let me ask you a question. Just one question. Can I ask you a question? Do you or do you not believe that Jerusalem should stay forever the undivided capital of the Jewish people?"

I should have been silent, but some devil possessed me. I looked back over my shoulder. His face changed, and the false smile disappeared. He looked more than angry—he looked enraged.

"No," I said.

He flared right up. "You're one of those, aren't you? One of those anti-Semitic Jewish parasites! That's what you are. Scumbags. People like you are the very worst: self-haters, racist, anti-Semitic Jews, the lowest of the low," he yelled at us from the bottom of the steps. "You should kill yourselves and the world would be better off!"

I could still hear him as we walked away. My heart was racing, as though we had been in danger. Simon was walking towards us, balancing four flimsy paper cups of fresh juice. He had heard only the end of the diatribe.

"What happened?" he said, and I said, "Nothing. A crazy person, that's all." My hands were sweaty, and I'd been holding the boys too tightly; I loosened my grip and Gabriel released his hand and said, "Ow. Why are we walking so fast?" But he wasn't really interested.

"Do you want to go home?" Simon said, but I shook

my head. "He should be arrested," I said, and my voice sounded tinny and mean. "They wouldn't let him stand there and do that if he was a Muslim. He'd be in jail in a minute. Only Jews are allowed to be that obnoxious here."

Past Jaffa Gate, low stone steps led into a warren of stalls, canopied with blue shade that was a relief after the white heat of the new city. And after the sterile promenade, the gaud and glitter of the market was also a solace. Beaded blouses and tapestries hung from the stalls; below them were velvet boards laden with necklaces, silver bowls of turquoise and jasper, baskets of miniature stuffed camels.

In the nineties, the Arab market was mostly off limits, under curfew and heavily policed. There were still men in navy girded with handguns, watchful behind their dark glasses, positioned on either side of the entrance like caryatids. But now the market was much more crowded—boys in black hats and *peyos* shortcutting their way back from the Western Wall, buses full of African tourists schlepping suitcases full of merchandise. The most dedicated shoppers and the most adept bargainers were these Africans on pilgrimage; they came by the busload, carrying large wheeled suitcases, and they bought blankets and toaster ovens, not the T-shirts and carved chess sets and belly dancing costumes that were for more dilettantish shoppers. They wore faded button-down shirts and slacks, rubber flip-flops, colourful *kente* cloth. I saw a woman standing impatiently outside a stall waiting for her husband to finish negotiating, her purchases perfectly balanced in a duffle bag on her head, her lips pressed together and her hands on her broad hips. They were the very best at bargaining, my friends at the market said. Better than Arabs, even. The sellers were too busy to notice us, and the boys too dazzled to stop, with their fingers crushed against our own. T-shirt stands sold Israeli Defence Forces camouflage next to images of Arafat and Obama in *keffiyehs*, endless variations of "I got stoned in Bethlehem," Coca-Cola slogans in Hebrew.

"The beauty never stops here, does it," Gabe said, impressed by the magpie's nest of heaped metals and glass beads. He was six years old and easily dazzled by everything shiny and small. He and his brother both bought plush camels with ornate beaded saddles, since Sam always needed what Gabe had. It would take years for them to realize that fairness did not mean having exactly the same thing.

"There's no lack of camels," Gabe said as he picked his out of a basket of identical, long-necked plush creatures. He had the inappropriate vocabulary of a child who was read to at length every night. He already delighted in indirect phrasing and unusual words, and in his slightly off-key, six-year-old understanding of understatement and irony.

The camels had luxurious eyelashes and human smiles. They were made in China, and when you pressed their stomachs they said "I love you" in English. Later, at home, the boys amused each other by throwing the camels at the floor and listening to them caterwaul like battered spouses until we said that the game was illegal. We were fond of laws in our house, though we tended to change them every morning. It was so much easier to have a rule than to make a request; you didn't have to explain the law. The boys were young enough that they took every rule for granted.

After the market, we went to the Tower of David. The museum on the grounds was shiny and expensive. We climbed the stairs up the tower and walked along the ramparts, and Sam tried to squeeze himself through the narrow slits in the wall. At the parapet, tourists jostled for the view. A woman in a long jean skirt, her hair entirely covered by a baseball cap, led a tour group of teenage girls who were occupied with their cellphones, heads leaning together over the tiny screens. It was a kind of atrocity tour; I listened, fascinated and horrified.

"Here," she said in a bored voice, pointing towards the cemetery, "is the place where the Jordanians desecrated Jewish graves, piling up tombstones to use as latrines. And there," her arm swung north, "in 1948, they murdered a convoy of doctors and nurses headed towards the Hadassah medical hospital."

The girls giggled and whispered, smelled like bubble-gum and shampoo. They weren't really listening, but there was this dark worm twisting into their consciousnesses that would grow on fear and distrust and gradually colour everything they assumed about this place. They would come to believe that they were surrounded by enemies.

Sam tried to scrabble up the parapet wall, and I pulled him back. "I can't see," he complained, and I lifted him to my hip while we looked over the old and new cities. There was a sheer drop down to the stones of the street.

He pointed to the gold in the distance and said, "That's the holy temple."

"That's the Dome of the Rock," I said.

His hand found the pewter dome of the Church of the Holy Sepulchre. "And there, that's the other holy temple!"

Two men hung back, talking to each other in low tones. The younger man wore a white shirt with pressed khakis; they both wore flip-flops on their feet. They followed us into the building. There wasn't much information in the exhibit, but there was a film, so we ducked into the dark, cool theatre and watched an animated short about Jerusalem that somehow managed to skip two thousand years of history, from the destruction of the Second Temple to the establishment of the state. I translated the Hebrew to Sam, whispering to him along with the narration. The men I had noticed sat behind us, and I could feel the heaviness of their disapproval.

The younger one leaned forward and said to me, "It wasn't really like that."

"I know," I whispered back, but it was too much for me to translate and critique at the same time.

The film concluded with a victory montage, swelling music, sunrise, a people finally in their homeland. The men left before the credits ran, and we headed down to the courtyard for ice cream. I thought of Jenna: would she have taken offence at the film, would she have been like the men sitting behind me, frustrated and mournful? But I knew the answer already. She would have assumed that the film was all lies, since that was her assumption about most of the world. She would have liked the tower, but would have complained about the stairs. She would have felt cheated at the lack of a gift shop.

We ended the day at the Western Wall. When you have always worshipped in the dark and cluttered interiors of synagogues it is strange to transition to a marble platform, an austere space exposed under the midday sun. There is a popular Israeli song about the Wall. The words are, "There are people with hearts of stone / and there are stones with hearts of men." I wondered what had happened to me; I had once found those lines beautiful and now I thought them obscene. Worshipping stones, wasn't that idolatry? Stones, places, nations. I tried to feel some of the old piety, but instead I looked around. The woman behind me wore a black headscarf that entirely covered her hair, a long black skirt, and a long-sleeved, high-necked maroon shirt. She was lightly moustached and sweating visibly and stood behind a man in a wheelchair who must have been her son. His arms were unusually short and bent at the elbows like wings, his face was slightly spastic, and his eyes were afraid. I wondered if she had come to pray for him.

Beyond me, women in long dresses and headscarves pressed their foreheads to the wall. Behind me, another group clustered around their cheap white plastic chairs and passed around pastry and small plastic cups of water, as if they were having a tea party. Beside me, another woman was barely visible, collapsed on her own lap so you could see just her headscarf and a bit of her skirt, her bags piled at her feet. It was very hot, and the platform seemed to magnify the heat. A woman in a sleeveless black dress, a lace shawl pulled across her shoulders for modesty, dialed her cellphone and said, "Yossi! Guess where I am? I'm at the Wall, Yossi, at the Wall. Pray, Yossi, pray!" She held the cellphone to the sweating stones.

The cracks of the wall overflowed with notes. I'd often wondered about what happened to them; they seemed like a cornucopia, endlessly replete. Simon told me they were swept up and burned at night. Obama had recently visited the Wall, and his note was stolen by a reporter and printed in the paper. "Protect my family," he wrote, "and guard me from pride and despair." It was so much the right thing to say that it made me wonder if he'd known it would be read.

I stood in front of the Wall with a pencil and my notebook. I didn't believe that the Wall was some kind of telegram to the divine, didn't think those were anything but pieces of paper, the motley scraps and wishes of a single day. But I was too nervous not to write. I might as well try to believe, like Pascal's Wager; I had nothing to lose. "Protect everyone," I scrawled quickly, "and please make me be happy." On the way home the boys played hide and seek among the Roman pillars. I wished I could believe in God again so I could have a God to protect them. Otherwise, I was far too vulnerable, with those children at the mercy of the vast and indifferent spinning world.

The next day, my mother's cousin Shira visited us

from Tel Aviv. Drinking tea on the cheap black leather couches, she lifted her penciled eyebrows dramatically when I told her we'd gone into the market.

"And why not have a nice Arab slip a knife right into your back," she trilled, in her high, accented English.

"It's fine," I said, "totally safe. And fine."

Her eyebrows rose even higher. "You do what you want," she said, in a tone that implied that what I wanted would always be precisely the wrong thing to do. "Why listen to an old lady like me?"

12.

And what would Shira have thought of Jenna? I knew better than to tell her where I planned to go the next day.

When Jenna told me that she had to go to the police station, I offered to accompany her. I thought I might be useful—I spoke Hebrew and she didn't, and besides, I was afraid of what would happen if she went without a translator, or a witness. She wasn't worried; she just wanted company. She treated it like it would be a morning out, while I had nightmares for three days running.

Jenna was going to the police station to complain about a series of obscene phone calls that she had received at her house. It was a man's voice, and she was pretty sure he knew her. She said that from his accent she could tell he was from her family. He said filthy things, but she refused to say what they were—"You know," she said, looking away, brushing her hands on her shirt as if she was brushing off dirt. He called late at night, often two or three times, and always while Aden was out, so it seemed he had some way of knowing she was alone. The calls were starting to scare her.

Jenna's family extended across Shuafat and lived in both the refugee camp and the houses around it. Low-lifes, mostly, she said. Drug addicts, terrorists, hicks. It surprised me when she spoke of her family that way.

They had a particular accent when they spoke Arabic, and it was that accent, the dips and intonations of her childhood, which she recognized in the whispered obscenities in the phone calls that came late at night. "Why would someone from your family hassle you like that?" I said, and she said, "That's just what they're like. You don't know them." But I had the feeling that there was something she wasn't telling me.

We went to the police straight from the daycare. Noor wouldn't sit in a car seat. Instead she wandered around and tried to clamber over the back of the driver's seat and onto her mother's lap.

"Jenna," I said, "do you want me to buckle Noor in?"

"No," Jenna said. "I tried that. She'll just cry."

"I can't believe you can drive around here without buckling your kid in," I said. "In America, you'd get arrested."

"I would never get a ticket for that," Jenna said. "It's different here. Everyone does it." In America, Britney Spears had just been caught by paparazzi, driving with her young son in the front, unbuckled and without a car seat. The media had been outraged, as they were at all displays of maternal negligence, which got so much more attention than bad fathers, since no one expected any better from them.

Noor grabbed a can of Red Bull from the cup holder next to the driver's seat and started to swig it like a truck driver. She picked up her mother's purse and began to cry when she couldn't unzip it. Jenna reached back without looking and grabbed the purse back, and Noor started to cry louder but without much fervour, all smoke and no heat. "No, Noor!" Jenna said loudly, and then in a lower tone to me, "Is that the police station?" She made a sloppy left turn across oncoming traffic into the lot. The sign said, "Mishmar Hagvul."

"Jenna, this is border patrol," I said. "This isn't what we want."

Border patrol looked like a parking lot. There was a woman in a glass booth, a long, low building, and an expanse of asphalt. Guards dressed in dark green paced back and forth. I was sure that they would throw us out of the country. The line between permitted and forbidden, between welcome and exiled, was so faint. I couldn't believe that Jenna trusted the border guards more than I did.

"They'll tell us how to get to the police station," she said, and pulled up by the soldier who had begun to walk towards us. The soldier was a woman; her small frame seemed weighed down by her security vest and by the Uzi hanging from her hip. Jenna slid open the window and Noor grinned toothlessly at the soldier.

That baby was totally indiscriminate, would smile at anyone.

"We're looking for the police station," Jenna said, and I waited for us all to be arrested for illegal immigration, or at the very least, for driving without our seat belts. Though we had done nothing, I was certain we were guilty.

"What a sweetie!" the soldier said, smiling at Noor. She gestured back to the road, "Take a right on Route 1."

I felt sick. Noor finished the Red Bull and threw the can between the seats.

"I told you they wouldn't care," Jenna said. "Now I remember where the station is."

As we drove out of the city centre Noor started crying again, and Jenna pulled her between the seats and onto her lap as she drove, releasing a small brown breast. Noor settled into the snuffling, satisfied sounds of nursing. Jenna smoked, drove, and nursed. Smoking punctuated Jenna's life; she seemed to exist in the interstices between cigarettes, the way that people had begun to live in the moments between checking their email. Smoking kept her thin and nervous, her long, nicotine-stained fingers trembling at the wheel.

Spending time with Jenna made me realize that back home, none of my friends smoked anymore. And all of my friends, every one of them, would have been appalled at Jenna's behaviour. When they became parents they instantly turned into puritans. The wilder they had been, the stricter they now were. They quit smoking, quit drinking; not only would they not smoke in front of their children, if a man was smoking on the street they would glare at him as if he was a war criminal. They started buying organic food, used water filters on their taps and air filters in their homes, since North American air and water were no longer clean enough for them. They subjected their houses to inquisitions in which every dangerous object was unearthed and expunged; one friend had even told another to get rid of her houseplants.

I tried to imagine their reaction to Jenna, the way Jenna let her children play with her cigarettes, or ride in the car unbuckled. It was a little like safety was a myth she didn't believe in. When I couldn't help myself, and some word of warning bubbled out of my mouth, she would look at me as if I was childishly naive, as if I had no understanding of the difference between real and false danger.

And I could understand that. For all of our careful parental pursuit of security, we could not keep our children safe. The organic baby food and the obsessive baby proofing had the quality of magical thinking. We might as well have hung charms against the evil eye on their doors, or tied red strings around their chubby wrists. I knew a child who'd swelled and sickened and died in a year, despite all efforts to save her. I knew a girl whose blood had decided she was a stranger. I lived in denial of something that Jenna seemed to understand: motherhood was a surrendering of control.

I looked out the window. We were passing the security wall, driving by a stretch that bordered right on the city. Young men with white T-shirts and blank gazes leaned against it, alone or in groups. They seemed like they had nowhere to go. They stared through us without expression, barely seeming to notice us, but as we passed them a rock skipped off the trunk like a pebble on the skin of a lake.

"They think I'm Jewish," Jenna said. "Losers. If Aden was here, he'd show them." Her eyes were distracted, scanning the road. "If they scratched the car, I'm going to go back there and run them over. We're here."

We pulled into a small white building next to a strip mall. I trailed behind Jenna, Noor on her hip. I had expected metal detectors, dramatic security, but there was only a secretary behind a messy desk, and a few bored people sitting on brown plastic chairs in the foyer.

"I have a complaint to file," Jenna said.

"Over there," the secretary said, without looking up from her newspaper. There was another waiting room, a smaller one, and a couple of offices with half-opened doors. The entire building had the sleepy aura of a provincial office on a Friday afternoon. Noor wandered the hallway, leaning on the plastic chairs for balance. After a while, a pudgy, walleyed man opened a door and motioned for us to come in. He wore a crocheted *kippa* on his balding head. It clung to a hank of hair at the side of his head and threatened to slip off entirely. His drifting eye made it difficult to see where he was looking. To my surprise, he spoke to us in English.

He beckoned us inside his office and motioned for us to sit down. My chair was a little bit broken, and I sat tentatively, afraid to settle my weight. He flipped open a pad of paper and held a pen cocked in his hand, but he didn't write anything down as he started to ask questions.

"And what is your name?"

"Jenna. Jenna al-Masri."

"And where do you live?"

"In Shuafat."

"In the camp?"

"No. I have a house."

"And this is?"

"This is my friend from Canada."

"And how do you know English?"

"I'm from Louisiana. I'm American."

"So what brings you to Shuafat?"

I looked around the room but there wasn't much, just a grey metal bookcase, a few filing cabinets, a window looking out onto the parking lot. I felt stupid. Because they were speaking English there was no reason for me to be in the office. And in his focus on her I had disappeared. Even his drifting eye seemed a little more focused, a little straighter. I wondered what it was like, to walk around the world that beautiful. She seemed to take it as her due.

The officer listened to her story, then leaned back in his seat. His shirt strained at the buttons, and he stuck his thumbs into his belt loops. It couldn't be easy to be a police officer, to sit all day and take complaints from people who didn't trust you. I wondered if he had someone to go home to at night, to laugh with about the girl who came in that day to complain about dirty phone calls.

"As your friend," he said, "I can tell you honestly, we can't do much about it. We get thousands of complaints. Do you think you are the only one to get calls like this? And worse, much worse. The truth is, you're lucky if this is all you have to complain about. It's too expensive to sit on your phone and wait for him to call. I doubt he's watching your house, though of course, you should call us if you see him. My advice for now is to change your number."

He leaned forward now, more intimately, as if they really were friends.

"You know, you live in a very traditional area. You are open-minded, men see you and how you dress, you dress nice, you are pretty, no head covering, they see the nose ring, they think that you are available." He looked at her intently. "They think you are a *sharmuta*, a whore. I'm just explaining to you how it is."

Jenna half-rose in her seat, clutching Noor to her chest.

"You see how it is," he said, shrugging his shoulders. "I'm just telling you how it is." He held the door for us as we left. "Come again if you have another problem."

In the lot Jenna said, "I knew they wouldn't do anything. Did you hear him call me a *sharmuta*?" I had never seen her so angry.

"I don't think he was calling you a *sharmuta*," I said, "I think he was saying that other people might mistake you for a *sharmuta*."

She shook her head, lips tight. She was right; I had sensed it too, without wanting to name it. He was glad to call her a *sharmuta*, looking at her breasts under her T-shirt with his two uneven eyes, pretending a courtesy that he did not feel.

"Why don't you change your number?" I said, getting into the car.

She looked at me as if I was an idiot. "Because I don't want Aden to know."

"Why not?"

"He'll kill him if he can find him. Or he'll kill me."

enna and I had decided to swap lessons: I was going to help her learn Hebrew, and she was going to help me with my Arabic. She had a primer in Hebrew transliterated into Arabic, and I had a Hebrew transliteration of Arabic; neither of us could read the other's language. But these lessons were colloquial and casual. She'd tutor me in what to say to the young assholes who hung around making catcalls near the walls of the Old City: "*inran tarbetac*," which meant "Damn your manners," as in, "Your mother didn't teach you to behave right." Or "*wachad uti*," which meant, "You low one, you low-class person." Mostly she was teaching me how to curse.

But I needed more formal lessons. I decided to sign up for a class in Palestinian Arabic, and I found a friend to take the class with me. The class was held one evening a week at the bilingual school in Beit Tsafafa. The school was called Yad V'yad, which meant "hand in hand." It was one of only a few bilingual schools in the entire country. The class was mostly meant for parents in the school so that they could try to keep up with their children's homework, but was also open to the public. It was oddly difficult to find beginner Arabic classes in Jerusalem; Al-Quds had a campus in the Old City somewhere, but I'd felt intimidated while trying to track it down one day among the twisting alleyways and the heavy, ornamented, and unnumbered closed doors of the Arab Quarter.

On the first day, Shayna and I shared a taxi to the empty school. Her son was in class with Gabe. Like me, she had spent a year after high school in Israel. At eighteen, I hesitated and left Israel; Shayna had leapt. Now this was her home.

We found the teacher in front of the locked door, wrestling with a keychain. The deserted school felt illicit by night. It was strange to walk down the empty corridors and flick the switch to illuminate the wide and vacant stairway, just for us.

Once in the classroom, we pulled our desks into a semicircle and learned how to introduce ourselves. There were about seven students in the room. Our teacher's name was Salem. He stood at the front, dressed like Mr. Rogers in his pressed slacks, tidy sweater, and the authority of his greying sideburns. Because I had once loved Mr. Rogers, I loved him immediately. I felt sorry for him, facing a desultory class of adult students late in the evening. We lacked seriousness. He was distinguished and a little weary and so obviously too good for us. He had us turn to one another and address our neighbours directly.

"My name is —. I live on — street. Pleased to meet you!"

"*Esmeee —. Ana sakne fi shaaree —. Sharafna!*"

The class was in Hebrew, and the textbook was transliterated into Hebrew. The family resemblance between the languages was startling; I'd been theoretically prepared for that but not prepared, I suppose, for how intimate the language would feel to me. The proximity of expression made it almost more confusing than a truly alien tongue. I kept slipping into Hebrew structures, cheating by borrowing Hebrew words I already knew and shifting the accent, making them more guttural, throatier. All wrong, of course. It was like when my son put on an exaggerated Inspector Clouseau accent and claimed he was speaking French.

The woman on my right sat with a straight back and a fallen face. She wore reading spectacles with a beaded cord that draped around her shoulders. Her lipstick had been applied with a tremulous hand. Later I found out that she was a volunteer for Machsom Watch, the human rights organization that monitored the checkpoints, and was taking Arabic so she could better communicate with some of the people coming through. I asked if I could join her one morning, and she peered over her spectacles and said, "It will not make you feel good. It does not make me feel good, and I do not believe that anything has really changed, or if it has changed it has changed only for the worse. It does not make me feel good, but I have been doing it for such a long time that I no longer know how to stop."

I didn't know what to say to that. I hadn't been expecting such a frank answer. I kept intending to join her anyway, but somehow, all year long, I never went.

"*Sharafna*," I said, the day I first met her, then turned to my right and introduced myself to an apple-cheeked New Zealander. "*Sharafna*." "Nice to meet you."

At the end of the room, two boys sat. They were college students, and ten years younger than anyone else. One of them was fascinatingly ugly: he had curly dark hair, fleshy lips, a long exaggerated nose, and pale jade-green eyes. They flushed with embarrassment as they introduced themselves to each other, and Salem leaned in to catch their exchange.

"*Sharafna!*" he said when they dropped the ritual end piece. "*sharafna!* How pleased we all are to meet each other. *Kul tamaam.*" The pleasantries were important. Salem said that if you didn't use them, you weren't just rude; you weren't even really speaking the language. He was trying to socialize us, and we needed it, desperately.

One of the boys, the green-eyed one, had grown up near Abu Tor and had a perfect accent, with breathy chs and glottal ayins. You used so much of your throat, it felt conspicuous. But of course I had to keep in mind that failing to pronounce those elongated vowels, those airy consonants, was far more blatant. It was hard to imagine myself a stranger in a language, though I was a stranger in all but one language. I thought of the many times I had made eye-blink judgments based on a thick accent or a careless sentence structure. And yet I willingly tumbled into Arabic, unashamed, the wrong sounds tripping off my tongue as lightly as if they were correct.

The only other man in the class was named Moshe.

He was pudgy and bearded, and wore a small crocheted *kippa*. He had served in the army for three years and was a week away from *miluim*. When we asked him why he was taking the class he said, "I want to learn how to say something in Arabic other than, 'Get out of the car,' and, 'Put your hands on the hood or I'll shoot.'"

Army soldiers were taught a little bit of Arabic; they called it "*machsomite*." "Checkpoint language." *Machsomite* was a language that consisted only of commands. "Open your bag. Take the car seat out of the car. Step outside. Hands up."

A friend of mine had served three years in the army. Later, while living in London, he'd taken an Arabic class to refine his language skills and increase his vocabulary. He didn't know why the teacher looked at him so coldly—he hadn't mentioned his army service to anyone—until one day she said, "Please, you need to stop addressing me in the imperative." He hadn't realized there was any other tense.

Soldiers often hitchhiked on the long bare stretches of road around the army bases. Hitchhiking was a relic of the early days of the state, when the roads were empty, and gas was dear.

"Say Pepsi," drivers would demand when they stopped to pick up young men, as a way of checking if they were Israeli, since "p" was a consonant that didn't exist in Arabic. It was a *shibboleth*, a way of exposing foreigners, after the story in Judges about the war between the Ephraimites and Gileadites. The Ephraimites were defeated, and the Gileadites blocked the crossing at the river Jordan. "Say *shibboleth*," they'd say when men came to ford the river, and if a man said "sibboleth" they killed him. Forty-two thousand were found that way, and each one drowned in the Jordan.

We were surrounded by *shibboleths*; they were everywhere.

Salem told us jokes in Yiddish. We drank tea and listened to him patiently repeat the same lessons over and over again. He brought herbs from his garden—something I'd never tasted before, a little bit like lemon and a little bit like mint—and we steeped them in hot water, adding large spoonfuls of sugar. The sugar was to keep us awake.

Our pace was very slow, and soon we lost half our students—the reservist with the short beard, the two boys who biked from Hebrew University. Only women were left in the class now. Me and my friend Shayna. Lynn from New Zealand, who was learning Arabic because she sometimes needed it for her work on a sexual assault hotline. And Bella, of course. She was the retiree I'd spoken to that first day, the volunteer for Machsom Watch. She came to pick us up for class sometimes, and we waited for her on the dark corner while the headlights streaked by. She was a nervous driver, and leaned forward towards the wheel. Bella was slow in class, but diligent. I was fast, but lazy.

Salem was painfully patient, but I thought he'd privately given up on us some time before. As the term went on, he told more stories and anecdotes in his fluid Hebrew in between our stilted efforts in Arabic. "Did you see the boy?" "Is your car broken?" "I am going to the airport." "I went to America on my vacation." "I do not speak Spanish."

I liked the many modes of greeting: "good morning," "bright morning," "rose morning," "jasmine morning." I liked it that when someone fed you, you "blessed their hands."

As well as a language teacher, Salem had been a tour guide in Jerusalem for twenty years. When he first took the course, there were very few Arab tour guides; he studied hard, said he knew the subject cold, but when he went to the tourism ministry to check his results he was told he'd failed the exam. He asked to see his test, and they wouldn't show it to him. He took the test three times, and failed again and again. The third time, a secretary took pity on him and showed him his exam. He had a near-perfect score. He confronted her supervisor, and she said there must have been a mistake, and sullenly, reluctantly granted him his license.

He rarely spoke about himself. We knew he had a wife, a home, two daughters, apricot trees that bloomed in season. But this story about the tourism ministry was the most intimate thing he had ever confided in us. We all sat in silence. What was there to say?

He was disappointed in us. We didn't do our homework, stalled when he asked us questions, were weeks behind where we should have been in the textbook. Next week, we would say. Next week we'll catch up. Next week we'll be prepared. "*Bukra fil mishmish*," he said, and we asked him what he meant. "It means, 'Tomorrow, in apricot season,' " he said.

"How shall I explain? It means, 'It's never going to happen.' Because apricot season is so short, it's over almost before it's even begun. So if someone says they're going to pay you back, for example, you might say, '*Bukra fil mishmish,*' meaning, 'You're never going to do it.' " We said no, no, we meant it. We were going to do it. We would be better the next time.

I tried to speak Arabic in the market. It took about five minutes to get to the limits of my conversational ability. I could buy things: when I didn't know the names, I pointed like a two-year-old and said, "That, please." The possessive was built into the names of objects; "my car," "my house," "my child," each a single word. I was trying to be wary of drawing sociological cues from the rules of the language, but if I had, it would have been something like this: Everything in this culture belongs to somebody. There are no objects without ownership.

When I came home after Arabic class, Simon was usually already asleep, or pretending to be asleep. He didn't ask me about my day; I didn't ask him about his work. Sometimes I thought it might be less lonely to be, in fact, alone.

14.

All my life, I had been told I belonged to Israel. But the reverse was also implied: I belonged to Israel because Israel belonged to me. Throughout my childhood, Israel was the lost dream and the true homeland. We studied modern Hebrew, we sang the Israeli anthem at camp and school events, that song about a cry in the heart. We prayed to the east. We sent money to Israel, cheques in paper envelopes that would be planted there in the form of trees and forests, like a reverse metamorphosis, the paper turning back into bark.

I bought it all. In my youth I went back again and again. At camp I sang Hebrew words to old Polish melodies under Adirondack stars. I would return to Israel, I would complete the *aliya* that my parents had aborted, I would raise my own family there. I had the kind of clarity about it that only belonged to the reckless imaginings of my youth, when my future was sharp-edged and shadowless.

Back then, I could have never met Jenna. I could never have even imagined Jenna, or anyone like Jenna. Her Jerusalem was a place I had never been and it did not fit, it did not fit at all, with the homeland of my childhood.

I was not a child anymore.

"Come over after we drop off the kids," Jenna said. "We'll have some breakfast, and I'll show you the orchard near my house—in Arabic you call it the 'kerem.' That's where we're building our new house. There's a little bungalow there now, but we have big plans—three stories, a garage."

Pigeons were clustering around a handful of crumbs on the marble stairs outside, their heads vanished into a bustle of backside and wing, and Noor charged at them to watch them scatter. Jenna looked tired, smoked nervously, her hand trembling.

"The kids all came into bed with me last night," she said. "I stayed up late, waiting for Aden. I made him a special supper and everything, maqluba—have you ever had it? —eggplant and meat and rice, like his mother makes it. I can tell you, it's a pain in the ass to cook. He didn't get home until eleven, and then when we finally sat down to eat his cellphone rang, it's his friend, asking him to come out, and he can't never say no to his friends, they pressure him. So he just left, and then I guess he slept in the house we have in the kerem. When he's not in bed all the kids come into bed with me. When I woke up, Noor was lying right across the bed like this, and Zac was kicking my ribs, and pulling Aisha's hair, and Aisha was crying, I swear these kids are going to kill me."

For all that her driving terrified me—Noor climbing in and out of the front seat, a book balanced on the steering wheel—Jenna was confident in the car. We drove north, past the Old City walls, and along the hills I could glimpse the half-finished grey mass of the wall, the cranes and diggers miniaturized like toy trucks in the distance.

"I know some people who live right there," Jenna said, gesturing towards the houses that huddled near the wall. "They were so happy when they built the wall. Their property values went up, just like that." She snapped her fingers. "Anyway, they don't like the people on the other side. A lot of criminals, you know, a lot of thieving. But they just climb over now, anyway. Like those kids—but at least, you know, their prices are better."

She gestured at the children running towards the car window. We had stopped at an intersection, and some Palestinian children ran up to us, clutching cigarettes and packets of gum. I couldn't imagine how they came over that steep, intransigent wall. Big-eyed and skinny, like my sons, they ran through traffic as if it was an obstacle course. Jenna rolled down the window, handed them a bill, and took a few packs of cigarettes with her long, pale fingers. Noor reached into her open purse and grabbed a fistful of bills, reached for the window too. Jenna caught her chubby fist, twisted the money back.

"Did you see that? Did you see that? She likes to throw money out the window, I mean, literally. She threw out a hundred shekels yesterday! Aden says I'm always losing money, but I swear it's not my fault." We pulled into the parking lot of a strip mall—white, shiny, new. "This is where I go to shop," Jenna said, "and my bank is here too.

It's more high class than the places in my neighbourhood."

It didn't look high class. It looked like a strip mall. Everyone in the bank was speaking Hebrew. Jenna stood in line, handed the teller a wad of cash, Noor on her hip.

Her phone rang, and she picked it up.

"Yes, yes, I'm there right now." She closed the phone. "He's driving me crazy," she said. "He doesn't trust me."

She pulled up again to buy long, narrow loops of bread from a street stand, and then drove up the hill to her house. The road was gouged in the centre for the tramline that had been under construction for the last three years. The street signs had changed from Hebrew to Arabic, and the buildings were lower and more spread out. On Jenna's corner there was an abandoned dirt lot strewn with garbage: abandoned television sets, plastic bags, broken bicycles.

"Disgusting," Jenna said. "The people here love to throw their garbage in the street."

She pulled up in front of a low bungalow. The house she rented had a large concrete patio, with an overhanging roof that had been half demolished. You could see the rebar protruding out of the concrete like broken bone. Beside the house was a pit and in the pit their neighbour's house was crushed and sunken like a shipwreck. I leaned over and saw the rusted carcass of an automobile in the rubble and plastic chairs upside down, their legs sticking up in the air like insects trapped on their backs.

"Two years it's been like that," Jenna said. "It's a pain in the ass. The children want to go play down there— they try to jump over the wall. It isn't our house, at least.

They started to break down this one, too, but then they stopped. I guess the landlord paid his taxes or talked them into it or something. He was supposed to fix the roof, but he doesn't do anything."

She unlocked the door, and we stepped into the cool shade of the house. Heavy curtains were drawn against the sun; the furniture was brocaded in shiny fabrics that reminded me of my grandmother's apartment in Brooklyn, when I was a child. On the wall was a massive picture of a boat in a gilded frame; when I came closer I could see that what I had mistaken for a kind of pointillism was actually a jigsaw puzzle, a reproduction of a Monet, broken up into tiny cardboard pieces and reassembled.

"My mother did that," she said, looking at me looking at the picture. "It's, like, a million pieces. We do those puzzles together. That was the last time she came to visit. And what was I going to do, break it apart after all that work?"

The house was smaller than I expected—there was one large room, kitchen and dining and living room at once, heavily furnished and dark, and then two bedrooms, both strewn with blankets, pillows, and toys. Jenna opened a closet to take out another basket of toys for Noor and had to push her hip against the door to wedge it back shut. She put spreads out on the counter—*labne*, hummus, salty fried eggplant. She made us sweet strong tea and smoked while she watched me eat.

"I'm never really hungry in the mornings," she said.

We heard the scratching of a key in the door, and a

woman let herself in. She was swathed in layers of skirts and shawls, and a scarf was draped around her face. She was broad, and her layers made her seem monumental, like a draped statue. She smiled at Noor, and gold glinted in the corners of her smile. Jenna got up and kissed her on the cheek. "This is my mother-in-law," she said. "Ummi, Hannah's studying Arabic. Say something to her in Arabic."

"Ismi Hannah," I said, stupidly.

She leaned on the counter, picked up a piece of eggplant with her fingers, and lowered it into her mouth. The eggplant was slick with oil.

"Hannah," She said. "Hannah—Jannah. Jannah—Hannah. Very nice." She laughed. In her voice, our names were almost the same. I had never noticed that strange propinquity.

She kept darting glances at me under lowered eyelids, as if she didn't want me to catch her watching me. When she saw I'd noticed she smiled at me again, tight-lipped this time.

"She really doesn't know any English," Jenna said. She said something to her mother-in-law, a stream of Arabic so fluid that I could only pick out a few words, like sticks rushing by in fast water—"son," and "friend," and "school."

"I told her that our kids go to the Y together," Jenna said, "but she knew that already. She likes to spy on me." I looked at her mother-in-law, worried that she'd heard, but she just smiled at me again, picking her teeth. Jenna noticed my empty plate and the tea that I had drunk to the bitter dregs.

"Shall we go to the *kerem*?"

Her mother-in-law followed us to the car, locking the door of the house ceremonially behind us. After the shade of the house the midday sun hurt. The cul-de-sac, with one house standing and the other buried in the pit, felt like the very end of the city, the end of the world; a dirt road led further into the hills. Jenna took a pair of sunglasses out of her purse; Noor grabbed them off her face, tried to perch them on her own small nose, cried when they slid off.

"She wants everything," Jenna said. I offered Jenna's mother-in-law the front passenger seat, and she and Jenna both shook their heads; we bumped up the hill and navigated two switchbacks and a gate. Jenna's mother-in-law got out of the car and slowly, fussily opened the latch. She stood back while Jenna swung the car around and backed in. "She isn't allowed to drive up here on her own anymore," Jenna said. "She can't handle it. She kept driving right into the gate."

"Why a gate?" I said. It had seemed more elaborate than anything this hillside could require: solid high unscalable bars, lights along the top like a prison. The other lots on the hillside were also enclosed, but for the most part with chain link fences, lower and less forbidding.

"People kept breaking in." Jenna said. "The first time Aden built a house here on our lot, they blew it up. He didn't want them to blow up this house too." She nodded at the low bungalow.

I said, "Why would someone blow up his house?"

"I know who it was," Jenna said.

Jenna's mother-in-law drew a broom, a mop, and a bucket out of the car, and headed to the bungalow. The exaggerated swivel of her hips and her broad back seemed somehow a rebuke. "She still cleans his house for him," Jenna said, "and he's thirty years old. Can't clean up after himself. And I refuse. Bad enough that he comes here and watches TV with his friends when he should be home with me. I'm not cleaning up after all those men. I told him that a long time ago. Anyway, all this is coming down when we build our new house. We're just waiting on the permits. Do you want to see?" She swung open the door. Her mother-in-law was polishing the counters with a rag and did not look up. A hallway kitchen, a bathroom, a room with a sofa and large television.

"It's bigger than our TV at home," Jenna said. "He sleeps out here sometimes, when it's too late to come home. I mean, you saw it, it takes five minutes, but in the dark you'll go right off the side of the mountain. No lights."

She held out a bag. "I brought us some fruit. Shall we go back outside? It depresses me in here." She called back to her mother-in-law over her shoulder, "I don't know why you'd want to stay in the dark on a beautiful day," and her mother-in-law, uncomprehending, flashed us her gold smile.

There were no lawn chairs, there was no outdoor furniture at all, so we sat on the ground. The fruit bag was filled with tiny sour-sweet yellow plums. The lot was large and built into the hillside, layered in terraces. Jenna stopped to finger the crisp dry petals of a rose on a bush, and the flower crumbled into dust. "I planted all these flowers, but he doesn't water them so they're all dead now." A funnel lined in plastic led to an empty pool. She followed my eyes and said, "He started to build a waterfall. He has a lot of ideas."

Noor grabbed a plum, and Jenna plucked it back, split it with a long fingernail, pulled out the stone, and gave back the fruit. Noor threw it away and reached for Jenna's fist, with that practiced, hiccupping cry. "Do you see her, she wants the pit?" Jenna drew back her arm and threw the plum pit, like the American softball player she had once been. Noor waddled towards the bushes to look for it.

"I told you she spies on me," Jenna said, nodding her head towards the bungalow. "She came over because she knew you were coming. She wants to see who I'm hanging out with. She doesn't usually wear the headscarf—she wore it for you. She's such a hypocrite. She lets herself in when I'm out and she looks around the house."

"Why does she have the key?" I said.

"I tried to take it away, but she cried to Aden, and she has him wrapped around her little finger. Anyway, let her look. I have nothing to hide. More than she can say."

"God, it's beautiful here," I said. "Who owns all this land? How long has this been in your family? Who owns the rest of it?"

The hillside was covered with fenced-off squares of

107

land. A few of the parcels had been cleared, but most of them were orchards of olive trees, so that the hillside resembled a chessboard in shades of green. Near the bottom, someone had built a three-story house, entirely tiled on the outside and slightly aslant, like a house in a fairy tale. In the distance, on a neighbouring hillside, a white stone apartment complex glittered in rectangles and cubes. An apartment in downtown Jerusalem, a small apartment, would cost hundreds of thousands of dollars. I had no way to calculate what this land was worth; it was beyond price, since those who owned it would never sell it, and those who wanted it would give anything to possess it.

Jenna shouted up to the scarfed figure in the house and her mother-in-law shouted back down. "She says two hundred years, maybe. And they belong to lots of different families, mostly related to us. They come pick the olives in season. My father's land is down that way. He hasn't been there for twelve years—he can't get a visa. He keeps applying every year, and every year they turn him down. We'll go visit it in a minute. But you can't get permission to build down there, near the bottom of the hill. This guy built a little shack, just to store his garden tools, and the army came and blew it up, said it was a security risk. They were worried he was going to hide something in there. And you see that"—she pointed at the glittering sugar cubes in the distance—"that's a Jewish settlement, and they don't want anyone building a house too close to it."

"These lots must be worth a fortune," I said, and she said, "Oh, they are. You'd be amazed at how much you can get for the olive oil."

We walked down the dirt road together. Jenna was awkward and unsteady in her high-heeled clogs, Noor on her hip again. "I wouldn't dare walk down here in the summer," she said. "Too hot. And there are snakes. They leap up and wrap themselves around your neck, like this"—she gestured at her collarbone. "I swear it."

One of the groves held a clearing with a plastic table, three chairs arranged around it, all facing west. "The men come in the evening," Jenna said. "They play cards and drink tea and watch the sunset."

"Only men?"

"Only men."

"Doesn't that bother you?"

She looked at me. "Why would I care? I don't play cards."

The sky was a deep aching blue, and the leaves of the olive trees glittered green and silver. It was quiet. Noor squirmed to be let down and ran ahead of us, looking over her shoulder and laughing as if she was getting away with something.

Two hundred years.

Jenna took a long contemplative drag of her cigarette and said, looking over the mountains, "You know, when the end of days comes, the blood is going to be up to here"—she swiped a hand across the jewelled denim of her calf.

Her father's fence was a less serious affair than her husband's. She reached over the top of the gate and unlatched it, and Noor stumbled inside. There were no chairs, no tables, not even a shed, just trees and rocks and the bare ground. The trunks of the olive trees looked like knotted muscles. I leaned my hand on one, and the bark was warm.

"I have to check on the land. My father asks me about it when he calls. I never come down here anymore—we used to come all the time when I was a kid, and have barbecues. I hated it."

"Hated it? Why?" The spot was lovely, paradisiacal, in the true sense, since "paradise" once meant "an orchard." There were thirty or forty trees, silver-green and regal. You could see straight down into the valley. The evenings must have been glorious.

"There was nothing to do. It was hot. Me and my cousins, we used to kill ants. That was all we had to entertain us. The red ones, they bite. They hide under the rocks. Look."

She kicked a large stone with her heel, twice, three times to dislodge it. Noor squatted down to watch the scurrying, miniature world. She reached out a chubby fist.

"No," Jenna said to Noor. "NO." And to me, "Look at her, she wants to eat them. We need to go or we'll be late."

She kicked the rock back over and covered the ants, restored their roof of shade.

Noor could not believe it. She wailed, scrabbled at the rock, trying to lift it back up with her fingers, crying for her lost world.

15.

At the *kerem*, my neck started to hurt, and for days after my visit the pain persisted and worsened. For years, my neck and shoulders had stored all the tension of my bad posture. My head stuck out several inches in front of my shoulders, as if I was always anticipating bad news. My shoulders slumped, and I spent all my time reading, which exaggerated both the curve of my neck and the hump in my back. I was so crooked that it felt crooked to pull myself straight.

When my father died, it suddenly became much worse. I developed a hacking cough that haunted me for months, and I couldn't turn my neck to either side. From then on, the pain had come and gone. I had started to think of it as a chronic condition. The worst of it was that it made me so aware of my body, which was most real to me when I was hurting. When I wasn't in pain I forgot about it, but when the pain came back it was all I really knew.

My osteopath was a parent at the school. Like everyone there, he was from somewhere else—Austria, someone said, but someone else said Switzerland, or Germany. He lived in a beautiful old stone house in a neighbourhood that had been abandoned in 1949 by wealthy Arab families who fled east when the city was cut in two. It was a beautiful, expensive area, the Ottoman houses graciously renovated, the streets lined with flowering trees. But I wondered about the ghosts.

A lemon tree grew in a pot by the door. The thin branches were bowed with the fresh, heavy fruit. I always wanted to pause there, by the lemons, to finger their smooth, bumpy flesh.

I would lie there on the treatment table, my shirt off. As he pushed and pulled at my limbs he asked me questions. How did I sit when I worked at the computer? How long since it started to hurt? Was it a burning pain or a stabbing pain? Did I believe in God? He showed me exercises to do, windmilling his long arms from his shoulders in demonstration, pushing my knees up to my chest and pressing them down in what my yoga teacher used to comically call "wind-relieving pose." He had the curly tight hair of a poodle in a colour neither blond nor brown nor grey, and dramatic, non-Jewish cheekbones. His age was indeterminable—somewhere between forty and sixty.

He told me that my back pain would vanish if I could believe in God again. He said that when I lost my father I also lost my faith and then had to carry that heaviness on my shoulders. All I had to do, he said, was ask God for forgiveness for my disbelief, and my pain would go away. He cradled my head in his hands and pulled back, as if it would pop off like a Lego head, and with it all of my old knots and tensions. When he put my head back on it would be on straight.

He leaned over, and I could see his grey teeth, could smell the mouthwash-clean of his breath. "You need to ask God to forgive you, because he loves you as you are."

He told me to eat breakfast, to try swimming, to walk over to the Old City whenever I had the time and to feel the sacredness of the stones. Try lemon with ginger, sit like this at the computer, start to pray again. He left the room as I put my shirt back on, though that seemed an odd modesty on both of our parts, and then he would stand by the door, arms loose at his sides, and duck his head at me as I left. He had the kind of face that always leaves you aware of the bone under the flesh, that plush, wrapped skull.

I did walk up to the Old City, sometimes, in the dreamlike intervals when the boys were both in school, when my time seemed to be briefly my own. There was a man who always sat near the entrance to Jaffa Gate, on a folding chair under an awning. He wore traditional Palestinian robes, and his hair was perfectly white, but his face was young and walnut brown. He called himself a poet of peace, and insisted I come up and have tea in his room over the square. It was spare: a single red rug, a wooden desk, a narrow bed, two rickety chairs. The tea was made from herbs he grew on his balcony, and he gave me a handful of them and told me they were very calming, good for the nervous system. He left the door open to the staircase as if to reassure me. He had photocopies of his one long poem, translated into English, French, and Spanish. He said he'd given copies to people who lived all over the world. He read it to me out loud; it didn't rhyme, though there was a generous use of repetition and refrain, birds flying free and children laughing in the street and finally the sons of Abraham and Moses, that sort of thing. Sunsets, rainbows. He gave me a copy in a manila envelope, along with a business card that had his name and title—"Poet of peace." I felt ambivalent about throwing it out, as if it was peace and poetry themselves that I was in danger of discarding. I found the envelope wedged behind the bookcase a few months later.

A beautiful park across the street from the daycare faced the walls of the Old City. A stretch of the park dipped below the level of the street. The green lawns and benches were mostly deserted during the day. I sat there one day with my notebook, trying to work on my dissertation, which felt a little like swimming in mud. A boy started hovering around me like a hummingbird—that same nervous energy, dips and feints towards the spot where I sat. He looked about seventeen years old, though I was old enough now that I had become bad at guessing ages.

"What are you doing?" he said finally. He spoke to me in careful, accented English.

"Writing," I said, and looked back down at my book.

He wore that uniform of youth in the developing world—the acid wash, the white T-shirt, the semi-mullet. He even wore a bleached jean jacket, the collar turned up.

"Where are you from?" he asked, and I said, "America." The blankness of my replies didn't dissuade him, though he seemed to have trouble coming up with the next question.

"But where do you live," he said.

I said, "I live here."

"Where?" he asked quickly, and I gestured back with my arm and said, "That way. And you?"

He looked panicked for a minute, and pointed towards Jaffa Gate.

"In the Old City?" I said.

He nodded, and then said in a breath, "Are you a Jew?"

"Yes," I said, taken aback. "Are you?"

He looked at me, glanced back towards the Old City.

"Yes," he said.

We both knew he was lying. "I have to go now," I said, standing up, and he looked startled but more relieved than disappointed. I could feel his eyes in my back as I walked away.

I couldn't figure out why he had lied to me. He couldn't have expected me to believe him. I was chronically, compulsively truthful; I didn't have the fortitude for lying. Once I had bumped into Jenna and Aden on the steps of the daycare. They were going on a date; their babysitter had come with them to take the children. When Zac and Aisha wept and clung they said, "We're going to a doctor. We're going to get a shot." Jenna had mimed the plunging of the needle, right into her ass. I'd asked her about it, and she'd looked at me in wonder. "We always say we're getting a shot when we need to get away from them," she said. "They hate shots. It works every time." "But don't you feel bad, lying to them?" I said, and she said, "How do you get anything done without lying to your children?"

I told Shayna about the incident in the park when we met the next day. "You should watch out," she said. "You think you can talk to anybody in this city. But that's naive. You have children to think about—you can't just be wandering around, talking to strange men. It's dangerous. How does Simon feel about it, anyway?"

"I don't think it's any of his business," I said quickly. "I'm not doing anything wrong." Even though I had spoken the truth, it felt a little like a lie.

Shayna was by far the most serious student in our Arabic class. She had two older children and a new baby and needed the intellectual stimulation.

"I just want to think about something else," she said, "not school lunches and what to make for dinner and when to clean the house. Did you know I was my high school valedictorian?"

We were having breakfast in Baka, at a cafe with old mosaic floors and cracked stained-glass windows and notoriously unfriendly staff, beautiful young women with long, haughty necks who wore slim black aprons. Breakfast was the best meal to eat out in Jerusalem. They brought a mezze of tiny plates; smoked salmon with dill, tiny moist cubes of feta, homemade apricot jam with thick chunks of fruit, baby tomatoes with fresh basil and wet white slices of mozzarella, a dark salad of shredded greens mixed with toasted walnuts, sour *labne* and honeyed dates, a basket of hot bread, an omelette cooked to order, a cappuccino dark and wakeful under a coverlet of foam, a jewel-like narrow glass of grapefruit juice. Shayna sighed happily as she gazed at her plate, and shivered a little bit in anticipation.

"Isn't it beautiful?"

Outside, the day was grey, but the glass threw coloured lozenges onto the floor and warmed the skies. The cold juice clattered against the top of my head as I drank it in a single gulp.

"I'll get breakfast," I said, and she said, "You will not."

"How are things with Elijah?" I said.

Her husband was looking for a job. Shayna's face showed no good news.

"Mmmm." She looked at the scattered, shifting light drops on the floor. "OK, I guess. Did you know he had an interview at the Ministry of Defence?"

"How did that go?" I said.

"Strange. They have a complex in Tel Aviv. It's a fortified bunker, but it's massive—they lead you underground, and then through a maze of hallways. He said there were two people at the interview, but only one of them asked questions. The other one just leaned on the side of the desk and stared at him. It was like some kind of mental kung fu. He thought they were trying to psych him out. He was pretty nervous."

"So what did they ask him?"

"He said they wanted to know how he would build a plane that was as light as possible, and could go as fast as possible. They gave him a number, and he looked it up when he got home—it was roughly the distance to Iran. He asked them about the weight of the pilot and they said, 'No, there's no pilot.' He said that he started to calculate the weight of the fuel, the drag on the plane, and then he said, 'Wait a minute, what about the weight of the landing gear?' 'No landing gear,' they said."

"What kind of plane doesn't need landing gear?" I said.

"Exactly. Then they took him to a small cubicle, and they gave him a pencil and a piece of paper and they told him to start writing a personal history. 'Anything compromising,' they said. 'If you've had an affair or you've ever been involved with any kind of radical politics, and every time you've taken drugs, any drugs. If you're not sure whether or not to include it, write it down. We know anyway.' Anyway, it's a good thing they asked him and not his brother, who's a total pothead. He said it was crazy."

"Does he want the job?" I said.

Shayna shrugged. "He wants a job. God knows this isn't what he trained for. He wanted to do green energy, but that whole industry collapsed six months after we got here. And do you know what the worst of it is? Weapons are a for-profit branch of the military. They sell the stuff."

She had stirred all the foam out of her cappuccino. She picked it up, took a sip and made a face. "It got cold," she said. "Anyway, enough about me. How's that girl?"

"Who?" I said.

"The one you're always talking about from the day-care. The Palestinian girl. What's her name? Anna."

"Jenna," I said. "I don't talk about her that much."

"Right," she said, and leaned in and lowered her voice. Beside us, a table over, was a group of women as raucous as crows and all dressed in black. Israelis took up so much space.

"You know, you wouldn't be friends with her at all if she wasn't Palestinian. You're nothing alike."

"That's not true," I said. "I like her. She's interesting."

"That's exactly what I mean," Shayna said. "*Interesting*. As if she's a science experiment. I'm sorry, that's not a friendship." She gave me a stare. "That's *anthropology*." She collapsed back in her seat. She looked at her watch. "I've got to go," she said. "The babysitter is leaving soon."

She left some money on the table. I scooped it up and handed it back to her.

"Fine," she said, a little angrily, "but I'll get it next time."

As she walked down the street I noticed that she led with her head, squinting and always tilting a little forward, as if she was at once leaning into the future and flinching in anticipation of it.

I was frustrated all afternoon, and I couldn't figure out why. Everything rubbed me raw. The streets looked dirty, and the traffic was even louder than usual, the people ruder, the day more wasted. I tried to shake it off, like a horse shakes off flies, but the feeling persisted. It was like a stain, this off-colour feeling, and everything felt desolate though nothing had changed.

When Simon got home, I asked him, "Do you think my friendship with Jenna is anthropological?"

"I don't know what that means," he said, but then he softened. "No. I think you're friends with her because you like her. And part of liking someone is being curious about them. I don't think there's anything wrong with that. Anyway, you like women like Jenna. You've always had friends like that."

"What do you mean?" I said.

"You know. Women with drama."

"No," I said. "I hate drama."

"You hate having drama. But you like people with drama." Then he started listing old friends and former friends until I begged him to stop. Sometimes I forgot how well he knew me. I couldn't fool him, and I couldn't fool myself when I talked to him, he had known me for too long. I had honestly forgotten about Lila, Andrea, Cindy—the various women I befriended right around the times they blew up their lives.

That week Bella couldn't pick us up, so I shared a taxi with Shayna. We both forgot to take the address, and after circling in the taxi for a few minutes we decided to have the driver drop us off in the general vicinity of the school. It was a mixed Muslim and Jewish neighbourhood, one of very few in Jerusalem. We saw a lighted courtyard and heard snatches of conversation and song. Inside the courtyard was a group of teenage boys, and they stopped talking when I leaned over.

"Where is Yad V'yad?" I asked, and one of them said, "Over there." He gestured with his hand, but the others stared at us in sullen silence. As we walked away, we heard laughter, and a song rising to follow us. I couldn't quite hear it, but Shayna gripped my arm and pulled me forward. "Just keep going," she said. About half a block away, the words came into focus, "*Maaaa-vet l'aravim*," "Death to Arabs." He chanted in a traditional tune, the way you would chant a line of the Torah, and he had a pure voice, a cantor's voice. I pulled back and Shayna gripped my arm tighter.

"It isn't going to help anything," she said.

Ahead of us was the school, lit up in the dark like a spaceship. A modernist architect had been commissioned to build this low, swooping structure in the middle of the green; there were bridges to signify the bridges that would be built among communities, large open windows to let in light and air. But it didn't fit with the modest stone row houses of the neighbourhood. We had been just a block away, but we had needed to turn the corner to see the building, glowing and silent and almost empty.

I was furious. How could everyone pretend that living like this was normal? I remembered once waiting on the platform of the subway in New York, on a foul August city day. The train was late and the platform was hazy—a fug of heat and sweat and foul temper. I kept thinking I could see rats in the shadows of the rails, and whether

I could see them or not I knew that the rats were down there. A skinny black man was whooping and gesticulating by one of the pillars. He lifted one leg like a crane, and then kicked into the air. He twisted from the waist, like he was wringing himself out, and let out a series of staccato grunts. Everyone was pretending not to look at him while tracking him warily, both out of curiosity and in an attempt to preserve their own safety, in case his performance suddenly turned more aggressive and violent. An invisible *cordon sanitaire* surrounded him, maybe two body lengths long on each side, as if everyone had together decided exactly how much space to keep between themselves and whatever madness he was carrying. Suddenly, he stopped his display or his calisthenics or whatever it was that he was doing, and stood still and looked straight at me. His clothing had all faded to the same dead shade of dull black.

"Y'all just pretending you don't want to jump out of your own skin," he said. His eyes were coals. "Y'all just like me, don't think you ain't."

He raised his arms again, elbows chest high, and started the twisting movements, and this time it looked almost like a private exorcism, and the train pulled into the station and everyone but him got on it.

16.

Though we had been in Jerusalem for three months, we barely knew any Israelis. It was too easy to join the community of immigrants and to float along the surface of the city. There were so many of us, especially in Jerusalem. In the streets I heard English and French; at the beach, French and Russian. Besides, the Israelis were all so busy, often working two jobs, trying to keep up in a country with low wages and an ever-rising cost of living. The Israel I remembered from my youth was austere and isolated. There weren't many imported products on the shelves, and most people lived modestly. Even the toilet paper was rough and poor. But the new Israel was hectic with acquisition, the stores overflowing with the same cornucopia of crap that I could get back home. Everyone complained about it, but nobody really wanted to go back to the old days.

Leah was one of the few Israeli mothers in the daycare. She intimidated me, though I really didn't know her well. When I first met her, I thought that perhaps she was one of the teachers. She projected authority. The first time she ever spoke to me she ordered me to give her my telephone number and my email, before she'd even introduced herself or asked my name. She was Class Mother, though I wasn't sure how real the position was, or if it carried with it the power she seemed to assume, of corralling the parents and telling them all how to behave.

The first time we arrived at the daycare, Leah had been sitting in a chair in front of the door, taking names and email addresses. By our second week she had put us on a rotation, helping the teachers at recess. During our third week she had told us each exactly what to bring for the holiday celebration. She should have been a general. Her talents were wasted on us.

Several months later Simon asked, "Do the classes even *have* class mothers?" "That didn't even occur to me," I said. "I don't know." Perhaps it was a fiction, like the time later that year when she told us that her brother had the ear of the Minister of Defence and would help implement our suggestions for ending the war. But equally, it might have been true.

When she told me that our sons were going to have a play date, it felt like an order.

"We will take you to our house," she said. "I have an extra car seat. They will eat an egg and then they will play. We will drive you home at four o'clock."

If the weather was fine, we might go to the park. I wasn't sure what to say, so I acquiesced. It seemed rude to do anything else in the face of her certainty.

She had large tragic dark eyes, heavily and inexpertly lined, and a face that might have looked soft without

124

makeup but with makeup looked harsh. And old: I wasn't sure how old she was, I just knew that she seemed an adult in a way that I was not, the weight of the world heavy on her rounded shoulders. She was tall and also heavy in an exaggerated, womanly fashion—pouched eyes and cheeks, full chest and hips. She wore tight clothes a size or two too small; her black pants cut in at the hip, and her majestic bosom spilled out of her jewel-coloured V-necked tops.

Her son was four years old and was her second child, from a second marriage; her first son was seventeen and lived with her first husband. She was separated from her second husband, and they were currently going through a slow, acrimonious divorce. Her son had a huge, moony smile, a big head, and a skinny, tiny body. In many ways, he seemed her opposite: timid, pale, slight. When I first met him I thought perhaps he was a little delayed—he had that slight epicanthic slant to his eyes, that broad head too heavy for his body, a goofy undirected smile. I saw his mirror when his father dropped him off one day, a rooster of a man with a large bald head and a barnyard strut.

She said to me once, "Tal's father is a bad person, but he is a genius and also a genius in bed."

Her voice was deep and full, and her English sounded gruff. Her Hebrew was beautiful and resonant, though I only caught every other sentence. Leah's aggressiveness and Tal's shyness formed a sharp contrast: she was the hawk and he was the white mouse.

Our sons rarely played together. At that point, my son had formed a little clique with the other English speakers in the class—embassy brats, UN kids, interracial internationalists. When the class ended at one in the afternoon and they spilled out onto the lawn in front of the daycare, they looked like an old Benetton ad. But Leah had decreed that our sons would have a play date, and in a way I admired that she was looking out for Tal; he was too timid to make friends on his own, and often seemed to play in the corners of the room, ensconced inside imaginary worlds.

After school that day, Leah was waiting for us and took us to her car, parked in the lot behind the YMCA. It was held together by rust and duct tape, and the two car seats in the back looked like they might date from the early eighties. The car smelled like cigarette smoke and sour milk. The back seat was littered with candy wrappers, plastic bags, old toys; in the front the dashboard was covered with a thick film of dust.

Her son and my son were buckled in—I couldn't manage the unfamiliar clasp, and with a snort she leaned over me and did it, her hot breath on my neck—and they babbled to each other in their respective languages, perfectly happy, mutually uncomprehending. Leah put the key in the ignition and said, "I hope that this time the car will start." There was a low rattle as the car pulled out, accompanied by lights on the dashboard that she seemed to ignore.

She said, "This car is so old, only the Arabs know how to fix it. I take it to East Jerusalem. A Jewish would not know what to do with it. They would say, 'Throw it in the garbage,' but I have no money to buy a new one."

We turned onto Gaza Street, where the traffic was barely moving.

She announced, "Today, I am very upset. This morning his father sent me a letter saying he will pay me no more money. So what will I do? I have looked for a job, but I tell them, 'I have a child, I will not work overtime, there are only certain hours I am willing to do,' so who will hire me?" She jerked her head towards the back seat, and lowered her voice to a pitch that anyone else would have considered loud.

"He doesn't want to pay me anymore. I have to go to court again. I was on the phone with my lawyer all morning. I am sorry, when we get to my house I need to make some more phone calls." She switched into Hebrew, and I tried to follow, but I was distracted by the way she moved in and out of lanes with the elbowing, signal-less certainty of a bully in line. That was why I couldn't quite translate a word that sounded familiar.

"You what?"

"We *fled*."

She leaned forward over the wheel like a race car driver and said, "He beat me. We went to my parents. I live with my parents. And they are too old for this, for a small child in the house, but they took me in. I had nowhere else to go! It is very difficult. It is not ideal, but what can I do: I have no job, I have no money, I am all by myself, and I need to look after him. Who will pick him up from school if I go to work? I am looking for a part-time job but I am too old. And I don't know what to do, because now Tal is afraid of his father, he doesn't want to go with him on weekends, he cries and cries, and I am worried that maybe he hits him. But I have no choice, because of the judge. And he has told the judge that I'm crazy, that I'm not fit, he's made up all kinds of lies about me."

She suddenly cut in front of a grey Saturn, and sped away to a chorus of honks.

"Hannah, you might have to testify for me, I need people to tell the judge I'm not crazy."

Leah pulled into the parking lot of a flat, white apartment building.

Her English was fluid, and she spoke through her mistakes so that they seemed somehow dignified due to her certainty. When I tried to speak Hebrew to her, she kept correcting me, so we switched back into English. But I hadn't said much, even though this was our first conversation; it didn't even seem like she was talking to me as much as to some sounding board for her grievances, for her life that she laid out so bare and lurid, like a carcass on a hook. She hauled her son and then my son out of the car. "We go upstairs now."

The apartment entrance was full of plants, clustered under a small skylight, overgrown and luxuriant amidst the oriental rugs and dark bookshelves. It looked like the apartment of an intellectual, an academic, or a writer: the universal language of carpets and books and shabby gentility. As soon as we came inside she told us to take off our shoes; before we sat down she was cleaning up, straightening a newspaper on the table, scooping a plastic toy off the floor. She looked down at a pair of jogging pants and underpants shed like snakeskin on the Oriental rug, picked them up, and yelled, "Tal!"

He came running from the hallway. He was completely bare except for his shirt, and laughing. He had a flat bottom and skinny bow-legs, and, to my surprise, he was uncircumcised.

"Tal, why are your pants off? Put them back on!"

Tal looked mutinous, and started to run away. Leah picked him up and his feet kept running, like those characters in cartoons who don't realize that they are already off the cliff. She tried to slide his pants back on and he kicked her. She dropped him and he disappeared back down the hallway.

"You see how it is for me? Raising him with no father."

My son appeared in the hallway, holding a red car half as big as he was, vanished into a doorway again. Leah said, "Now we'll have some tea," and backed into the small kitchen.

The kitchen was tidy and well organized. There wasn't much room for me so I stood in a corner by the doorway while she boiled the water and wiped the countertop. A man came into the room. He was shirtless, big-bellied, and had suspenders hanging from the waistband of his pants down to his knees. "This is my father," Leah said. "Abba. Abba!" She turned to me and shrugged. "He isn't wearing his hearing aids." She swept a pair of flesh-coloured buttons from the counter and held them out to him, her palm open. I had noticed the intimate, curled shape of them earlier without registering what they were. "Abba, put your hearing aids in."

He ignored her, and leaned into the fridge, his stomach threatening to tip him over. He pulled out a plate covered in Saran wrap, grabbed a fork from the dish-rack, lumbered out of the kitchen, looking down all the while. It wasn't that he didn't say hello; it was as if he hadn't even seen us. Down the hallway, I heard a door slam.

"Pass me the tea that you would like," Leah said. I couldn't find the tea at all, and she gestured towards a drawer, then impatiently reached over me and yanked it open. All the while she talked over the hiss of the kettle.

"I have a boyfriend now, in Ma'ale Adumim. Can you imagine me with a boyfriend in the territories? I tell him, I could never live there. But that is not the problem. The problem is he has a son and the son is very disabled, he has serious problems. So, you know. It is a big problem," she said. "Because that kid will eat all our money. It will always have to be his son first. Not me, or my son. Well, my sons, but my other son is already almost an adult, he is going to the army this year. I was married before, you know. To a diplomat. Also a genius. We lived in Brazil together. After we broke up he moved to Switzerland. My son went with him. When my son came back, he told me I was vulgar. What can I do? We have all become vulgar here."

"Let's go outside," she said, pointing to the large balcony. Her son had returned from his bedroom, still in just his long shirt, the skinny gooseflesh of his legs exposed.

"Put your pants on!" she ordered and he stood there shaking his head, braced to run. She bent down and caught him and as he struggled in her arms she seemed to change her mind and loosened her grip. "You will be cold," she warned, opening the sliding doors and ushering us out.

The day was overcast, and there was nowhere to sit. The balcony was immense, almost as large as the living room, and lined with wilted geraniums; you could see the highway, and beyond it, the green of the university campus. I leaned on the railing, shivering, while the boys rode tricycles and plastic cars in circles and Leah disappeared inside. I wanted to be let back in, to be offered a cup of tea, to be allowed to sit on the low sofas and eat tangerines from the bowl on the coffee table. But it was clear that I had been sent outside to watch the children while Leah did whatever she was doing inside; through the window I heard snatches of a rapid, one-sided conversation, and assumed she was talking on the phone.

Tal careened around in a plastic Flintstone car, his legs the motor. My son, meantime, was chasing him and trying to climb onto the roof of the toy car while it was still in motion. The car was irresistible and unsharable. I tried to negotiate with them, but they paid no attention to me. Leah came outside as they both were crying and yanked her son out of the seat. My son stopped wailing and sat in the driver's position, his face smiling though still wet with tears. Tal wailed for another few minutes, then mounted his tricycle, still bare-assed and shivering.

"I had to call my lawyer," Leah said. "Sam, would you

like to see Tal's room? Time to come inside." The boys followed her, no more inclined to disobey than I would have been. "Now put your pants on!" she said to Tal, gesturing towards the pair of sweatpants, empty and formless on the rug.

Leah held her son by the shoulders and as soon as she let go he ran towards his room, looking back at her and cackling. My son looked at him, then looked at me, and followed him, the car forgotten. We walked back outside and Leah lit a cigarette. Below us was the green expanse of Givat Ram. "Over there was the partition road," she said, pointing towards the highway. "I remember them shooting at us. I cannot forget that. And I tell you if you ask me to choose between my child and their children I choose my child, I am sorry."

She took a long drag on her cigarette.

"I had a boyfriend, he was Palestinian. We lived together, before Tal's father. Even my father liked him although my father is a religious. This is what my family is like—we are patriots, we are very high in the army. But my brother does his *miluim* at the checkpoint one week and then checks for human rights abuses at the same checkpoint the next week. We are all like that. My boyfriend was good to me. Then the Second Intifada came, and my boyfriend said, 'Now we will push you Jews into the sea, but I will save you and your family, only you must become Muslim.' That was it!"

She stubbed out her cigarette in a tub of geraniums.

"I left him, after that. Lunch now," she said, and

walked back inside.

In the kitchen, Leah cracked an egg one-handed and fried it in a slick of oil, wiped the counter down, chopped tomatoes into a fine wet dice. She slid the fried egg off the pan—she had used so much oil, there was no need to unstick it with a spatula. The egg slid unctuously onto a plate, and she cracked another, all the while dicing cucumbers and tomatoes in the classic, precise style of the Israeli salad. I'd once offered to make a salad while visiting my Israeli cousin, and she'd taken one look at my hand-torn lettuce and said, "Are you making that for horses?"

I was getting hungry, but I didn't want to ask for food. Instead I took my cold cup of tea over to the couch while Leah put placemats on the table, called the children to lunch, pulled in their chairs, put a coaster under my cup of tea with a disapproving look.

I picked a few pieces of tomato off Sam's plate with my fingers. They were perfect. When I left Israel later that year, and people asked me what I missed, I thought, I miss tomatoes.

When the boys came back into the living room Tal had managed to find a new pair of pants and now they hung droopily off his legs. "Hummus!" my son cried happily—the most Israeli thing about him. A fork had rolled off the edge of the table and onto the floor.

"Come on," Leah said. "Be a bit more careful!"

Behind her Tal was taking oranges out of the bowl on the coffee table and lining them up in rows, humming "*Rosh hashana, rosh hashana.*" The boys were getting along well—each maintaining a constant stream of chatter in his separate language. Leah pressed a video into the VCR, and the television came to life somewhere in the middle of *Beauty and the Beast*.

There was a photograph of Leah on the wall, a portrait, her face younger and softer and seeming less angry. Beside her photograph were pictures of a tall dark man in uniform—perhaps the brother she had spoken about.

Leah noticed the oranges.

"What is this?" she said, towering over Tal, her hands on her hips. "You need to put this all back, every one. Why do you do this? Why do you always do this kind of thing?" Tal kept his back turned to her, spacing the oranges evenly along the rim of the table. "Enough now," she said, lifting him up and putting him on the chair beside Sam, who had already finished his omelette, and then sweeping vigorously underneath their feet.

"This is what I tell you. If I had anywhere else to go, I would go. I would even go back to Brazil. It is very hard here, all the time. Even my son, my older son, he has become racist. He used to have a girlfriend from Ramallah! He used to have friends who were Palestinian! And now he can't wait to go into the army, he won't talk to his old friends, he calls his uncle, the one who does checkpoint watch, a traitor. This is not how I raised him, this is not how he was when we lived in Europe. This country, it drives people crazy. But where can I go, with no money? And besides, my life is here. Why should I have to leave?"

"After I clean up this mess," she said, "it will be time

to go." There was no mess, only a doily slightly askew on the television, two dishes still on the table, near three forlorn oranges.

On the way home, I decided I was being too hard on Simon. He was doing the best he could. It was difficult to be in a new country, at a new job. I didn't have to navigate work and nasty colleagues. I was lucky. I should be grateful. He provided for our family, that was more than Leah's husband had done, more than a lot of men.

I felt clear and righteous, but my resolution faded when I walked in the door. Simon's things were strewn across the hallway, the kitchen looked like the bread basket had exploded, Gabriel was slack-jawed in front of the television, and the door to the bedroom was firmly closed. Sam dashed in front of the television—it was unusual for it to be on mid-afternoon and he could not believe his luck. I walked into the bedroom. "Hey," Simon said without looking up, "I'm just finishing this class for tomorrow. Will you close the door, please, on your way out?"

17.

After Leah's house, spending time with Jenna felt like a relief. Jenna had offered to take us to the zoo one day after school. We didn't have a car, and the zoo was on the outskirts of the city, which made it a bus ride and a long hot walk. We could get almost everywhere in the centre of the city by foot, but that slowed our days right down, and when I think about that year it seems to me that we were always walking. The buses were slow and lurching, and while large trenches had been dug in Jaffa Road for the new light rail, it was still years from completion. I felt a little like a teenager, dependent on the kindness of friends with cars. Being a stranger in a country was already like being a child; having no car reinforced that feeling, so when Jenna drove me around I felt like a kid, though I was perhaps a decade her senior.

Jenna had left her car in a handicapped spot outside the Y. She had the same disdain for parking rules as the consulate women did, but she didn't have the diplomatic sticker; she harvested tickets. She pulled another one off the windshield and into a glove compartment already bristling with paper. "It drives Aden crazy," she said, "that I get so many tickets, and then I don't pay them. I tell him, 'You drive the kids, and then I won't get tickets.' What am I supposed to do when the parking lot is full? And with all three kids?"

When we came to the car, Zac was making a fuss—his bottle was empty, or he wanted a pacifier, something to plug his mouth. It was hard to believe he was nearly four years old. He seemed to always be sucking or crying; she was worried, she had told me, because he didn't talk much yet. I wanted to tell her that perhaps he didn't talk much because his mouth was always full, but I didn't want to be that friend, the one who always knew better. And I was a little bit tentative with Jenna. She would laugh and ignore me or she would tell me to fuck off and, after all, who was I to tell anyone how to parent? She loved her children. That was clear.

Jenna leaned over and hissed at Zac, "*Inran umec itmut.*"

"It means, 'Your mother should die,' " she explained to me. "But you can only say it to your own kid. Never say it to anyone else—it would be a terrible insult. Unless you want to start a war. You can also say, '*Inran abec itmut,*' 'Your father should die,' but people don't use it as often. You know, like, 'You're going to kill me with your behaviour, and then you'll be sorry.' "

"That's so Jewish," I said. "Like a caricature of a Jewish mother. 'God, you kids are killing me! You're going to kill your poor mother and then you'll be happy!' That kind of thing."

Jenna looked at me. "No, it's nothing like that," she said.

I buckled Sam in as she slipped a DVD into the entertainment system. *Dora the Explorer* came on in Arabic, and from the back I could hear, "*Wakaf, Swiper, Wakaf!*" Zac leaned forward, sucking his bottle dry; he cried when it was empty, and she reached back, grabbed it, unscrewed the top, and poured the rest of her can of Red Bull inside.

"He likes it," she said, shrugging.

Noor wobbled off the seat, grabbed the can, threw her head back like a sailor and tried to chug it; when nothing but a trickle came out she screwed up her face and started a fake and practiced cry too high and uniform to be unintentional. She tried to climb over the seat back onto her mother's lap. Jenna wove in and out of traffic, leaning on her horn.

Jenna cut in front of a small truck. "No offence," she said, "but Jews are the worst drivers. Worse than they are in Jordan, even." Noor reached an arm over the back seat, and Jenna pulled her over and onto her lap, nursing under the wheel, smoking out the window.

"This one is driving me crazy," she said. "She always wants to nurse. I've done everything to make her stop. I even put that stuff on my nipples, you know, to make them bitter. She didn't care. She sucked on them anyway. I think she liked it."

"You could leave town," I said. "You could go away. That's what I did. I just couldn't wean in person; it was too difficult to say no. I needed an ocean between us. It took a week."

"Are you kidding?" Jenna said. "And who would

watch the kids? There's no way I could go away for a week. Aden couldn't handle it. He's not like Simon." She said it with a little bit of disdain, as if it was unmanly for Simon to be competent with children.

Zac, in the back seat, grinned at something in the video. His front teeth were still missing, leaving a broad gap that made him look reptilian. My son leaned forward to watch. His eyes were glazed and his mouth was slack. They were both zombied by the screen.

"Zac loves animals," Jenna said. "This is one of his favourite places. You know, I took his cousin here the other week, because I wanted him to get a chance to see it. He's lived in Jerusalem all his life, and his family has never taken him to the zoo. Some people are so lazy."

The zoo was the most visited tourist spot in Jerusalem. That didn't make any sense to me, until I realized that the tourist board only counted the sites that charged admission. There were lions, elephants, a reptile house, a sculpture garden. The zoo was also one of those rare places where everyone mingled: secular Jews, Chasidim, Christians, and Muslims, monkeys, lions, and rhinos. We edged around each other as the zebra skirts the elephant, stood next to one another in line for soda and ice cream or on the viewing decks. It would have been encouraging if it weren't so unusual. Black hats on the monkey bridge, headscarves among the parakeets, a menagerie of languages.

We pulled in at the lot. As soon as we came in through the gate, Zac started pointing and whining at the concession stand, a glassed-in booth of plastic and stuffed animals, cheap binoculars, T-shirts and hats. "They always get something here," she said. "They're used to it. You coming in?"

"We'll wait," I said. We had a rule, in our family. No gift shops. But my son looked longingly at the gaudy store window.

Jenna flounced in, Noor on her hip, Aisha by the hand, Zac trailing behind her. They came out a few minutes later looking happier. Zac held a plastic bag of tiny animals, and Aisha and Noor both had stuffed bears cradled near their faces.

Jenna held out another bag of animals in her manicured fingernails.

"I didn't want him to be the only one not to get anything."

"He doesn't—" I said, but Sam grabbed the bag with a happy cry.

"Ice cream?" she said to her children, and walked over to the counter. A woman was standing there, waiting as the man behind the counter prepared her fries. She wore a long maroon coat dress, buttoned all the way down, her hair tightly covered. Her husband and children, waiting at the picnic table, were far more casually dressed. He wore a white T-shirt and jeans faded in patches; the kids wore shorts and T-shirts. It was thirty degrees at least, but her sleeves reached her wrists, and her headscarf was black. I was hot in a T-shirt dress and sandals. It seemed unfair that she should swelter alone.

"I used to dress like that," Jenna said under her breath, inclining her head. Jenna was wearing a low-cut, pale yellow T-shirt with bleached jeans jewelled at the pockets, and high-heeled clogs. She wore nothing on her head. I waited for her to say more.

"When I first came back from Louisiana. Because, you know, I wanted to try to be more religious. And I was worried about what people would say. I mean, I knew that because of my mom, and because I was from America, they would talk about me anyway, but I thought I might as well look right."

"Isn't it hot? What are those made of?"

"They can make them out of anything. Wool, silk, cotton. Mostly polyester. That one looks like polyester. It *is* hot. In the summer I wouldn't wear nothing under it."

I laughed. The robe had brass buttons, like a military coat. It was fitted on top and swept out at the skirt. I had seen women similarly garbed in the Old City. Not a dress but a uniform, like the Chasidic girls who all wore long navy skirts, long-sleeved white blouses.

"Why did you stop?"

"Aden didn't like it. He wouldn't let me wear it. He said it wasn't modern. He likes how I dress now. Anyway, dressed like this, I never get stopped at the checkpoints, not even once. Well, once. When my friend's mom was with me. Wearing one of those on her head."

"I find it hard to imagine you dressed like that," I said.

But the truth was, I didn't find it that hard to imagine, because I had once made a similar decision, though a less drastic one. When I came back from spending my first year of university in Israel I was only eighteen. Leaving felt like a failure. I went to see the rabbi who led the program and asked him what I could do to keep my faith. I don't even know the girl who visited that rabbi anymore; she seems to have nothing to do with me, that self-important, falsely pious *naïf*.

He said, "You should make a change, a physical change. Stop wearing pants and only wear skirts. That will remind you of who you are; it will serve as a promise to yourself." Promise of what, I did not ask. Instead, I listened to him, for a year at least, the year I met Simon. What a fool.

Jenna looked back at the woman in the maroon robe, heading to her table, a large tray stacked with snacks and drinks precariously balanced on her arms. Her husband looked at her, didn't get up, his eyes black and flat. They studiously ignored us—our pity, our voyeurism, and our interest. We didn't exist.

"You know what they say," Jenna said. "The tighter the headscarf, the worse the person. Just because someone looks religious doesn't mean they act right. Usually, it means the opposite. Look at him. He's not even getting up to help her."

Sam's mouth was smeared with chocolate. He seemed in a stupor over his ice cream, as if he would fall asleep. Jenna wet a tissue with her water bottle and wiped his mouth. He looked up at her, mildly surprised. He was still young enough that I would wet my finger with my tongue to rub a spot off of his cheek.

Once when we were driving with the window open a bug had become trapped in his eye and he'd screamed so loudly we almost crashed the car. We pulled over to the side of the road and I tried to look at his eye, but he was closing it so tightly that I couldn't see anything, couldn't pull the lid apart with my fingers. Finally I held his wet, snot-smeared face between my hands and leaned over and licked his eye, his eyelids parting with the pressure, my tongue against the hot salt of his tears and the slick rubber of the cornea. I hadn't been prepared for the visceral grooming of parenting: the stroking, licking, nit-picking animal love.

We walked by the murky green pond, where black swans spun slowly in lazy ovals. The swans had sinister red eyes. A group of ultra-orthodox schoolchildren sat on the grass in their black jackets, black pants, leaning on their palms, their *peyos* flapping weakly in the wind. "Those black hats must collect the sunshine like a magnifying glass," Jenna said. "God, look at them. They must be so hot." They ate bags of Bamba—the peanut-flavoured snack that looked like Styrofoam and was so beloved by Israeli children—discarding the plastic on the green manicured grass. A few of the boys leaned over the water, throwing Bamba at the swans, calling to them in loud, raucous voices. The swans drifted over disdainfully and inclined their long necks into the water to retrieve the snacks. That was the first word for a lot of Israeli children: not "Abba," or "Daddy," but "Bamba." Nobody had ever heard of peanut allergies.

"I can't imagine that's good for the animals," I said.

Jenna said, "They don't know how to behave."

On an island in the middle of the lake, a spider monkey hunched on the roof of the monkey hut, then reached out a powerful hand and swung out on the rope hung from a nearby tree, his armpit like a sail. My son reached up his arm in unconscious imitation, as if he too could fly out over the water on a rope. The schoolchildren on the grass were speaking Yiddish, though fewer and fewer did, I'd heard; even in Meah Shearim, that long linguistic resistance had begun to shift. A teacher, thin and hunched in his suit, walked over to the boys and shook a finger at the trash on the lawn. Another teacher circulated with a cardboard box of juice packets—silver pouches to puncture with a straw—made of colour and sugar and more thirst-inducing than thirst-quenching. Aisha started whining, pointing towards the box of drinks and pulling on her mother's hand. Jenna yanked her back, harder. "It's not for you," she said. "You just had a drink."

"I have to say one thing," Jenna said as we headed up the path towards the park in the centre of the zoo. "The Israelis, they do know how to do zoos. I mean, have you ever been to a zoo in Jordan? Pathetic."

At the park my son looked longingly at the swings where two Arab girls, on the very cusp of being teenagers, sat side-by-side dragging their feet along the sand. They weren't even swinging, they were rocking, heads leaning towards each other and against the rope, hair covered in white shawls. After a few minutes I felt that bullying, parental compulsion to intervene.

"*Asfeh,*" I said, in my halting, odd Arabic, "*il-walad bidi aruch,*" "the boy would like to go." I didn't know the word for "turn," didn't know if "go" would indicate what I meant, and was pretty sure that I was conjugating everything wrong. The girls looked at me. One of them dimpled into a smile, her eyes pale green and her cheeks plump. "You speak Arabic!" she said, as if that was as strange as anything in the zoo. She stood up and her friend reluctantly followed, dragging her hand away from the rope. Sam ran to the swing and grabbed it.

"Does he know Arabic too?" she pointed at my son.

"Not really," I said, "*shwaya shwaya,*" which meant, "just a little bit."

"Mmmhmm" she said, her gaze sweeping me up and down, and her friend pulled her away by the hand. Their voices behind me were musical, amused.

The children were happiest in the petting zoo beside the park. Noor tried to feed the baby goat the car keys, but Jenna stopped her. Past the sculpture garden were the hills of Jerusalem, brown now after the long summer. On the bench two girls were taking off their robes and headscarves. They were part of a school group; as I looked around I could see a number of the girls disrobing. The robes and scarves were Arab dress, but the girls were speaking Hebrew, sighing with relief as they divested themselves of their hot, cumbersome layers. I went over to one of the girls on the bench. She was finger-combing her curly dark hair, and with her walnut skin she could have passed for Palestinian before the scarf came off.

"What's up?" I said. "Why were you all dressed up?"

She looked up at me, surprised to be addressed. "You know, it's one of those things. Dress like them, see how it feels. And then we have to write an essay." Her friends were calling to her, flashing mocking glances at me. She rolled the robe into her backpack, slipped it over her shoulders, and stood up. She wore a long skirt now, and the three-quarter length sleeves of an orthodox schoolgirl. She leaned over and grabbed Sam's chin. Sam, resistant to being claimed, shook his head away.

"What a sweetie! A blondie!" she said, looking at my son and then at my dark hair. She rejoined her friends.

I knew a man who had survived the Holocaust because of his blond hair. He had false papers, and because of his pale skin, his blue eyes, his blond hair, he was able to pass as a non-Jewish child and stayed at the house of a farmer who had been a friend of his father's. I had never imagined having a blond child.

"Not blond," Sam told me once. "I have *gold* hair."

These religious Jewish girls dressed as Arabs at the zoo could have easily walked through the Arab market in the middle of the day in their costumes without anyone realizing they were Jews. At least, I thought they could have done. They had the same Semitic features: dark, thickly lined eyes, long black hair peeking out under their headscarves. Did it make it worse, that we looked like sisters and brothers? And Jenna, dressed as she was in jeans and a

T-shirt, just looked American.

I wondered what people saw when they saw Jenna and me together, what they imagined we *were*. Even before I opened my mouth, people addressed me in English. How did they know? I asked Jenna, and she said, "Well, look at you. It's obvious." She refused to explain herself further.

We stopped to see the lion tamarins in the monkey house before we left, in an indoor enclosure where the air was heavy and stank. They were a new acquisition at the zoo—tiny golden monkeys with leonine manes who stared at us, gripping their bars, their faces masks of accusation. Zac clung to the rope and would not move. Suddenly he was laughing as I had never seen him laugh before. He was delighted by the monkeys, and their acrobatic flips and feints. He pointed and hooted at them, and ducked under the rope to get closer to their cage.

"Out," said Jenna. "Out."

She pulled on his arm and he darted down with his toothless mouth and bit her. Her other arm flashed out, fast as a snake, and slapped him.

"You bite me, I'll break your arm," she leaned down and hissed. She saw me watching, shrugged her shoulders. "They have to learn," she said. Without thinking, I had covered Sam's ears. He hadn't taken it in, anyway, was still looking at the monkeys.

Zac wasn't crying, which surprised me, but he gazed at his mother in black fury. I wasn't sure what to say. I thought about taking Sam home but we were stranded— we were in a zoo in the middle of Malha. Even the bus was a hot walk up the hill.

I tried, "Aren't you worried that you'll scare him?"

"He's used to it," she said. "Come on, he doesn't think I'll actually do it. But the threat, you know, it gets him to stop biting. He's too old to bite."

Too old to use a pacifier, I thought, looking at his mouth, now stopped up again in the constant suck. Too old to drink from a bottle. Too young to drink Red Bull. Too old to be silent.

And me?

18

I t felt as if someone was taking me apart, brick by brick. It suited my mood that all of central Jerusalem was under construction. Clouds of yellow dust hung in the air and it seemed that every other block some building was in the process of being destroyed or rebuilt. Down the street from the YMCA a massive hotel was rising from the ground. The builders had been told by the city to preserve the historic Ottoman façade, so the outer wall still stood, arches onto nothingness. You could look through and see the pit. The air was loud with the sound of diggers and cranes, and on the safety wall around the construction site the builders had wrapped a banner depicting the street as it would appear when the hotel was completed. The dream of the city was wrapped around the incomplete skeleton of the real one.

Then every so often, in the middle of a golden mile, beside a condo of multi-million dollar apartments and a four-star hotel, was an abandoned lot, overgrown and strewn with rubbish. The empty plots were contested land: in some cases, they had been in the courts for decades. And many of the beautiful apartments were empty.

They called them ghost apartments, because they were inhabited for only a few months a year, Passover, summertime, when their wealthy French or American or Canadian owners came to Israel on vacation. The new mayor had said he'd impose a special tax on the ghost apartments and empty neighbourhoods in order to dissuade these wealthy squatters, who had left no space for local residents. Prices in the city were unaffordable, and University students had been driven to live on the very outskirts of Jerusalem in ultra-orthodox areas where they were often unwelcome.

To get downtown from the YMCA, I often cut through the old Muslim cemetery. It was in a shocking state of dilapidation, the ground hairy with weeds and sparkling with broken glass. Plastic bags were caught on the branches of leafless shrubs, and gravestones were tilted and tattooed with the faded, ineradicable markings of old graffiti—"*maavet l'aravim*," "death to Arabs"—which seemed, in this case, redundant. There was a small mausoleum with a domed roof, and on the wall someone had drawn the ghostly outline of the figure of a man. At night, it was a hot spot for pick-ups. Even in the day I saw young men lurking off the path, their gazes filled with dark intent.

The Wiesenthal Centre had appropriated part of the cemetery to build a museum of tolerance: it was like the punchline of a joke. So far they had disinterred four layers of bodies, and the bulldozers plowed up gravestones by night. Their defence had a kind of kettle logic—Freud has a story about a man who borrows a kettle and returns it with a hole, claiming he's returned the kettle undamaged, and the hole has always been there, and that he never borrowed the kettle in the first place. The Wiesenthal Centre said the museum was not to be built on the cemetery, but would be adjacent to the cemetery; that those weren't real bodies under those tombstones, but tombs placed over empty ground to claim the land; and that the cemetery had been desacralized by the mufti long ago, when part of it was sold to build the Palace Hotel, and moreover, that the cemetery was shamefully neglected by the Waqf, who only cared about it now to spite the Wiesenthal Centre. Anyway, they said, they weren't building the museum over the cemetery but over what used to be an old parking lot.

I'm guessing the bones disagreed.

Frank Gehry had been commissioned to build the new museum in the shape of a fruit bowl. Simon started a petition and wrote them a letter of protest against the desecration of the cemetery. In response they had put him on their email list and now sent him fundraising pleas.

Sometimes I walked through the cemetery, past downtown, and all the way to the market. The fruit market was one of my favourite places in Jerusalem. Back home in the winter almost all of the fruit and vegetables were imported, and I was accustomed to carrying pineapples home in the snow. In Montreal in the wintertime none of the fruit tasted right; it tasted like a thin, watery approximation of itself—tomatoesque, or mangoish. In Jerusalem the produce was like the weather; it swept through the stalls and then vanished like a cloud. It was frustrating when you needed a zucchini, say, or a lime, but it was exciting to see oranges give way to pomelos. And there were fruits that I had never tasted, or because I had only had imported versions, had never *really* tasted: guavas for instance, which I had never understood before, peppery and sweet, perfuming my hands and my house.

A neighbour came by in guava season and saw a bowl of the pale, green fruit on the table.

"Ugh," he said, "I hate guavas. I can't stand the smell of them. My wife buys them occasionally, but she keeps them wrapped in the fridge. You have to be careful with guavas or the smell will take over the whole house."

But that was precisely what I wanted: to fill my house with these delicate, vanishing smells—jasmine when it was in bloom, guavas when they were in season. I could not retain the scent or taste of a guava when it was gone, so I gorged on them when they were available, frequently bringing my hands to my face to sniff the perfumed, intimate scent because it made me so absurdly happy.

For a long time, people were afraid to go to the central market in Jerusalem. There were frequent terrorist attacks, documented with graphic pictures in the newspaper, and the destruction seemed more devastating surrounded by all of that abundance, the gorgeous, ripe, indifferent pyramids of fruit. And then there were the bodies in the aisles, surrounded by fallen fruit from the toppled stalls: a foot, an orange, a head, and the broken carcass of a melon. But it had been several years since the last bomb, and the market was now full again.

I went on Fridays, when the foot traffic was shoulder

to shoulder. There was a cheese store, where they sold two hundred kinds of cheese and held giddy wine tastings on Friday mornings; there were candy shops with long tables of brightly wrapped sweets, and bins filled with jellybeans that looked like rocks, jawbreakers that looked like eyeballs, sweet and sour worms.

The night before, when the children were finally in bed, I had sat down at the kitchen table, the laptop in front of me. I wasn't writing but I was trying to ready myself for writing, or for not writing, which I'd been doing much more of recently. Simon came in and went straight to the fridge. "You won't believe who I saw today," he said, scattering sandwich supplies over the counter.

"I'm working," I said.

"Right," he said. I could hear the flinch in his voice. "You're working."

"What's that supposed to mean?" I said, too quickly. "You know I have to finish this by the summer. I'm not going to get another extension."

"I didn't say anything," he said. "Get back to work, that's fine." His voice was like the voice of a stranger.

In the market there was an "*etrog* man," who sold elixirs based on what he claimed were rabbinic recipes that promised to restore fertility, end insomnia, cure temper. The next day I stopped and bought the *etrog* juice for marital harmony, a thick, bright green citron potion that was more bitter than sweet. I didn't believe in it, but it couldn't hurt.

In the early years of our marriage, Simon and I had

this game we played where we imagined being other people—the Lycra-clad couple speeding past us on matching bikes as we walked in the park, their bodies greyhound-sleek, bent forward in mutual diligence; the old man and lady with their matching berets and walking sticks, strolling slowly in companionable silence. We saw ourselves especially in the couples with young children, back before we had children, tossing a ball, pushing a stroller up the street. And then life got busy and we didn't have any time to play those games, couldn't imagine being other people, it was so exhausting being ourselves. Though I kept playing the game on my own, trying on other lives like other outfits, slipping them on and off in the secret chamber of my head. As I drank the syrupy, bittersweet juice I wondered if we had been better off when we imagined being other people together.

The market had shifting, kaleidoscopic displays of produce, and darker seamier alleyways that smelled like death, where stripped carcasses hung from hooks and butchers wiped their hands on blood-stained aprons. Boys carried samples of *halva* on trays with their arms raised high like waiters in a Chaplin film, men played backgammon in the alleys, and tourists with cameras hunted Chasidim buying *challah*. There were baskets of rose petals, heaped cones of spices, and dizzy, lucky, glutted flies.

One day a mild drizzle meant the lanes were almost empty. Strawberries had just come into season, and the bins were overflowing with that red, beefy, heart-shaped fruit. Squashed strawberries stained my sandals underfoot. I heard a man singing from behind his stall. He didn't have any customers; there was no custom to be had. He just sang for the pleasure of it, for his strawberries—"*Tut Sadeh, tut sadeh, gam bezol vegam yafeh*...."— "Strawberries, strawberries, both cheap and beautiful...."

I was about to leave the market when I saw an old woman standing on the sidewalk, looking lost, her hands full of shopping bags. She was as wide as she was tall, though she only reached about up to my chest. Her face was like a piece of paper that had been creased again and again. She was overdressed for the weather, but it was difficult to tell if that was out of modesty or just old age, hidden under layers and layers of clothing.

"Do you need help?" I said. I had an hour before I needed to be back at the daycare.

The woman looked up at me from under her wool beret. Her eyes were pale blue and bulbous, like a toad. She also had a toad's wide mouth, leathery skin, and disapproving glare. Her voice was hoarse and low.

"Yes," she said. "Thank you. Thank you."

We were speaking Hebrew, and her voice was so thick and deep that it was difficult to understand her, though her words were simple. "Take these bags for me," she said. "I live right here, near the market, not far. It won't take long, no, it won't take long."

She dropped her bags and dug her fingers into my arm, and I was shocked at her strength. The bags were heavier than I had expected. I sagged under them and under the pressure of her fingers. She pulled me down the street, and for a moment the stalls on the street were like the trees in a forest, and I was like a child in a fairy tale, led to some obscure destiny.

After a few blocks, she stopped at a small blue door. There was no number; it was so unobtrusive I would have never noticed that there was a door at all. I dropped the bags, my fingers cramped, tie-dyed red and white from the weight of the plastic. "Have a good day," I said nervously, but instead of picking up the bags the woman said, "Please, can't you take them upstairs for me? I'm a very old woman."

Her staircase was dark and windowless and smelled of shoes and garbage. The woman had an enormous keychain, and it seemed like it took every key she had to unlock the door at the top of the stairs. "You can put the bags in the kitchen," she said, and gestured into the gloom of the apartment. The curtains were drawn, and the lights were off. But I could see that the walls were covered in newspaper, and there were piles of newspapers and letters on the floor. The sink was full of dishes, and the table was also covered in books and papers. She cleared a space for the bags with her hand. The room was sad and reeked of old age and neglect. I couldn't wait to get back outside.

But the woman grabbed my wrist again. I would wear those circular marks for the next three days. "Come," she said, "let me show you my son."

Instead of pulling me deeper into the apartment she pulled me to the wall, where I realized that the yellowed newspaper was not many pages but one page, taped again and again and again so that it papered the room. There was a faded photograph of a boy in a soldier's uniform. The headline said he had been killed. I couldn't read the date.

"My son," she said, and stood there, hanging onto my arm like a dog with a bone.

I stood still, as if I had been turned to stone. "I'm sorry about your son," I said. "I'm very sorry." I stood there, thinking of Gabriel and of Sam. I was going to be late to pick them up, and though it wasn't reasonable, I was suddenly afraid for them.

"You're sorry?" The woman said. "Is that all you can say, that you're sorry?" Her eyes seemed to grow ever larger in her face and out of her mouth poured a torrent of words, an excremental river in which I could catch only passing curses and phrases as I backed away towards the door and down the long staircase and into the lemon sunshine and clean air of the street. The next week I looked for her blue door again and could not find it.

But few of my days were that dramatic. Sometimes instead of going downtown or to the market I'd walk down through Yemin Moshe and up the ramp to Jaffa Gate. Yemin Moshe hugged the hillside and was impossibly picturesque; no matter how many times I walked through the alleyways I never saw an actual resident, as if real life would mar the perfection of the miniature stone houses, the famously colourful doors, the flowerboxes overflowing with geraniums and laburnum and the walls feathered with vines. I did bump into tour groups, often on photo safaris, each angling towards the same iron-grilled

157

window collared in pansies, ignoring the equally lovely cactus or passageway behind their broad, camera-bag laden backs. But it didn't matter which way they turned: each inch of Yemin Moshe had been photographed repeatedly, by so many different people, at every time of day, that it presented itself to their lenses as already framed.

I picked up one of the brochures off the cobblestones. The text read, "Yemin Moshe is especially lovely in the late afternoon, when the golden light warms the walls and casts long shadows on the cobblestones." But in the late afternoon it was so crowded with camera-wielding Cyclopean tourists that it was difficult to get a clear shot. I preferred the late morning, when everyone else had fled the sun, even though the light was bad for pictures. I wasn't immune to the picturesque: I took a picture of a rose cooling its flushed cheeks against a cream wall, a cat napping in the shade of an old stone archway. When I came home I posted the pictures on Facebook and I waited. It took less than a minute for the first thumbs up. I refreshed the page again and again for the sugar rush, one person, now two, now five. Cats and flowers, those were the pictures that got approval, rather than the photographs that I found unexpected or interesting, like the boy in the market leaning his arm on the decapitated head of a lipsticked mannequin wrapped in a *keffiyeh*. I could piggyback on that inherent unfair beauty. How was it, I wondered, that we didn't get tired of this clichéd loveliness, so familiar that only its outlines needed to be sketched for us to say, "Ah, there it is." Blue door, stone steps, eucalyptus. Late afternoon.

I had other associations with Yemin Moshe. Once, when I was very young, and living on my own for the first time, I had a desperate conversation by moonlight with a boy in its terraced, spiky gardens. I had forgotten the content of the conversation, had forgotten his name, and had even forgotten the face of this boy that I'd thought I loved, but I remembered the abyssal, hollow-hearted feeling of our encounter every time I walked down those paths, like a cloud covering the sun. Even though it was hot and crowded and the beginning of the day, somewhere in my memory it was night and deserted and the end of the world.

19

We finally hit a spell of bad weather, and the skies, grey and spectral, contributed to my feeling that I was drifting ghostly through the city. I kept going back to the Old City in the day, when Simon was working and Sam and Gabriel were in school, drawn by its haunted charisma.

Jenna didn't like the Old City. "Too many ghosts," she said. "You can tell terrible things have happened there." She shuddered even thinking about it, though she offered to come with me if there was anything I needed to buy. Jenna was convinced I was being constantly ripped off. She was always asking me how much I'd paid for some trinket or bag of spices, and then she would tell me how much it should have cost.

I loved trying to practice Arabic with the vendors, who were the only strangers who would talk to me, I suppose since there was profit in it. The one time Jenna did come with me, as she bargained in Arabic too quickly for me to follow, I saw men looking at each other behind her back, grabbing their crotches and winking. I wondered if that was what they'd been doing behind my back all the time, if what I had mistaken as curiosity and friendliness was in fact contempt and casual lust.

It reminded me of a trip I'd taken before I was married, to Turkey, where making a pass at a foreign woman was a courtesy, like offering tea or opening a door. I was hit on incessantly and impersonally. I had never received so many phone numbers scrawled on the backs of business cards and scraps of paper, had never been given so many lines, delivered without inflection or irony. As I walked down the street men would try to guess my nationality, knowing only that I was not from Turkey; they needed to know which language to use when they approached me. They had lines ready in English, in French, and in Spanish.

Some of the lines were sweet, if musty, "Is your father a candy maker?" Others were more direct, but never crude. When I had traveled other places alone the constant passes had been obscene and sometimes aggressive, and seemed in some way a means of exacting revenge on me for journeying, free and untrammeled, through places where few women had the social freedom to move around without a chaperone and few men had the financial freedom to travel to other countries for pleasure. But in Turkey they were dispassionate and businesslike. Flirting was another part of the commerce between foreign women and Turkish men. As one man said to me, "If you will not go out with me to the disco, at least you will buy my carpets."

Back then, none of the men were particularly

persistent, except for George Michael. George Michael was not his real name, but it was almost the first thing he said to me: "I look like George Michael." He then added, "Not like now, like he used to look, before he got old and fat." He didn't look like George Michael, except that he had dark hair streaked blond and eighties-style bleached jeans. He wore a dark sweater and a black pashmina knotted around his neck. As I wandered through the stalls I had smiled aimlessly at nothing in particular, out of pleasure in the beauty of the market and the day. Then George Michael stepped forward and announced, "You smiled at my friend and now you have to smile at me."

Without asking my permission, he took out his cellphone and snapped a picture of me. He held it at arm's length, frowning slightly. "Not a good likeness. Smile this time." He handed his friend the phone and stood beside me. The phone came up again, and this time I smiled. He looked at the picture and said, "This one is better. You licked your lips. I like that." Then, again without permission or invitation, he was at my side, striding through the market.

I love markets. I love the labyrinth of treasure, the promise of hidden bounty. The Grand Bazaar in Istanbul has been there for hundreds of years, a shrine to the pleasure of commerce. Stall after stall of slippers curled at the toe, absurdly ornate ottomans, antique wooden spice boxes from Tibet, patchworked tapestries from Uzbekistan, tea sets made of glass, vases made of stone, lanterns made of copper, carpets carpets carpets. Also perfume, Tupperware, and Teflon frying pans, but I stayed away from those galleries in favour of the exotica. I didn't know enough to tell the cheap and tacky from the common and lovely from the truly extraordinary, but I knew that the market held all of those categories of object and much that fell somewhere in-between. It was my third day in Turkey and I still could not find my way in and out of the same entrances, or back to the Aladdin's cave of jewelry and illuminated manuscripts I had stumbled on my first day. George Michael appointed himself my guide. He said, "I grew up in this market, I can find you anything you like."

Then he proceeded to tell me what I should like. Not the expensive colour-blocked weavings I had been admiring, row after row of subtle variations of red or blue that reminded me of the soothing vistas of Rothko paintings.

"What does that shit have to do with Turkish art? That has nothing to do with our traditions. They make it only for the tourists. It is extremely ugly."

And not the small *kilim* I had bought that morning after what felt like hours of agonizing. "The colours are too bright. Not natural dye. This is nothing special. You should have waited until you met me to buy a carpet. But it is not bad. Don't worry, you can tell your friends when you get home that some village girl wasted her eyes on this carpet for two or three months."

George Michael said, "I'll show you something special. I have a stand of my own. SVA-ROS-key. You know SVA-ROS-key?"

I didn't. He led me weaving through the stalls, away

from the tapestries and wall hangings and into a forest of crystal, stand after stand of hanging beads and fussy little ornaments, carefully poised rabbits and eagles forever about to take flight. I stopped walking. Swarovski. Now I knew what he was talking about. He gestured possessively at a stand that looked to me just like five other stands around it. Crystal drops threw twitching rainbows onto the cold pale floor.

"See. SVA-ROS-key."

"I'm sorry." I said. "I don't really like this kind of stuff."

For a moment he looked mortally offended. "Everyone loves SVAROS-key."

I shook my head. "I guess I'm just too clumsy. I'd always be worried about breaking it."

Something like rage flickered across his face. Then he shrugged his shoulders.

"No problem. I will show you my father's stall. That one is more Turkish. The old-fashioned stuff you like."

He pointed to the rug under my arm, which I kept hoping he would offer to carry, "Like that. Only more nice."

As we walked through the market, he'd nod his head or casually wave at many other salesmen, men like him who were in their twenties or thirties. I recognized some of them from my forays through the market, but this time, none of them tried to talk to me. It was as if, simply by walking at my side, he had taken possession of me. He kept telling me I had to go with him and his cousins to the disco, and I kept saying that I could not.

His father's stall was in one of the oldest parts of the market, and held carpets, cushions, tapestries. He unlocked it for me and gestured with his hand to a boy to bring us tea, one of the boys who spent all day with silver trays balanced on their palms, weaving through the labyrinth of the market. We sat on stools in the cramped space and drank the sweet acidic tea that smelled of apples and came from a white powder. You could buy it in the market, of course; box after box, with pictures of idyllic orchards on the front, arranged next to glass and metal tea sets and seven different grades of Turkish delight. He held the cup delicately, with the tips of his fingers, from the top of the glass, and I did the same, taking small careful sips. One of his eyes was blue and the other was deep seaweed green.

George Michael showed me a carpet on his wall. "Now this one is a beautiful carpet, I would sell it to you except you already bought a carpet today. A shame, really, since this one is more special." He went through a quick version of his spiel—the knotwork, the colours, the meaning of the pattern—but his heart wasn't really in it and he was right: I had already bought a carpet that day. He said, "Only you must promise me that if you buy another carpet you will come back to me."

I was ready to go. The indoor air of the market was beginning to give me a headache, and I wanted to walk outside. "Thank you for the tea," I said, standing up. I had to stoop a little in the stall. He smoothly stood up too.

"And where will you go now?"

"I'm going to walk a bit, maybe into Beyoglu."

"Then let's go," he said, and locked his father's stall behind me.

It was at once a grey and golden afternoon, the light filtering through the clouds and turning the waters of the Bosphorus luminous. Fishermen bordered the bridge elbow to elbow, their long multi-hooked lines studded with fish like silver nails. George Michael kept up a steady patter about his foreign girlfriends. Mostly I didn't believe him. The night before, at the hotel, the clerk had confided in me about his girlfriend in England. He was working, he said, to make enough money to join her there. They met at the hotel the previous summer; she stayed in my room. He was upset because he kept trying to call her but she was not at home, and didn't call him back. This had been going on for days. I told him there was probably a good explanation, knowing there probably was not, or that the explanation was the simple explanation, the one he did not want to hear. And at the restaurant where I'd had dinner the previous day the owner had sat down at my table and told me about the German ex-wife who broke his heart.

But George Michael's stories were not sincere or bittersweet; his were a list of scores, of notches on his studded, oversized belt. At one point he paused and said, "I am only telling you this because you already said you will not go out with me. If you were going out with me, of course I would not tell you. Actually, I am not sure why I am bothering with you except that, unfortunately, you are my type." He sighed an extravagant, exaggerated sigh.

We were in Beyoglu, walking along the wide boule-vard, when he stopped. Behind an iron gate was the open crater a bomb had left the month before.

"All the tourists want to see this," he said, gesturing with his arm as though he were showing off something that was his possession. "Why, I can't say. It is a sick thing to want to see. Also has nothing to do with Turkey. Just another way to say we are not ready to join the EU, even though we are the victims here. So many tourists can-celled their trips because they did not feel safe, but what choice do we have? We live here. Now everybody in the market is having money trouble because this is the time of year, around Christmas, when we usually sell the most, and now a whole day can go by and nobody will stop in my stall. Then the tourists who do come, this is what they all want to see. Except there is nothing to see. Only a hole in the ground. Are you finished?"

I was remembering the newscasts from the month be-fore, the stumbling bandaged bodies being led from the scene, the bodies that lay still on the ground. The week before the consulate and bank were bombed, two syna-gogues were attacked. I had meant to go see them, but it was almost impossible to get in since they had tightened up security.

I hadn't mentioned to George Michael that I was Jewish, although a few things he said made me think that he knew. So I looked, in response to him and in defiance of him, at the hole in the ground. There were no signs of reconstruction, no guards posted, no people at all; it could have been abandoned for one year or ten.

Impatiently, George Michael lit a cigarette and stamped his feet to keep warm. "Lunch?" he said.

There was a small vegetarian restaurant off Istiklal Caddesi. From inside, you could have been in Paris or Barcelona or San Francisco except for the language of the menu; women in jeans and hippie scarves and sweaters drinking smoothies and eating salads. George Michael was irritated with the lack of meat on the menu; he seemed to see vegetarianism as essentially un-Turkish, like the Rothko weavings or militant fundamentalism, and said he didn't want anything to eat. I ordered lentil soup, which was thin and lukewarm when it arrived, and a salad.

George Michael took tea and lit another cigarette, watching me eat a little too closely. He took out his cellphone and began to fiddle with it. I was starting to feel exhausted and irritable. He showed me the picture he had taken of me in the market. My hair was wild and my eyes looked crazy. "Not very flattering," he said. "I will erase it for you. This one is better."

He showed me the next picture, the one his friend had taken of the two of us, standing stiff and awkward side by side. He began thumbing through the other pictures and said, "Ah, here is a picture of my girlfriend from Australia, but maybe you do not want to see it."

"I do," I said, curious about the corroboration for something I thought he had invented.

"Very well," he said. "My girlfriend and me—a certain part of me—that I will cover with my thumb." He turned the phone around and there were the cartoonish startled eyes, the lipsticked top of the open mouth.

"That's not your girlfriend," I said. "You took that off the internet."

I was gathering my coat, looking for my wallet.

"It is my girlfriend," he said. "She is very attractive, much more attractive than you, and will be coming back in the summer."

George Michael had become desperate and insistent, as if something more was at stake than my belief.

It is difficult to leave a vegetarian restaurant in a hurry; one quality that seems universal to vegetarian restaurants is slow service. I hailed a cab at the door. George Michael had recovered his composure. "Look for me in the market," he said. The rest of the trip, I avoided his corner.

For a long time I thought I had gotten the better of our encounter. I hadn't been convinced or compelled to go out with him; I had bought nothing at his stall and bought little of our conversation. I told Jenna about it one day. "He got exactly what he wanted," she said. "You don't understand. Guys like that, they don't get to talk about sex. They can't do that with girls from their neighbourhood. And you know he told all his friends you slept with him anyway."

I thought about what Jenna said, and remembered the photograph on his phone. With a sinking heart I said, "Well, you don't know that." She said, "What do you care anyway what people think? You're never going to see him again."

20

If the days were for wandering and getting lost, then the afternoons and evenings were all about home, feeding the children, straightening up, getting ready for bed, all that relentless domestic Sisyphean labor. We had just come back from the grocery store, and I was unloading groceries and cleaning up the breakfast dishes. The boys were watching *Tom and Jerry* on the television, lying on the cold, hard terrazzo floor, which always seemed covered in a fine layer of grit no matter how often I mopped. We had bought the *Tom and Jerry* DVDs in Hebrew, hoping it would help them learn the language. Of course, I had forgotten how little dialogue there was, just the trill of the piano and the cat and mouse in their endless chase. Gabriel and Sam were addicted, and I was sick to death of both Tom and Jerry, especially that smug immortal mouse.

The phone rang. As I walked past the television to answer it, Jerry dropped a hundred-pound weight on Tom; the children snickered as Tom re-emerged, flat as a pancake, and walked on bowed legs back to his former roundness.

"Can't they be friends once in a while?" I said, and

Gabriel, who was like a Talmudic scholar of *Tom and Jerry*, said, "They are, in that one when the baby runs away." As Gabriel took a deep breath to begin what I knew would be a long and detailed narrative of pursuit and escape and near-death I stepped over him and said, "Sorry, Gabe, I should get the phone," and picked up the receiver, relieved to be spared.

"Hello," I said, "*shalom*?"

"Hannah," Jenna said, and her voice was urgent, "I need to bring the children over, something's wrong with Aden."

"Of course," I said, "is everything alright?"

"I'll explain when I get there," Jenna said. "He's at the hospital waiting for tests, I got to go. Of course his mother, stupid cow, can't be found just when I need her. She's probably going to think it's my fault anyway."

"What's your fault?" I said, but Jenna had hung up.

She must have been calling from the road because the buzzer sounded five minutes later. She hauled the children up the stairs, the little one on her hip. Noor kept reaching over with her skinny hand to slap Jenna on the face, and Jenna kept catching her hand before she made contact.

"She's mad at me," Jenna said. "She wanted to stay in the car and watch her show—here, I brought it. Look, Noor, you can watch it here."

Noor toddled over to the television and stood right in front of it, her ruffled skirt the exact breadth of the screen, her hands in fists on her hips.

"Hey!" Sam said, and Jenna reached forward, swept Noor off the floor and onto the couch. Sam sat back.

"I hope I won't be long," Jenna said, "I'll call you. He started having these awful stomach pains, like an appendix or something. I brought the bottles and the pacifier, that's right here, and some snacks 'cause I didn't know if you had the food they like, thanks, I'll call you, I got to go."

"All right," I said, taking a deep breath. "Anyone hungry?"

I looked at the cover of the DVD. Jenna had brought me *Robocop*.

"I don't want to watch this baby show," Zac said, glaring at the screen, "I want to watch my movie."

"It's broken," I said, hoping he didn't know how to check, and he looked at me as if he didn't believe me but settled on the couch anyway, his skinny arms crossed in front of his chest. Jenna had brought a bagful of chips and candy, food I never had in the house. The children pounced on it.

After *Tom and Jerry* the kids watched a Japanese cartoon dubbed into Hebrew that Zac seemed to recognize. As he watched, he laughed, his mouth open wide, his toothless gums shining. I hadn't ever seen him laugh at the daycare. Simon came home and sat on the couch, sandwiched between the children, so we were two adults and five children, all of us waiting for Jenna.

Then there was a knock on the door.

"That must be her," I said, but when I opened the door it was my neighbour. She was squat and short and had blond hair so stiff, so permed and bleached, that it stood out around her head like a wig. Come to think of it, it may have been a wig.

"You have some children over!" Daphna said. "How nice! Are they from the school?"

"Yes," I said. I could sense that she was trying to look around me, into the apartment, but my shoulders blocked her view.

"That's good!" she said. "It's good for the children to have friends!"

She had a son, too, a dark, sullen boy with a pre-adolescent hint of moustache whose shirts were always a little tight. I had never seen him with any friends. I stood there, waiting.

"Right," she said. "So the *mashkanta* is due at the end of the month."

I wasn't sure how the most unpleasant person in the co-op ended up being the one to collect the housing payment, or why she wanted the position, since I often heard her complaining about it. Simon said it was because she liked to spy on everybody. As I turned to get the checkbook, I could feel her small eyes on my back, could feel her desire to be asked inside almost as a physical pressure. I grabbed the checkbook, and came back to the door.

"What nice children!" she said again. "What are their names?"

She had never asked the names of my own children. I pretended not to hear her. "See you later Daphna," I said heartily, and though I didn't quite shut the door in her face I came close.

"What was that about?" I said.

"Shhh," Gabe said. He was enraptured by the television. Usually we turned it off after half an hour.

Three *Pokémon* episodes, two snacks, and half a tantrum later the phone rang.

Simon held the phone tightly to his ear. "Uh huh. Ok. That's good," he said, and put the phone down. "She's on her way," Simon said. "Everything is fine. But she wants the kids to be ready, because Aden is in the car, and they're both pretty tired."

When Jenna came upstairs, she looked exhausted. "Men are such babies," she said. "He kept yelling that he was dying. Anyway, they couldn't find anything wrong with him. Good thing we're the ones who have the children, right? They could never handle the pain."

When the house was quiet again and the children were in bed I turned to Simon. He was sitting at the kitchen table, his face lit by the spectral glow of the computer.

"What do you think Daphna wanted?" I said.

He shrugged, his face tight. He hated Daphna.

"What does she always want?" he said. "To be a pain in the ass."

"Do you think she was trying to figure out who they were?" I said. "If they were Arabs?"

"I thought of that," he said. "But who cares. It's none of her business. Anyway, it'll make her happy, give her something to gossip about."

For some reason, when I was lying in bed that night,

I remembered something that had happened years earlier. When Simon and I first moved in together, we were living in the East Village. We had a tiny third-floor apartment. It was a hot August day, the air thick and heavy. I was walking home when a girl approached me. She had blue hair, a safety pin in her ear. Back then there were always punk kids hanging out on our street. She was standing with a friend whose head was half-shaved, half-bleached and spiked.

"Excuse me," she said, and her voice was nothing like her appearance. It was soft and well-bred, like the girl who sits at the front of the classroom, not the girl who sits on the sidewalk on St. Mark's Place.

"Yes," I said, caught by surprise. I was never hard enough for New York.

"Do you have a tampon?" she said. "Or a couple of tampons?" Under the pale blue hair, her face was miserable. She had light freckles, I remember, sprinkled across her nose and cheekbones. Sam has the same kind of freckles.

"I'm sorry," I said. "I don't." But suddenly I had an idea. "I live right here," I said. "In this building. If you want to come up, I have some tampons, and you can use the bathroom. Also, I've got ice cream if you want some."

"Ice cream!" she said, and for a moment I could hear the kid she had been. I suppose she still was a kid, and I was too, barely twenty-one and living with someone for the first time.

"Come on, Deb," she said, and her friend shrugged, and followed her up the stairs to my apartment. But somehow, everything felt wrong. As we climbed the stairs, the air grew heavier and hotter, and when we arrived at the door Simon was running the electric saw, working on the bed he had decided to build us in order to save space in the tiny apartment.

The saw was loud, and the air was full of sawdust.

"What the hell is that?" Deb said, and my face grew hot.

"God, I'm really sorry," I said, "I didn't know he'd be working on it, that's my boyfriend. He's building us a bed."

"That's so cute!" the blue-haired girl said. She hadn't told me her name. "This place is really cute! You live here together?"

Deb cut her eyes at me and then said to her friend, "Why don't you get the tampons, we should go."

"But the ice cream!" the blue-haired girl said, and Deb sighed and followed me to our tiny kitchen. Our freezer was full of frost, and the ice cream had half-melted; Simon kept the saw running in the next room so it sounded a little like we were standing on an airport runway.

The blue-haired girl disappeared into the bathroom and I stood leaning against the fridge, awkwardly, as Deb smashed her ice cream with a spoon, leaving most of it in the bowl.

"You're bleeding," she said, and I said, "What?"

She pointed at my hand. I'd cut myself cooking a couple of days earlier, and somehow I must have pulled off the scab. My whole hand looked bloody, though it was just a scratch, and as I ran it under the sink the blue-haired girl came out of the bathroom and said, "Your bathroom is so nice!"

"We have to go," Deb said. "Thanks a lot for the ice cream." She said it flatly, and without inflection.

"You guys are so nice," the blue-haired girl said sadly, but they were already out the door.

Later that day, our neighbour Pete accosted me. "You can't do that," he said. He was a real New Yorker, born and bred in Stuyvesant Town.

"What?" I said. "They were just girls."

"They're not just girls," he said, "don't be naive. This is New York, you can't just let these people into your house. You don't know what they're like. You can't do that again."

Later on I realized that Deb's stiffness had not been un-friendliness but fear. She was inside a strange apartment, with a man running an electric saw and a woman whose hand was bleeding. It must have been terrifying. It was a day before I thought to check the medicine in the bathroom, but as far as I could tell nothing had been taken, except for the Advil that the blue-haired girl had requested on her way out. A month later we left Pete our keys and instructions to water our plants; we came back to find our plants dead and our whiskey bottle empty.

The night after the girls came over Simon finished our bed. There was a rough ladder and a platform, enough room to sit up on the bed but not to kneel.

"Wow," I said, hollowly.

"Come on," he said, boyish and excited, "let's try it!"

I climbed up the ladder carefully. My legs were shaking. It felt five degrees hotter in the bed. Simon climbed up and lay beside me, and the room grew hotter still. The ceiling seemed too close, as if it was pressing down on me; I was nauseous and short of breath. He put his hand on my hip and I lay there, still and sullen.

"I don't think I can sleep here," I said. "It's so hot."

His hand twitched back, off my hip.

"I'm sorry," I said miserably. "Maybe when it's cooler. I'm really sorry. I'll sleep on the couch tonight."

He said nothing, and I climbed over him as he lay there in silence. I slept on the couch that night and I slept badly, with the window open and the night sounds of the New York street in my living room. In the morning, Simon looked exhausted and wasn't speaking to me. But in the afternoon, when I got back from school, the apartment was full of sawdust and the bed on truncated legs on the floor. A pile of lumber was leaning near the front door, and Simon himself was nowhere to be found.

21.

Being a mother puts you into contact with all kinds of people you never would have known; it makes you part of a world of shared identity and responsibilities. It's like having a passport to another country, one you barely knew existed, though it's hardly glamorous, filled as it is with domestic cares and anxieties. And it is easy to get lost in the role. When Gabriel and Sam were small, I felt like my mind was a Rolodex of things to remember: the next vaccination, the need to buy milk, the laundry waiting to be folded. It was all I could do to clear some space for thought.

Leah decided that we—the unemployed mothers of the daycare—should have a program of activities to edify us in the hours between nine in the morning and one in the afternoon. We should go to East Jerusalem: it was important for us—me, Yumiko, Katie, the non-Israelis of the group—to see the real Jerusalem.

"What's *really* going on in this city," Leah said gruffly, beetling her brows. "It isn't all lattes and Liberty Bell Park."

Leah was trickily proprietary, even of what she loudly

claimed were the wrongs of her country; she knew them better than you did and would berate you with them, but if you picked up her cue she would turn around and accuse you of disloyalty, or worse, of not having a stake.

"Easy for you to say," she'd sniff, "you have somewhere to go. You understand, there is nowhere for my children. This is all we have. This is our home."

Everyone carried the tension of the country differently. I met a woman named Maia at the daycare. She told me that in the worst days of the Intifada, when buses blew up every day, when every backfiring car was cause for panic, she placed a note in her purse that said, "If I am killed, you may not blame my death on terrorism or Palestinians. I died for the sins of an inequitable political system, and the government of Israel is fully responsible for my murder."

I said, "That seems a little extreme," and she said, "Everyone here becomes extreme."

Jenna offered to drive us to East Jerusalem—she knew the roads, had family there. Again that mysterious and vaguely threatening word, *family*. "The roads are awful," she said, "and my car has four-wheel drive. Afterwards we'll get tea and sweets at this place I know in Shuafat. They have the best *knafeh*."

"I die for *knafeh*," Leah said.

This was before they each decided that the other was irredeemably crazy, back when they had built an odd and unlikely friendship. When they walked down the street Leah seemed like a mastiff, and Jenna a companion poodle.

Jenna left Noor with her mother-in-law, and we piled

into the car, Leah in front, Jenna driving. All of these women, except Leah, of course, had massive, bloated cars; riding in them was like floating in a zeppelin over the city. Jenna and Leah both seemed to want to play tour guide, Leah quoting us statistics about the lack of classrooms in East Jerusalem, the appalling absence of city services, the general nefarious neglect, Jenna telling us where the best place was to buy hummus and *fuls*—fava beans mashed with lemon juice and garlic. I couldn't believe the levels of enthusiasm and nuance people could muster when talking about hummus. I mean, hummus was just—hummus.

"Pull up here," Leah ordered, "here. Look!" She pointed to a pyramid of trash on the side of the road, almost as tall as a man. "Look!" she cried, pointing at the blown-out streetlights. "Look!" she said, pointing at a woman enveloped in black cloth from head to foot. "We have a lot to be ashamed of," she announced, pressing her hands to her generous bosom. Her voice echoed in the car like an organ in a church. "A lot."

A woman in a headscarf clutched her son's hand and glared at us suspiciously as she crossed the street; I took a photograph of another in the blind tent of her *niqab*. I pressed the display button: the shutter speed was too slow and she had moved, so she seemed like a black ghost against the sharp backdrop of rubbish and fence. "Did you get your picture? Did you get your picture?" Leah asked hysterically, gesturing back at the pile of garbage.

The road switchbacked up the hill. The streets turned to dirt, and the houses crowded together like crooked teeth, leaning against one another. No signs, no side-walks, and there were only a few women out, scuttling like hermit crabs along the edges of the road and swathed in layers of fabric.

"Just a little farther up," Leah said, "if I haven't for-gotten. I hope I'm not taking us to the wrong place." We were headed to a Jewish settler's house in the middle of the Arab quarter. The houses were outposts, established in Muslim neighbourhoods to root a Jewish presence that would make it impossible to divide Jerusalem. They were often funded by donors, and inhabited by young religious families reckless in their zeal.

Jenna was starting to get nervous. "All I need is for someone from my family to see me here," she said. "They think I'm a spy already. Anyway, I'm getting hungry. Can we go eat pastry?"

"There it is," Leah announced, ignoring her.

A tall white building rose up among the crooked little houses, straight sides and shining walls. An Israeli flag hung out like a banner from a priapic pole.

"Unbelievable." Leah said. "Stop the car. Stop the car, Jenna, I'm going to get out and tell them what I think."

"There's nowhere to stop," Jenna said, but she pulled into a narrow niche on the side of the road. A low stone wall separated the makeshift lot from a precipitous drop down the crumbling hillside, littered with plastic bags and empty water bottles.

Leah got out, stomped across the road, and knocked loudly on the heavy door. "*Shalom*," she yelled up to the shuttered windows. "*Shalom*! Open up the door, please!"

Jenna leaned on the car, lit a cigarette. "She's going to fucking get us killed." More faces started to appear in the windows of the houses around us, expressions both hostile and curious.

"Let's go, Leah," Yumiko called. "Nobody's there, let's go already. I'm not even supposed to be here," she confessed to me, "the consulate would not be happy about this."

The door suddenly swung open and closed again behind the straight back of a man in uniform. He was Ethiopian, with a kind, long face, and he wore an Uzi slung across his narrow chest. He smiled at Leah like someone humouring a child or an insane person, said something to her quietly before he vanished behind the door again. She swayed heavily back across the road, her face flushed.

Jenna had already started the car and swung it around. "Get in, come on, get in," she said, and Leah huffed at her like an insulted hippopotamus.

"Our tax dollars," she said, "our tax dollars guarding that house, picking up that garbage. Nobody else gets their garbage picked up around here."

"Nobody here pays their taxes," Jenna said.

I leaned forward, "What did he say?"

"He said that nobody was home," Leah said. "A lie, I could hear them behind the door. He told me not to make trouble."

"He's right," Jenna said. "Satisfied now? Had enough?" She turned the wheel a little harder than she needed to, and Yumiko flew into me, her bony elbow in my stomach. "Are we done?"

The bakery was empty, except for the salesmen and the rows and rows of pastries under glass cases and neon lights. The cakes were dyed lurid colours, mint green and mandarin orange, and were gleaming with oil and honey. I took a picture of Jenna in her grey V-necked T-shirt, holding a cigarette and looking off into the distance, and another of Yumiko in the very dark sunglasses.

"Take a picture of me," Leah said. "I need it for a dating site. I'm tired of my boyfriend. I need to find someone new."

"Don't you want to fix your hair, to put on some lipstick?" Jenna said. She reached into her purse.

"No," Leah said. "They should see me as I am. Just, please, take the picture." She squared her shoulders at the camera and smiled at me, her mouth closed, her eyes soft. I passed her the camera.

"That will do," she said, passing it back to me. "You will email it to me tonight. That's fine."

I stayed away from Leah after that trip. I had still not invited her son back to my house, so the reciprocal, cyclical potlatch of play dates had been broken. And it was a shame, in a way, because her son was sweet, though I was bothered by the way that every morning he came up to me with a huge smile on his face and a toy gun in his hand and said, "Boom!" But she was exhausting.

I still saw her dropping her son off and picking him up sometimes, her shoulders rounded, her step heavy.

Yumiko told me about some of Leah's other escapades: she had written a rude, aggressive email to one father in the group; she had told Jenna that her husband was "as tall as a boot and as dumb as a shoelace," in front of her mother-in-law, no less. The women of the daycare, in a reflex of protection, had stopped bitching about their husbands in response to her constant attacks on them.

Slowly, the other women that Leah had so forcefully befriended began to drop away from her, to make excuses when she invited their children over to play. And I began to see her less and less; she dropped her son off late, and didn't loiter anymore at pickup, when earlier that year her booming voice was often the first I heard as I headed down the hallway to the classroom. She looked paler too, more distressed, her face shorn of the war paint that had marked it when I met her; I heard that she was having more trouble with her ex-husband and that her son cried when it was his turn to stay with his father. He told his mother he was afraid, that his father yelled, and hit him. She had been looking into a restraining order, then she had given up, and the child had stopped complaining.

I was relieved that she had abandoned the idea of my testifying on behalf of her sanity, though I felt guilty when I saw her. And she had less and less money, and then one day her car was stolen. "By Arabs of course, who else would take such a crappy car," she shrugged on one of the few occasions I spoke to her. Although her father replaced her car, the new one used more gas and she could not afford to fill the tank. Some days she stayed home with her son instead of buying the gas to get to the daycare.

I saw her away from the daycare once, walking on the street with bags of groceries in her hands. I didn't recognize her at first, without her son, without the car; she was muttering to herself and looked a little mad, her lipstick cracked, her mascara smeared. She saw me, and her eyes widened. For a moment it seemed she was going to say something, but then she lowered her head and plowed right past me, like someone who had somewhere important to go.

22

I t wasn't until we left Jerusalem that we realized just how claustrophobic the city had sometimes been with its inescapable sun and glittering stone. On the weekends, we fled the city. The school didn't have Sundays off but we took them off anyway; the children were young enough not to notice, and Simon only started teaching on Tuesdays. The cars we rented were tiny and battered. Back home, when you rented a car, the staff would inspect it from head to tail to testify to its shining immaculateness, but here the cars were all so dented that nobody bothered to vet them. Some young man would drive up in front of us too fast, from wherever they hid the rental cars in the dense central labyrinth of Jerusalem, after we'd been waiting so long we'd nearly given up. He would toss us the keys and vanish again, leaving us hoping that all the seat belts worked. We piled in.

And here is the thing: we could travel. We could go anywhere we wanted, we could go places the Palestinians couldn't go, of course, but also places the Israelis couldn't go, our foreign passports offered us that easy access. We could spend the morning in Bethlehem and the afternoon in Jerusalem, could go out for lunch in the West Bank and have dinner in South Tel Aviv. We could go anywhere, a privilege afforded only to those who did not call the land their home.

One day we decided to play hooky and head to the Dead Sea. On the way down, the hills were salt-white and glittering. Sam started to complain that he felt sick; we pulled over by a desolate bus stop. Next to a sign that said we were at the lowest point on earth Sam vomited into the dirt. It was hotter than Jerusalem, and the desert shimmered.

The Dead Sea was dying, or at least, drying up. The salt in the water was becoming more concentrated, and we had seen photos of the receding shores, crusted with arabesques of salt. There was talk of piping in fresh water to keep the resorts along the shores of the Dead Sea functional. The Jordanian side, we were told, was even more beautiful, and we could see the hills of Jordan across the water, hazy and dreamlike.

It was something I had always heard when I was a child: the Jewish pioneers made the desert bloom. It seemed like such a miraculous accomplishment, draining the swamps, banishing malaria, growing oranges and grapefruits where once there had been only sand and rock. Only, as it turned out, perhaps the desert wasn't meant to bloom. There had been unintended consequences to the agricultural miracle, and now more than ever Israel was a country addicted to water, exporting it in the form of grapefruits, oranges, and lemons while the Galilee dried up and the Dead Sea grew ever saltier.

Because Sunday was a workday we had expected the resort to be empty, but it was full of people. The signs were all in Russian as well as in Hebrew, and there were blond women in tiny bikinis, matrons in house dresses, and men whose stomachs pouched over their Speedos and who had caked their bodies in the medicinal mud of the Dead Sea. One sat in a white-slatted plastic beach chair, holding his cellphone gingerly away from his anointed flesh. An old woman in floral underpants and a stretched-out beige bra stood blissfully thigh deep in the water. Occasionally, she scooped up handfuls of the salty water and rubbed her soft, freckled shoulders, her large, creviced bosom. There was something fascinating and childlike about her utter lack of self-consciousness.

The children refused to jump into the mud pit and cover their bodies in the black slime, but I did, passing an Israeli who rubbed handfuls of mud over his hairy legs and chest and then grinned at me, saying, "When you go black, you never go back!" Simon threw handfuls of mud at the children and we must have looked just like a happy family on vacation.

But the mud burned, and then itched as it dried. The boys went into the water, but complained: it hurt and then felt icky, they said. A group of tourists were all using the same soggy newspaper as a prop for photographs. Nobody actually read it, they just held it up and looked towards the camera. There was a separate mineral pool, with a large sign extolling its therapeutic powers; I went in for a while, but it smelled strongly of sulphur, and was crowded along the edges with the heavy-lidded faces of swimmers whose resigned, long-suffering expressions announced them devoted patients of this vile, eggy therapy.

I had forgotten, somehow, that the Dead Sea was always disappointing, as if whatever concentrated the heat and salt also served to intensify emotion so that it was a place of melancholy and tantrum. The first time I went to the Dead Sea I was thirteen. I had my period, but went in the water anyway. I had been warned about going in with scratches on my legs, but nobody had warned me about this; the salt burned, and I was too embarrassed to tell anyone, but spent the rest of the day cross-legged and miserable on a beach chair.

The next time we left the city, we rented a cabin on the Galilee in a small resort. The resort had an ostrich farm; the long-lashed, peg-legged creatures gazed at us haughtily from behind their fence. A sign warned that we risked getting kicked if we ventured too close. Their long sharp nails were like knives. In 1918, Theodore Roosevelt had written about how to respond if confronted by an ostrich: "If, when assailed by the ostrich, the man stands erect, he is in great danger. But by the simple expedient of lying down, he escapes all danger." There were metal ostriches for the children to ride, ones that wouldn't eviscerate them; we fed shekels into their necks and watched the children buck and lean. In the activity hut nearby we pasted feathers and fragments of coloured mosaic onto hollowed ostrich eggs. They were the colour of ivory, and felt thick and smooth.

You could see the Galilee from our windows. The water was clear as glass.

The lake was shrinking; the yards and yards of brush that stretched from our cabin had once been covered in water. We had to walk ten minutes to reach the water's edge. We stripped down to our swimsuits in the late afternoon light, the hills around the lake stained umber and purple, the colour of the waves deepening. I was distracted, wrestling with my swimsuit under my dress; I twisted my head and realized Gabe was in the water, neck deep. I ran into the lake, fished him out, sputtering. He was calm.

"What were you doing?" I said.

"I just wanted to see if I could swim," he replied.

The wind picked up; the waves curled on the sand like fingers reaching for the old shoreline. I tried to take a picture of the boys in front of the lake, but it wasn't right. I looked at the back of the camera and pressed the button to delete it, thinking, as I always did, that I would press the wrong button and just like that all our photographs would be gone. "Let me see that," Simon said. He held the camera up. "Try shifting the focus point," he said. "You were focusing on the horizon. Pick something closer. Put the focus on your subject—in this case, that's the children. There." I pressed down and the lens whirred and fixed. I held the camera out to look at the image. "That's better," he said. It was.

On our way back to Jerusalem, we passed burning towers of garbage. The smell was black and poisonous, and coated our nostrils, the insides of our throat. Arriving in Jerusalem from the north always felt treacherous; the roads were high and narrow, and the hillsides were littered with the carcasses of tanks from the old wars, rusted and ensnared in flowers and weeds.

But still, it was starting to feel like coming home. We were finally accustomed to the city. We had settled into our new routines, and even things that had seemed abrasive or beautiful or extraordinary had dulled for us, as if our eyes had grown calloused. My older son had sat in a classroom for three months without understanding Hebrew, and then one day the language had shifted into place for him, like an optic puzzle. He was more comfortable now, and we were more comfortable too, in our safe corral of school, daycare, coffee shop, and library, the corners of our life so sharply demarcated that even walking had become automatic. As our friends had predicted, I'd stopped reading the papers.

And my son was in love. There was another new child in his class, a little girl. She was the youngest of seven, and her family had just moved from Britain. She was named Aliya, her very name an echo of her family's aspirations to come to Israel. Her mother was pretty and scattered, always watching too many children, with a baby on her hip, though she looked like a college student with her long brown hair and her faded T-shirts.

"I have something I want to tell you," Gabe said. "But I also don't want to tell you."

"What is it?" I said, and he blushed.

"It's about a person ...oh, never mind."

"A girl person?"

He had been talking about her a lot. He said that she was crazy, but he laughed when he said it, and seemed impressed. They had a Hebrew tutor twice a week, he and Aliya and an Ethiopian girl whose mother had a faded tattoo of a cross on her forehead. I wondered what it was like, walking around Jerusalem with that enduring mark. Aliya was naughty in class, he said. But funny, she was always funny.

"Is it Aliya?" I asked. "Do you like her?"

"Well, of course I like her," he said impatiently. "I like lots of people. It isn't just that."

"Do you want to marry her?" I said.

We didn't have vocabulary for a crush yet, and asking if he loved her seemed too strong. It was a child's game, wanting to marry; they knew about marriage, not about boyfriends and girlfriends, not yet. I was only half-listening anyway, though I knew my curiosity was pushing him farther than he'd wanted to go.

His face cracked, and he wailed, "I didn't want to tell you!"

For the next two hours he stayed under the bed, curled away from us. I lay on the floor and tried to talk to him, but he told me to go away. Every so often he would wail again, and this also was new, this unfamiliar grief. It was as if these new emotions were too large for his body. It was as if he was possessed. I knew I had screwed up, and didn't want to tell Simon, but it was clear that something was wrong. When he came home and I explained it to him, he looked at me, and his face flickered between amusement and disgust.

"What is wrong with you?" he said. "Why didn't you just leave him alone?" But he sounded satisfied when he said it; he liked being the reasonable one.

Simon took his turn lying on the floor, trying to coax Gabriel out. As he lay beside the bed, his long legs reaching foolishly past the doorway into the hall, his voice low and soft, I felt a sudden rush of affection. He had so much patience with Gabriel, with Sam. When he got up I leaned forward and kissed his cheek, and he looked boyish suddenly, surprised and grateful.

"What was that for?" he said, and I said, "Just because."

My younger son still believed that he would marry me. He liked to put his head under my shirt, so that it looked like I was pregnant. I let him; after all, he was only three. We were lying in his room like that one day, his head on my stomach while I was trying to put him to bed, and he said, "Can I just see the gate?"

"What gate?" I said.

"I just want to see the gate, where I came out," he said. "Can you just let me back in the gate, just for a minute?"

A few days later Aliya's mother had a terrible accident. She fell off the stone balcony of her apartment; for weeks she lay motionless, her entire body encased in a cast. She had been acting out the balcony scene from Romeo and Juliet for her children, or at least that was what she said, later, when she was miraculously well again. But I wondered if it wasn't the end of the play that she had been practicing, and if she hadn't been disappointed when she woke up in the hospital, to find that she had only been pretending and now she had to return to real life.

When I was doing the dishes that night Simon had come up behind me and put his hands on my waist. "You smell good," he said. "Like the sun." The dishes had piled up all day and the sink was so full that the soapy water slopped out of the sink and down the front of my dress. He kissed my neck and then I felt the cool air on my back as his body withdrew, felt him walk away, and heard the door close.

I turned off the tap and followed Simon into the bedroom. He was lying on the bed, his eyes closed. "What is it you want?" he said. "I'm tired of guessing. You let me know when you figure it out."

I sat on the bed beside him. "I don't know," I said. "I mean, this is what I wanted. It just isn't anything like I thought it would be." I lay down beside him on top of the covers, my clothes on, my shoes dangling over the side of the bed, and when I took his hand he did not pull away.

"Simon," I said. "Let's go away, just the two of us. I'll find something."

He nodded without opening his eyes. I curled onto my side and held onto him, I held on.

23.

While we were up north, I kept thinking about my old friend Raquel. When I was seventeen years old we had gone north together. She had thick, long honey-streaked hair, a pronounced swayback, and gappy teeth, and she was as close to sexy as anyone I had ever met, probably because she'd actually had sex. I mistook her confusion for sophistication, and she mistook my inexperience for innocence. She'd followed the Grateful Dead on tour with her boyfriend, and drew psychedelic, detailed miniatures where looping lines underwent metamorphosis into unearthly creatures. She had a strange, cracked voice that abruptly shifted registers, and spoke with an unearned world-weariness.

Halfway through the long bus trip to Mount Hermon, we were thoroughly sick of one another. I looked out the smoked window at the furred green of the mountains—it looked like Scotland, I thought, having never been to Scotland. When we arrived, the hostel was cold and bare and empty, and a mist had settled over the small vacation town. The heat was off and the room was freezing. In the night I woke up to the smell of burning: I had draped my wet clothes on the radiator and it had coughed to life, scorching my only pants.

But the morning was better. The mist burned off by nine o'clock, and after a spare breakfast of weak instant coffee, blue-white milk and soggy cereal, we took a walk. The streets were deserted: it felt like a place that people had fled. Beyond a knee-high wire fence was a field of flowers: daisies, narcissus, chamomile, and the silky red flag known as the humble poppy. We waded through, the sun hot on our uncovered heads, feeling drowsy and sated as bumblebees.

But then we heard shouts from the road. Two men, red-faced, were gesturing at us, circling their arms as if to pull us in.

"What's the problem?" I shouted in Hebrew, feeling defensive and inconvenienced. They pointed to a sign we had walked right past. It was bright yellow and showed a stick figure flying from a cartoon blast. We picked our way back, trying to retrace our steps although the long grass hid the path, and the flowers suddenly held the menace of tiny bombs.

"Didn't you see?" the taller man shouted at us as we stepped back over the fence to the road. "What, do you have a death wish?"

The top of his head was bald, and had pinked in the sun. The second man, smaller, his eyes behind mirrored sunglasses, just shook his head as if we were further evidence of the world's stupidity. It was hard to walk back to the hostel after that, even though we were safe. I found myself testing the road nervously with the tips of my toes before laying my feet flat on the ground, as if that would have helped, as if I would have known. We had left our brief feeling of lightness back in the blooming minefield. The bus didn't arrive until the next day: there was little to eat, nothing to do. Raquel spent the rest of the trip doodling in her journal, her Walkman firmly locked into her ears. I read Henry James and slept for fourteen hours.

We had also visited Kfar Chabad together that year, a small town in Israel that was confusingly modeled after the neighbourhood in Brooklyn where the Lubavitch *Rebbe* lived. The Lubavitchers who had built the settlement believed he was the Messiah. Eight miles outside of Tel Aviv, boys scurried to *Cheder* in their white shirts and black coats, speaking Yiddish and looking at their feet. In the middle of the town, alien and monumental, was an exact replica of 770, the brick mansion in Crown Heights where the *Rebbe* made his home. The brick house was as incongruous in the landscape as the heavy black coats were in the climate.

Somehow, though, inside the town, the architecture seemed less strange. Our eyes quickly adjusted to the way the Mediterranean sun flattened the village palate of black and white. Laundry lines hung out the windows with that same monotonous array, white shirt, black pants, white shirt, black pants, black pants, black coat, flapping in the wind like a murder of crows. The *Rebbe* wasn't dead yet, and his picture was on every wall. It was always the same photograph, the one where the *Rebbe* is looking into the distance in three-quarter profile, the colours as tea-stained and saturated as a Rembrandt portrait. "His eyes follow you when you move," they said, and the idea frightened me, but it wasn't true; I tracked the picture as I walked across a room and the eyes stayed as fixed and unblinking as a taxidermied corpse, each iris pierced by a single point of light. Children were everywhere, accompanied by immaculate women with their heads wrapped and their skirts to their ankles. At dinner a draped white table laden with Sabbath food glittered in the candlelight like an apparition from a fairy tale.

I couldn't wait to get out of there and Raquel couldn't stop talking about how peaceful she felt. It had made me feel the opposite of peaceful; it had made me feel enraged. Perhaps I should have known back then: this was the picture of order that she craved. All weekend, I had felt choked, like I couldn't take a full breath. "They all seemed so happy, so at peace," Raquel said wistfully.

"So cloistered," I sputtered, "so self-satisfied, so ignorant, so closed."

"How could you know that?" Raquel said. "Perhaps they're just exactly where they want to be. Perhaps what you cannot stand is the fact that they are at peace, and they don't need the rest," her hand fluttered at her wrist, vaguely, jostling my arm, "the rest of the world." We had both taken the visit far too personally.

After that trip, we began spending less time together. She began travelling to the Chabad village, and to a Jerusalem hostel that took in students for *Shabbat*, feeding them and hosting them at long tables set with paper plates and plastic cloths. The students got *cholent* and sweet grape juice and a free place to stay in the Old City in exchange for listening to rabbis give long and ranting speeches. At the time, I was young enough to think that was a fair exchange.

I did accompany her to the Old City once, and bumped into a boy whom I had met a couple of months earlier in a sleazy dance club in downtown Jerusalem. He was a film student from NYU, on exchange for the semester; he had tried to kiss me in the dark. Now he was wearing the white shirt and black pants of a *Chasid*; flaccid *tsitsis* hung out of the corners of his shirt. His parents were visiting from North America. As far as I could tell, they had come to try to convince him to return home. There were these honeytraps set up all over Israel, to catch the secular and the unaffiliated. If he stayed, he would be married within a year's time, studying full-time at one of the *yeshivot* hidden behind the closed doors of the Old City; he would have many children, who would know nothing of New York or film school or dancing in the dark; he would be lost to his parents forever, dead to his old life.

Raquel and I stayed in touch for a few years after we left Israel. We both went to college and to graduate school. She kicked up her heels at my wedding. I knew— vaguely knew—that she had become more and more involved with the Chabad branch on her campus. It was the kind of organization that offered a home to the lost souls of Judaism. At any rate, they would try to convince you that you were a lost soul.

The last time I spoke to her I caught her on the way out the door to a date. Not a date; a *shidduch*. She sounded awkward and distant. Six weeks later she was married. I was not invited to the wedding.

For a long time this vanished friendship hurt just a little bit, like a sensitive tooth when you bite down on foil. Then mostly I forgot. But when we went up north, Raquel was beside me at every turn in the road, a silent and sullen presence. After our family's trip north, I decided to find out where she lived.

Nobody vanishes anymore. I had expected to have difficulty locating her; I didn't know her parents, didn't know her married name, and didn't even know if she was in the United States anymore. But Google found her on Facebook under her maiden name. Surely she'd changed it? And her picture on the page, the size of a postage stamp, was crowded with children but showed no man. Her hair was tightly covered under a scarf wound like a turban; she wore a long denim skirt, Keds, a T-shirt that covered her collarbones and wrists, that bland uniform of orthodoxy. It was hard to imagine all those children belonging to her. I sent a friend request, winged out into the night; when she accepted, Simon hung over my shoulder as we scrolled down her wall for clues. Four—no, five kids. No husband in any of the photographs. An old picture of her in a bikini top and cut-offs from our university years, which seemed shocking in the context of all of that heavy religious camouflage. All that year, she had been living a half hour away from us, just over the Green Line.

And halfway down the wall was a link to an organization that helped Jewish women whose husbands would not give them divorces and a status update that seemed at once too intimate and coyly indirect: "I cannot believe a certain someone will not give me a *get*." A "*get*," the Jewish divorce document that was the only way to sever a *halachic* marriage. Indeed, the only way to sever a Jewish marriage in Israel at all.

Oh.

We spoke on the phone the next day, and her voice was the same as it ever had been, flushed and uneven with emotion. We didn't speak about our shared past. Instead we spoke about the last few years. She had decided to leave her husband when she became pregnant with her last child. It was hard to describe, Raquel said—it was as if he had tried to destroy her, and she had barely survived him. Somehow the last pregnancy had given her the strength to leave. But he had not made it easy. He had accused her of cheating on him, of being an abusive mother, of not loving the children. The small neighbourhood they lived in had divided over the split; she had lost friends, lost her community. There was a restraining order against him now because the social worker had witnessed him grabbing her arm in the driveway; that was lucky, she said. But for a long time he had refused to leave the house and even now retained control of most of their assets. It had been a long battle but he had finally, possibly, agreed to an appointment for a divorce, although he had agreed before and had failed to show up at court. She was paying him off, with money her parents had sent: she was, of course, penniless. And she had to give him custody of the three oldest children. It was strategic; he wanted it only because the *yeshiva* would pay him more to study if he had custody of the children, and once the divorce was in hand she would fight to reverse the custody decision.

"Why just the three oldest children?" I said, and there was a pause at the other end of the line before her voice came back, crackling with the poor connection.

"Because he doesn't believe the other two are his."

We met in town the next day. Her hair was wrapped in a turquoise scarf, as it had been in the photograph; she noticed me looking and her hand fluttered towards her head.

"I'll miss this when I'm not married. I like this style of headcovering. It makes me feel like a queen."

We met at a cafe that I loved, hidden in a small courtyard. The walls were stone and the tables and chairs were crooked and shabby. Books lined the walls, and the placemats were printed with stories and poetry, commissioned specially by the owners. The cafe held readings, and served strong cappuccinos in exquisite ceramic cups, intensely coloured in scarlet and cerulean and saffron, and with handmade smooth uneven edges.

More of the story emerged: her mother had flown to Israel a year earlier to try to help her. They had spent tens of thousands of dollars on a lawyer who hadn't been able to get her the papers; now she had a legal aid lawyer, but he wasn't much use. She had been meeting a friend in the back alleys of Geulah to receive money that her parents wired, so that her husband didn't steal it. They had an appointment for the *get*; it was the next month.

"And how strange," she said, "that so many years after falling out of touch you should re-appear a few weeks before this finally happens. Almost *bashert*. Meant to be."

"Do you have anyone to go to court with you?" I asked, and she looked at me tentatively. "I mean, would you like me to go to court with you?"

Raquel told me that she'd had to submit her marriage certificate as part of the paperwork for the divorce. Her rabbi had written it himself. He was the one who had first set her up with Samson. At the time of their marriage her husband was a personal indemnities lawyer. He'd donated a lot of money to the synagogue. A *gantse machor*—a "big man." He had fallen into Chabad even faster than she had, although she didn't realize it at the time; in two months his religious practice had escalated radically. He wasn't who he'd seemed: soon after their wedding, his partner was arrested at their law firm. She was vague about the charges, but he and his partner had both lost their licenses to practice law. He'd taught at a school for a little while, and then he'd just studied in a *yeshiva*. He was a member of the John Birch Society; in some bastardized way he'd hoped to bring their message together with that of the Lubavitch *Rebbe*. For a while, they'd thought of moving to a *Noahide* community in Vermont. He would have been their rabbi.

"We could have had a beautiful house," Raquel the

former architecture student said dreamily, "Queen Anne style. You know, those colourful wood shingles, stained-glass bay windows. We could have had a porch."

"You were going to live with members of the John Birch Society?" I said, incredulous. "Aren't they anti-Semitic? What were you thinking?"

"Only some of them are anti-Semitic," she said. "Anyway, that group weren't Birchers, they just had some similar views, you know, about the federal reserve. Anyway, it didn't happen. But we would have had a beautiful house."

The rabbi who married them had been a kind of surrogate father to her: looking after her in graduate school, hosting her at his house, feeding her, picking her up from the airport, and finally, marrying her off. Marriage bound all of these new *baal teshuvas*, these "returnees to the faith," to each other and the community. Each child anchored them deeper. There was a hierarchy in matchmaking: the sons of scholars married the daughters of scholars. And these *baal teshuvas*, of course, they married, or were married to, each other. They were part of the community now, but they would never be insiders. Their children, too, would carry that taint.

Her neighbour took the marriage certificate into court for her. He called her that night, livid.

"Who wrote this?" he demanded.

She was confused. "My rabbi from home," she said.

"Did you give him some reason, was there some reason, what could possibly be the reason?" he asked, incoherent.

It turned out that the rabbi had left the word *betula*, "virgin," off her marriage certificate. He had branded her, and had branded her children, since it was standard practice in a *shidduch*, an "arranged marriage," to submit the wedding certificate of the parents to the prospective in-laws. Her children would have to disclose her *ketuba* when they were later vetted by their own prospective spouses. He had labeled her a whore, and marked her family for generations.

She had not been a virgin. But she'd never told him that.

n December the lobby of the YMCA was taken over by the biggest Christmas tree I had ever seen, hung with glittering garlands and old-fashioned silken balls. It was always a shock to see the tree when I walked into the daycare in the morning, and then I realized that it wasn't that the tree was large, it was that I hadn't noticed Christmas decorations anywhere else in the city. No strings of lights, no tinsel candy canes, no Christmas carols rushing out with the warm air when you opened the door into the grocery store. I was so used to the rhythm of the calendar back home that missing Christmas was like missing snow, even though it had never been my holiday. The absence disturbed my equilibrium just a little bit. And then when I went into the lobby and saw the Christmas tree, something familiar clicked back into place, and I felt at once intruded upon and at home again.

Chanuka and Christmas came close together that year, in the shifting two-step of the Jewish and Christian holidays, the elliptical calendar of the moon and the metronome of the sun. Gabe's class took a field trip to the Valley of the Cross. They were learning about ecology, and those hills were full of olive trees. It was almost Chanuka: they would pick olives and then press them, in one of the old stone presses in the park.

It was a perfect day. The sky was a lucid blue; the clouds were *flaneurs*. The children hiked up the hill, then scattered, climbing the gnarled, knobby trunks of the olive trees. They climbed like monkeys, hands and feet and nearly prehensile toes, their socks off for grip, leaving sweaters and shirts strewn on branches as the day grew warmer. It was hard to imagine a first grade class in Montreal having a field trip that included tree climbing, and one of the most alluring things about Israel was that they hadn't yet fetishized safety, that children could just play. A few of the children, the daring ones, were already at the spindly tops, balancing on the narrow branches. We parents held white buckets for the hard green pellets and the children tossed them down.

I had been to the Valley of the Cross a few weeks earlier. There was a monastery, a courtyard, and a small museum. The monastery had been there for nearly a thousand years, squatting at the bottom of the valley. We could see it from where we stood. The museum was random and dank and smelled of urine. There were stiff mannequins dressed in national costume, their plastic, lipsticked faces swathed in headscarves that dangled rich coins.

A group of Russian pilgrims had come to see the church. The women wrapped shawls around their naked heads and shoulders and legs. When they stepped out into the light, you could see the shapes of their bodies through the gauzy fabric. They moved in clusters, caught in portals and on doorways as if they were not many bodies but a single body moving together, too large to gracefully navigate the narrow stone portico. They were business-like in their devotion. Each in turn put a coin in the jar, took and lit a candle, covered her eyes for a second or two and then moved to let her neighbour take her place. An assembly line of pilgrims; but in the sun outside they dissolved into individuals again, laughing and smoking and spreading out into the air.

The courtyard was beautiful, stone and spacious and walled in bougainvillea. There were giant birdcages lining the walls, made of curlicued green-blue metal. Inside the cages tropical birds flaunted their plumage at one another, and took sudden, swooping flights from corner to corner. The Russian women pressed up against the cages, twittering at the birds. I went into the gift shop: olive-wood sculptures, olive-wood plaques, olive-wood magnets, olive-wood crosses.

"Do the birds have something to do with the Saint?" I asked the woman behind the counter. Her eyebrows met in her forehead in a scowl. "Not at all," she said haughtily, but gave me no further explanation. I thought of how fun it would be to take the children to see the birds, though there was something a little sad in all of their penned-up brightness.

The teacher called us over to the olive press. "Valley of the Cross," she kept saying, but none of the children knew what a cross was or knew what significance the place might have for the people who once named it. It was a word denuded of content; it had become just a name. The monastery below her might have been invisible. She did not mention it and nobody asked. Instead the talk was all olive trees and Maccabees and a long-ago miracle, and Eleazar piercing the belly of the elephant, and Mordechai overturning the carcass of the pig. She took a plastic bag of olives and spilled them on the press, and then one of the fathers volunteered to turn it, flexing his shoulders under his short-sleeved shirt. Donkeys once turned the olive press; the father did his best. He leaned in and the olive press wouldn't budge; he tried again, digging in his feet and putting his shoulder to it, and backed off with an abashed smile, his eyes invisible behind the mirrored lenses of his sunglasses. "Anyone going to help me out?" he asked, and two other fathers stepped forward. Pushing together, they managed to shift the stone wheel just over the pebbled fruit. "Now, seven more times, and we will have olive oil," the teacher said, laughing at their alarm.

She handed out jelly donuts. There was everything to like about Chanuka, a holiday you celebrated with jelly donuts, and the city was full of them, in a kaleidoscope of colours and flavours that I had never seen. We sat in the sun, peeling the donuts off the thin napkins, our lips white with powdered sugar and our throats thick with the slightly acrid taste of the red jelly. The children finished first, and started walking along the stone wall that surrounded the press, as high as a man. Their heads cut off the sky. "*Die, die,*" the teacher exclaimed, which meant "enough" but always gave me pause. We carpooled back home, and in my car we had to stop so one child could spew sweet red vomit on the side of the road.

It took me a while to wonder about the presses. Who had built them? Who had used them? Who had abandoned them to be toys for children and props for field trips in a grove of two-hundred-year-old trees that had been bearing fruit for somebody for generations?

Sam also had an olive-picking field trip, to his teacher's house in Beit Safafa. The trees outside Jameelah's building were laden, and the branches low enough that the children could reach up and pick the fruit for themselves. Upstairs, in her apartment, she showed us how to crush the olives with the flat of a dull knife, to cut lemons and squeeze them over the olives, to add crushed red peppers and finally olive oil before tossing it all with our hands in a large bowl. We each took home a small jar. They had to age in our pantries for a few weeks before we could eat them. A few of the children put the raw olives in their mouths; their faces puckered from the astringency and bitterness.

We had decided to go to Bethlehem to see the Christmas decorations and to visit a family that Simon had met a couple of weeks earlier. He'd gone on a program which brought tourists to meet Palestinian families in the West Bank, and when he came back he was invigorated. "They were so nice," he said. "Such a lovely family. But you won't believe how they have to live. I mean, I knew it in theory, but it's different to see close up. You've got to come meet them." "I'd love to," I said, caught up in his excitement. This was what he'd been like when we first met; bursting with ideas and experiences that he wanted to share with me.

Bethlehem was just south of the city, past the wall. I'd never been there, though really it was right beside Jerusalem, just on the other side of the Green Line. We took a taxi through the back streets—there was still a way to evade the checkpoint on the way in—although different taxi companies operated in Bethlehem and Jerusalem, and the taxi driver charged us extra for the risk he claimed he took in bringing us over the invisible border.

The wall hadn't been there the last time I was in Israel: there was nothing subtle about it. Everywhere you went you came up against its brute facticity. In the distance, the wall looked like a snake, curling against the dry hills and valleys; up close, it was a behemoth, thick, impermeable, doing its best to block the sky.

I stopped in a gift shop to buy a present for the family we were visiting. The store was full of tiny vials of myrrh and frankincense and hundreds of olive-wood carvings, blunted abstract sculptures, from the size of a thumbnail to the length of an arm. I picked up a figure of the Mother and Child and ran my finger down its lacquered smoothness.

The owner was bored and friendly. He sat on a low stool, his knees high and akimbo. Business, he said, was slow. I asked him if he had anything for a local family, and he laughed.

"For a local? Not here," he said. "Go buy them a nice

bottle of wine."

The day was overcast and dull, and the square felt empty. Small drifts of tourists crossed aimlessly. The streetlights were strung with tinsel, but on that cloudy day even the tinsel looked drab. We wandered into the church and pressed with the crowd towards the star on the floor that marked the nativity. The Church of Mary was down a side street; the gates were locked, but a group of Filipino women were pressing at the fence and calling out in high voices. Finally a monk came out, looking crabby. He handed them Ziploc bags of white liquid through the fence, and they passed him folded bills. He seemed tired and rumpled, as though he had been caught napping in a pew.

"Mary's milk," Fatimah told me later. "They believe it comes from the walls. The women want to get pregnant. They think that the milk makes them fertile. These trips are pilgrimages, and the pilgrims are looking for miracles; busloads of them, mostly from the Philippines, women who can't get pregnant." She shrugged her shoulders. "Ignorant."

Fatimah el Khairi was a Christian, but not the kind that believed in miracles. She met us in the square and brought us to her apartment. She and her husband had built a small building with their family; his mother and brothers lived on the other floors. Her mother-in-law came down to lunch, dressed in a pale blue velour housecoat with small, embroidered flowers on the collar.

We sat down at the table, spread with pita, nuts, and

fruit. The apartment was large, clean, and impersonal. There were no family photographs on the wall, not much to look at except for the wide windows and a large TV in the very centre of the room.

Fatimah was distracted. She was worried about her son; he had gone to university in Greece, and there were strikes and riots at the school. He was stranded there, waiting for classes to start, hoping not to get caught in the middle of trouble. I couldn't imagine leaving Bethlehem only to find chaos in the place you'd gone to pursue your education in peace. He would come home for Christmas if he could, but coming home took days; you couldn't fly directly to the West Bank. He would have to fly from Greece to Amman, maybe through Abu Dhabi. Then they would have to drive to Amman to pick him up, a drive that took fifteen hours at least because it traversed several checkpoints and took the roundabout roads the Palestinians were allowed to travel. Ben Gurion airport was less than two hours away and had direct flights to Greece every single day. But that route was no longer possible.

Fatimah had thick dark hair and skin that looked scoured and red. By looking at her daughters you could see she had been beautiful. The girls sat on the couch watching TV. They were dressed identically in jeans and hooded sweatshirts. "Princeton," one of the sweatshirts said. The other two said "Notre Dame" and "Columbia." The oldest daughter would leave for school abroad the next year. There were some scholarships at American universities marked specifically for Palestinian students.

But that was very far away; she lit up talking about it, then glanced at her mother, hesitated, fell quiet again. Or maybe Greece, like her brother. The only thing that was clear was that she would not stay.

Because it was Christmas season, the family had applied for permits to visit Jerusalem. All the men were denied a permit; they had expected it. But their grandmother was also turned down. Of all the members of the family, she had wanted to go the most. She lived in Jerusalem when she was a child and her neighbour and best friend was a Jewish girl. They were blood sisters; when they were six they had cut their fingers and rubbed them together so that they were kin.

"Why they turned me down? What can I say, I am terrorist," the grandmother said, smiling. She said that during the last Intifada she had seen some soldiers beating a boy and she had told them to stop. They had arrested her, held her for a few hours, taken down her name and let her go. Perhaps, she speculated, that was why she'd been denied the permit. All her childhood memories lived in Jerusalem; they were so close.

Her hair was thin and lifted like a cloud on her scalp, in the unconvincing perm of the elderly—my grandmother also had hair like that.

The family laughed and so she repeated it again, enjoying her audience, "I must be terrorist, then!"

She would have visited some of those old friends from her childhood, would have gone, maybe, to the church, only it was so crowded during the holiday season.

The girls had their permits, and they were excited to go shopping, to go to the mall. The stores in Bethlehem were boring; there was nothing nice to buy.

In the Bethlehem market there were card tables spread with photographs of bosomy singers with long full hair in heart-shaped frames. There were cable sweaters that looked like something I might have owned in 1986. There were animal carcasses on hooks, flayed and head-less, sheathed in pink muscle and white fat against the turquoise of a door. The produce was more meager than the markets in Jerusalem, and the prices were higher; Fatimah stopped to weigh a cauliflower, to finger the blackened outer leaves of a giant lettuce.

Fatimah took us for a tour of the wall, since that had become the thing to see in Bethlehem. It was obvious that she'd taken visitors on this tour before; there were highlights, familiar spots. The security wall bordered one house on three sides so that the windows looked out onto the dull concrete (not that the residents were allowed to open their shades). There was a massive *trompe l'oeil* of a rhinoceros blasting through the concrete, and a series of oversized black-and-white portraits of grimacing faces.

"That has nothing to do with us," Fatimah said dismissively. "Some foreign artist who wants to be famous. That has nothing to do with Palestinians."

Banksy had recently been to Bethlehem. He'd taken an expanse of the wall as his canvas. He'd also decorated the wall of a nearby building whose owner then sold it to a gallery in London: it was carted off, brick by brick, and

216

the wall rebuilt. The owner of that wall made hundreds of thousands of dollars, the rumour said.

A restaurateur had written out his menu in giant painted letters, using the wall as his billboard. "Seafood," it said. "Denise. Crouper. Mullet. Beef Fillet. Desert." I remembered the rule: two "s"s in "dessert," because you want it to last longer; one "s" in "desert," because you are eager to escape.

Aside from the celebrity graffiti, there was lots of ordinary tagging, smaller-scale and somehow more touching: "Ghetto Pimp" in block letters, and slogans of solidarity, "Minnesota with Palestine" and "Berlin with Palestine" and "Detroit with Palestine" and "Boise, Idaho with Palestine." Most of the tags were Arabic or English, but one tag in Hebrew said, "*milhama lo hummus*," "war is not hummus." Nearby, in childish handwriting, was a plaintive phrase, written by an unsteady hand at about chest height: "Can I have my ball back please?" In the car Fatimah's children seemed bored and restless and I felt sorry for them, sacrificing their Sunday for us.

At the checkpoint we lined up along a long, fenced corridor; it felt like a pathway for livestock, as though we were lambs being led to slaughter. It wasn't a hot day, but the tin ceiling of the walkway seemed to concentrate and focus the heat as we moved slowly towards the booth. We took off our belts, our shoes, and our bags. The guards yelled at an old woman in Hebrew, telling her to take off her shoes. She had no idea what they were asking. "What are you, an idiot?" the guard said roughly. Simon took my hand.

At the security booth, the soldiers sat behind plexiglass barriers. A family of three waited ahead of us. While the guard looked down to check the father's handprint, the father's tongue flickered in and out so quickly that I wasn't sure I had even seen it; when she looked back up at him his face was still but his eyes were laughing. I remembered a friend who had told me that checkpoint was the worst duty; the most dreadful combination of boredom and threat. It took all afternoon to shake off the misery of the place.

When the El Khairis came to Jerusalem to visit us on their visas the next week, one of the daughters was missing.

"She didn't want to go through the checkpoint," her sister, Mouna, said.

Mouna, too, was furious. When Mouna had passed through the checkpoint, the metal detector had kept beeping, and the guard had forced her to take off her shoes, her belt, her hair clip.

"And they were watching me, and laughing," Mouna cried. "All those men, watching me undress!"

25

Although the children were getting older, the demands of childcare still felt incessant, especially when anything went wrong—an illness, a sudden deadline, an unexpected day off school. I missed my children when I wasn't home, but being home often made me claustrophobic. It was as if I'd lost the ability to be fully with them or fully alone. At home I was often distracted, and my distraction was a kind of lazy rebellion, an attempt to carve out a private space in my head. And then, when I was on my own for too long, I felt suddenly, wildly, lonely.

One day I walked down to the Old City to take a break from looking after Sam, who had been battling a virus. I'd been inside with him for three days. The climb up to Jaffa Gate was hot and tiring after the cool, long descent through the shadowed alleys of Yemin Moshe. The gate was crowded with juice sellers, tour guides, beggars, merchants, and always tourists. Locals who had walked through the gate a thousand times or more strode past as if it was any busy urban intersection. Visitors craned their necks like animals readied for sacrifice in order to decipher the inscriptions on the gate and to pose for photographs, which was a frustrating experience because someone was always walking through the picture on their way to an errand or appointment.

In Arabic, the gate was called Bab-el-Halil. Suleiman had built the gate in the sixteenth century; the entrance was enlarged at the end of the nineteenth century for Kaiser Wilhelm II so he could remain in his imperial carriage as he entered the Old City. When General Allenby came in 1917, he swung off his horse and walked in on foot to show respect for the Holy City. Now the gate was an ingress for a lazy, snub-nosed fleet of black-and-yellow taxis that pulled into parking spots just inside like a herd of stabled donkeys.

You descended into the market on broad stone steps, and even on the hottest days when the sun burned the street white, the alley was striped in blue shade. It was crowded from ten in the morning to around sundown, and all kinds of people passed through. *Yeshiva* boys rushed three or four abreast, *peyos* and *tsitsis* and elbows all flying. There were painted carts being bumped up and down the steps, boys with silver trays filled with glass cups of hot tea, women in veils and headscarves or niqabs and women in short shorts, children on their way to class, soldiers on their way to guard duty. There were trays of dried rose petals, saffron, sumac, bowls of irregular, cracked brilliant turquoise, teardrop pendants of amber encasing splayed and immobilized insects, rosaries in cedar, sculptures of the Virgin in stone, Jesus on black velvet.

A shuffling man with a three-day beard and pouches under his eyes sold me a scarf, then told me I was naive to think that the Americans hadn't planned the attacks of September 11th or that Netanyahu hadn't poisoned Arafat in his Ramallah mansion. "You don't have to believe me," he shrugged, folding his scarves for display, striped and floral and cotton and silk. "But then you are a fool."

"Why would you think that?" I said.

Glancing at me, he said, "Why are you asking me questions, anyway? Are you a spy?"

There were spies all over the market, he said. There were spies everywhere. He offered to sell me a scarf. I reminded him that I had just bought a scarf and he shrugged his shoulders, sighed heavily, and turned his back. He had no more use for me.

Deeper in the market was a merchant who wore an enormous belt buckle with his jeans and had a "Don't Mess with Texas" plaque over his shop. Inside, framed pictures of Clinton showed the two of them posing against his bricolage of carpets and mirrors.

"Did you see Rahmy, baby?" he said.

Rahm Emmanuel had come through the market that morning, flanked by security, posing for pictures and buying souvenirs. The merchant now had a new photograph for his wall; he showed it to me on the back of his camera. The two of them had identical toothy smiles.

A staircase at the end of his alley led up to the rooftops of the Old City. I walked up and the babble of the market receded behind me as if someone had shut a door.

The rooftops fit together like puzzle pieces. They were crowded places, with shacks built on the flat surfaces, old bicycles leaning against doorways, laundry unfurling like sails, and through a lattice of television antennas the bright yellow cap on the Dome of the Rock. A barbed wire fence enclosed a playground and a row of Israeli flags; that was the Jewish settlement built in the Arab quarter. I had seen some of its residents earlier, vanishing behind a heavy door. The women wore long sweeping skirts and twisted their headscarves like turbans, and the men had long beards, long hair, and *kippas* the size of soup plates. I'd noticed them because the men all wore Uzis strapped across their hips, though none of them had uniforms. The women had an elegant, stiff-necked haughtiness and swept through the market as if none of it existed, in a bright, rigid bubble of their own righteousness.

"But why shouldn't they live anywhere they want to in Jerusalem?" a friend of mine had asked, and even while trying to explain myself I felt the empty hopelessness that always accompanied conversations about Israeli politics, the dazzle and abyss of complication that so quickly festered into insult and attack, that felt like pouring glitter into an open wound.

And all along the street, every storefront was a snare. I could see confused couples attempting to extricate themselves from the promise of just one cup of tea, trying to reconcile their politeness, their curiosity, and their greed with their sense of privacy and their desire to move through the streets unencumbered. I was practiced at dodging and deferring and smiling at a distance, but sometimes I was also caught by even the most obvious displays of pathos.

On my way home that day a merchant convinced me to come into his store down the street by claiming he was very sick, his wife was sick, he needed to make one last sale before going to the hospital. I followed him into his shuttered shop, which was further than he'd claimed, and stood both empty and unlit. Each time I thought about turning back to the main road he held my arm at the elbow, steering me inside, not exactly forcefully but with insistence. He babbled on about his health, his wife, his family, and then suddenly he was making plans for me to open an outlet for his jewelry in Canada, to set up a website for him—"Canadians," he said dramatically, opening up the dog-eared black-covered book of testimonials that every merchant kept like a bible, "they love my work." On the blue-lined page, Anne from Toronto, Ontario, rhapsodized about her lovely new scarf.

"No," I said. "No. I can't open a business."

He looked at me in profound disappointment and disgust.

"I can see that you have no head for business or you would not miss this wonderful opportunity," he said. "But at least you will buy something or else you have wasted my time."

"Your time!" I angrily started, but he had moved away. A long glass case held necklaces, and he opened the case and took them out, watching me watch the jewelry—"Ah—this one I see you do not like—but this one you like, this one is my own design." The necklace he chose was made of Roman glass, and the silver chain—if it was silver—was oxidized, so it didn't have the arrogant gleam of the others. The piece of glass itself, small and modest, had the glint of mosaic but was also less glittery and elaborate.

"I have to go," I said, "my son is sick, I have to go home." I suddenly felt trapped, as if I might never make it back to Sam and Gabe.

He looked at me again and said, "I see all your thoughts are with your son, and look, now you are crying."

And it was true. My eyes had started tearing as I spoke, as if saying it out loud—my son is sick—had brought back the anxiety of the last few days. He'd been running a fever, was strangely listless; it was just a virus but he had been sleeping badly, and I had been waking up with him. I was weary and felt unsettled.

The clerk put the necklace down and his fat moist hands reached for my forehead. With two thumbs he stroked my eyebrows, from the centre to the hollows on the side of my head. He then rested his thumbs in the hollows and rotated them. I didn't know what to do.

"I know how to do this because my sister is a therapist," he announced. "Your husband should do this for you when you are home." He stood back and rolled up his sleeve. "The truth is," he said, "I am also very sick. I was just in the hospital, for my kidney—they gave me two injections—look, here." In the crook of his elbow were two bruised holes, like the twin fangs of a serpent bite.

"And even, it is hurting me now," he said, reaching his hands behind his thick waist.

"You should go home and rest," I said.

"I will. I am. I was going home. But you see, I cannot go home with no money."

He opened his wallet and showed me, but shut it again quickly, because there was money in there, more than I carried on me.

"Do you know how many sales I made today?" he said to me. "One. Only one! So tell me if you want to buy this necklace and make your mother happy. I will give you a very good deal, since you are not buying it for yourself—a lady never buys jewelry for herself."

I had in my bag a pendant I'd bought for myself earlier that day. The man's eyes bulged, and the whites were the thick, curdled creamy yellow of pudding. It seemed that he was at once looking at me and looking at the door, my only way out. I wanted to protest that it was my time, my time that had been wasted, that he had drawn me by the elbow like a child into this deserted store. I should have known better than to follow him, and how far away was the street and would anyone hear me if I cried out? But he was rolling up his sleeve and showing me the puncture wounds again and the bruising all the way up his arms and telling me about the hospital procedures that involved—could I be remembering this correctly?—removing his blood and replacing it, so I picked out a necklace from a dusty case and he spread out his fingers and held it out to me, and then insisted on putting it around my neck.

His cold, thick fingers fumbled as he closed the clasp, and I could see his face behind mine in the mirror, but his eyes were somewhere else. I handed him a hundred-shekel bill—he asked for more, but accepted it—and I stumbled back out of the musty, dark shop into the glare and noise of Jaffa Street, discomfited, unraped. I didn't even look at the necklace properly until I was a few blocks away, when I stopped and leaned against the wall and took it off my neck. The setting was antiqued silver and the pendant was Roman glass, that blued, lacquered opalescence that time had crafted like a pearl around the grit in an oyster. The Old City was full of Roman glass, real and fake, and I assumed that this too was fraudulent. But a year later it was still opaque and glimmering while the larger Roman glass pendant I had bought from a seller I knew and trusted, who I visited and drank tea and practiced Arabic with almost every time I went to the market, had proved to be a fake, the sheen peeling off with wear like foil off a gimcrack ring to reveal the plain new glass underneath.

I was late coming home, and Simon was angry.

"I need to get to work," he said. "Sam was asking for you. It took two hours to get him to take a nap. He's sick, you know."

"Of course I know," I said, "I've been home with him all week. Anyway, this strange thing happened to me in the Old City. It's kind of a funny thing…."

I started to explain the story to Simon but he was gathering his papers and putting on his jacket, and his mouth twisted as he turned back to face me. "What did you think you were doing?" he said. "You can't just pretend that you're going to be protected by your—stupidity. You have to stop walking around as if you're untouchable, as if nothing could possibly happen to you. What would you have done if he hadn't let you leave? I don't know where your head is these days. You're acting like a child, and you have to stop."

"Or what?" I said. My throat filled with salt.

He shrugged. "Or—I don't know. I don't know where you are these days, but one thing's for sure, even when you're here you aren't here. He's awake—" Simon said, gesturing towards the closed bedroom door. "I have to go."

I went to the osteopath the day after that trip to the Old City and he noticed that my shoes were uneven. He said one leg was longer than the other, and that I was dragging one foot. He suggested I switch my shoes. I dreamed that instead of walking heavily on one leg and dragging the other, I was walking with only one leg and the other was treading on the air. Even in the dream, it was very difficult, and as I walked on air I could feel the strain.

It made me think of this Hebrew phrase I'd recently learned, "*maka yevesha*," which in English would mean something like "a dry bruise." It refers to a blow that is deeply painful but leaves no mark, under the armpit, for instance. The kind of blow you feel but do not see. It is the kind of punch that is used in secret interrogations.

PART 3

26

Right after Christmas the war began. I woke up to a friend's one-line Facebook status: "My country breaks my heart."

Many years earlier, when I was in college in Israel in the tense days leading up to the Gulf War, my parents told me to come home. I was seventeen, and I thought of defying them. I had damp visions of heroism and courage, mostly formed by my vague memories of First World War memoirs. What was it that Freud said when the First World War started—"All my libido is dedicated to Austria-Hungary"? I was up all night in a friend's room, drunk on the excitement. When I came back to my room there were ten messages on my desk telling me to call my parents—back then there was no email, there were no cellphones. They said I had to come home, and I nearly hung up on them. My mother was crying. I asked the administrator at the college if I could stay at the school, and he said that they were closing the dormitories. Everyone was going home but I had no home in Israel. I had missed the gas mask distribution; the stores were out of tape for the windows. I called my parents back and took a midnight flight from a chaotic airport that was the closest I've ever been to an evacuation. I was envious of the friends who stayed. My plane left the day before the Scuds started falling. When I stepped out of the plane into the unfamiliar cold of a sudden winter, jet-lagged and ragged, I thought my heart had frozen.

I spent most of the war in my basement in front of the television. I'd watch the news with my father, chest tight as the rockets fell. They were hard to see; just small, bright red dots on the screen, like the tip of my father's cigarette, which flared up as he inhaled. In the week between the commencement of the war and my return he'd started smoking again; that was on my conscience.

This time I would not leave. Life in wartime was just like peacetime in Jerusalem. I dropped my sons off at school, sat in a coffee shop in the weak January sunshine, tried to get some work done, did some grocery shopping, and kept stubbornly hanging my clothes outside despite the technical arrival of winter. We got worried emails from our families back in the States, and sent back calm, unruffled responses. The weather was unaffected by the conflict in the south of the country. I remembered meeting an Australian girl in India, years earlier, who had just been surfing in Sri Lanka during the darkest days of the civil war. "But isn't there a war?" I'd asked her. "Isn't it unsafe?" In her nasal drawl she said, "The waaah's in the south, and the saaa-rfing's in the north."

Everyone everywhere seemed entirely immersed in the everyday. It was as if we had collectively agreed not to talk about it, without ever having spoken at all.

Jenna held Zac's fourth birthday party at her house. Most of the families from the daycare were already there when I arrived, hanging out on the terrace. The tables in the living room were covered with food, and the children sat on the couch in front of bowls of chips and candy and two-litre bottles of soda. They'd started loading as much food as they could onto plastic plates, as if it was a famine year and their very last chance to eat.

Jenna's mother-in-law wandered in, brushing the table with her broad hips. Jenna said her mother-in-law had been absolutely useless planning the party. She'd had demands: they needed to serve this kind of cake and this kind of meat, needed to invite this many of her friends. She was nervous, perhaps rightly so, about Jenna's friends coming into the neighbourhood and making her look bad. But she hadn't offered to watch the kids, to pick up food, or to cook. She looked at us suspiciously and then smiled widely, gold teeth glinting. I couldn't quite get over the distance between her and her tall, thin, modern son. Had she made him that way, to live in a world that she couldn't inhabit? Or did he feel like a stranger to her in his pressed jeans, his Ray-Bans, his polo shirts?

The children were shuttled out onto the large concrete terrace so that Jenna could straighten up the room and bring out the cake. I was nervous about the pit next door. The wall that separated the properties was hip high, seductively jumpable. The children milled in the centre of the terrace and the adults leaned against the wall.

Katie's husband, Roger, was home on leave from Iraq, where he'd been transferred after leaving the Jerusalem consulate. I was curious about him; he'd been away most of the year, and we'd never met. Katie told me that since he'd come back, he seemed to spend all his time in the shower and in bed. He roused himself for a few hours to play with the boys, then lapsed into wordlessness as soon as she went to bed, channel surfing until long after Katie had gone to sleep. Sometimes he slept on the couch but even when he came to bed they slept on opposite sides, back to back, curled away from each other. Once or twice he'd woken up shouting, but he didn't want to talk about his dreams, didn't want to talk about Iraq, didn't want to talk at all except about the general details of housekeeping or parenting: who was dropping the boys off, who was picking the boys up, what they would eat for dinner. And neither of them wanted to talk about that, not really, but it needed to happen.

As the shadows grew long and the air cooled down, Roger told me about living in Iraq.

"If this war triggers a war with Iran," he said, "just get out. Don't wait to see what's happening, don't assume they're not a threat. It isn't a risk that you should take."

I wanted to ask him more, but he was distracted and tight-lipped, looking far away. I wanted to know what he knew. We'd been out on the terrace for a long time. Sam had a helium balloon and was dragging it along the sky like a pet on a leash. I wanted to leave, but it was rude to leave before the cake, and we still weren't being allowed inside. Jenna was having some kind of debate with her mother-in-law near the door, her arms flying, and then her mother-in-law produced an enormous key ring and unlocked it. We all pressed in to ooh and aaah at the cake.

Later, Jenna said, "Do you know what she did? She locked us out! While I was on the terrace. She was mad at me from before, so she locked us out of the party, and refused to let us back in!"

"Mad at you for what?" I said, but she shrugged her narrow shoulders and raised her hands, open-palmed, as if it was beyond her power to say, as if it was always everything and nothing at all.

Jenna was full of wild rumours about the war. She said that Israel had poisoned the water supply in Gaza City; she said they'd put something in it to make the men impotent. I said that couldn't possibly be true. It seemed, if anything, much milder than the truth; over a million people trapped between the desert and the sea, and the bombs falling day and night. I couldn't talk to Jenna because she was full of insane urban myths, and I couldn't talk to my Israeli neighbours because they felt their position to be unassailable; after all, my neighbours insisted, Hamas had been shooting rockets at Israel for three years. And we—that furtive, usurping "we"—we had no choice.

The war was always on television, a constant, hysterical stream of coverage. Simon and I tried not to turn it on too often. There was a sentimental documentary piece about a centre for the disabled near Sderot. They didn't have a bomb shelter that was handicapped-accessible.

There was nowhere for the residents to go if a Katyusha rocket fell on the building. The camera held long lingering shots on wasted limbs, hands clutching the armrests of wheelchairs, sympathetic faces. The children of Sderot had nowhere to play; the residents were trying to build a playground in a bomb shelter, in case the children needed to spend a lot of time underground.

But a bomb had not fallen on the centre. The war would end three weeks later, the casualties a hundred in Gaza to every single Israeli.

It wasn't as if there was a lack of suffering in Sderot; it wasn't as though I doubted the nightmares, the strained nerves, the frightened children, the fear while living under siege. But the absences in the Israeli news were most striking: the flattened buildings of Gaza City, the children without water, the hundreds—soon over a thousand—Palestinians dead. The radical unevenness of force.

"Don't you think they'd do the same if they had the weapons?" Shayna argued when I broached the subject. "Don't you think they would be worse? What kind of country allows another country to aim rockets at their civilians again and again? What are we supposed to do, wait for their aim to improve? What choice have they given us?"

I was reminded of a man I had once met, an aggrieved professor who considered himself perpetually wronged. "If you hit me," he said, "I will CRUSH you," stretching a thin smile over grey teeth.

As the war dragged on, the daycare became strangely

dull and silent. I could see the wear and worry on the teachers' faces. Jameelah and Sarah had worked together for fifteen years and once again had something they could not talk about. The silence at the daycare was a tacit pact; let us not disturb the fragile equilibrium we have found together. But the war was more than an elephant in the room, it was like a raging fire in the building, sucking the oxygen out of casual, everyday interactions. The children didn't notice, but the parents looked at one another suspiciously and hurried more at drop-off and pick-up.

One day a siren sounded and Leah started screaming, "It's the Katyushas! It's beginning here! They are trying to kill us all!" The siren—it was a car alarm—subsided, and we were left in the silent classroom, us and them, when weeks before we had just been parents and teachers and children, worried about toilet training and our children eating vegetables and how to fill the long hours between pick-up at the daycare and dinner.

While sipping tea in Jenna's living room, Leah told her that the war in Gaza was justified because Palestinian life was worth less than Israeli life. Again she repeated that strange formulation she had used to me. "If it is my child, or one of theirs, I choose my child."

It was a hypothetical question, like the one about the sinking ship, when you have to save the baby or the Mona Lisa. Who asked her to choose?

Provoked, Jenna said, "Then I hope the IDF bombs my house right now, where your kid is playing." At that moment the radio announced that rockets had begun to fall on the north of Israel and Jenna raised her eyes to the ceiling and cried, "God has heard my prayer!"

Jenna said that because of the war, the women in Gaza had become more fertile, a pregnancy for every casualty. She called it a miracle.

My friends were fighting a war on Facebook. One had dedicated her status to a Katyusha count, while another was tracking the casualties in Gaza. We received a mass email from Fatimah in Bethlehem with atrocity photographs of children that could have been from any conflict. There were rumours in the paper of a new weapon, a kind of bomb that left a whitish residue and made limbs vanish, like a witch's curse, leaving a sealed stump behind.

In Gabriel's school, some of the fathers were called up to fight. They came to drop off their children while dressed in uniform and then drove directly from the school to their army bases. A psychologist came to talk to the first grade. He asked them to draw a picture of war. My son drew a flying creature in shades of phoenix orange and red, half-dragon half-bird, a small figure carrying a large sword standing on its back. In his scratchy beginner's handwriting he etched the Hebrew word "*milchama*," "war," along the top of the page. In his picture, the figures all seemed so happy—the dragon flew along with a smile stretched across his face, the figure standing on the dragon's back was grinning broadly. He had no idea, and I was glad, though I overheard other children his age casually talking about the war. Being a stranger had protected him from that knowledge.

"I'm worried about the boys," I said to Simon and he said, "If things get worse we'll leave, we can do that." As the country grew more chaotic Simon seemed calmer and steadier. His class was over and it had gone well; he'd had an article accepted; he spent more time with the boys again, throwing a ball in the park, reading them books for hours. Since the war had started Simon was the only person I could talk to without becoming defensive or outraged. There was also some kind of urgency the war unlocked. We stayed up late at night, drinking wine, talking about the war, and when we woke up in the morning we would resume our conversation as if it had never been interrupted. It was good for us to focus on something other than our mundane unhappiness. We had a common enemy: the hysteria that had gripped the entire country.

I had been to Gaza years before. We'd stayed in a resort hotel on the beach. It was cheap because even then going to Gaza carried a small element of risk; we traveled in a special armoured bus. Tourism was one of the primary industries of the Jewish settlement in Gaza; the other was flowers. When Israelis talked about the pullout from Gaza they always mentioned that the Palestinians had smashed the greenhouses, as if that was proof that the Palestinians did not deserve their independence and had no willingness for industry, only a desire for destruction. But the Israelis had pulled out infrastructure with their people; how would you run industrial greenhouses when you didn't have enough electricity or clean water for the people of Gaza City?

I never saw Gaza City, but I remember the shoreline in Gaza as beautiful. The sand was gold and the sea was a deep purple-blue. We went for a walk on *Shabbat* and reached the end of the resort quickly, a wall of barbed wire that stretched from the sand to the sea. But the tide was out; we walked past the wire on the wet sand and stopped abruptly. A family was sitting on a blanket, women and children grouped together on the sand, a rough tent, a man on a horse in the background. It felt as if we had walked into a private gathering, a birthday party or celebration. They all looked at us together, steadily and without either hostility or welcome, their holiday chatter silenced. The children began to walk towards us, but the man spoke harshly to them and then lashed his horse and rode straight at us. At the last moment, he turned and galloped into the blue, broken light of the waves. As we turned back we could feel the salt spray from the horse's hooves, could feel the salt taste in our own mouths.

27.

The war posed another problem, a petty one, which preoccupied me nonetheless. I was supposed to be going on a vacation with Simon. My mother was coming all the way from New York and had volunteered to watch the children; our reservations to Eilat were booked and non-refundable. We hadn't been anywhere alone for nearly seven years, since my first pregnancy. This vacation would be our chance to be alone again.

I monitored the papers every day, watching for travel warnings, signs of escalation. I was afraid of getting cut off from the children, of having them in one part of the country and being trapped in another. And then there was the plain tackiness of going on vacation while other people were suffering. It seemed callous, beyond callous, unfeeling.

I caught myself rehearsing various rationalizations: after all, someone, somewhere, was always suffering, and this was only a little more proximate. I vacillated until it was time to leave. I remembered my friend Rebecca, who had initially planned to stay in Israel during the Gulf War.

She left a week later, out of boredom. She was staying in a stranger's house, she said. There was nothing to do. They spent all day in the basement with five screaming children, watching movies she'd already seen. Eventually she went home to Colorado to ski. I thought of her now as we drove south.

We were driving towards the war, though we would skirt it to the east. But the closer we came the farther away it seemed; the war receded, like the vanishing lines on the highway. The road was empty. We rolled down the windows. I looked at Simon, his hands relaxed on the steering wheel, his face in profile, side-lit by the sun, and he glanced towards me and half-smiled. His eyes were brown but there were pools of green around his pupils that I could only see in the sun. I had always liked it so much that his eyes changed colour depending on the light. It took me a second to remember to smile back, as if that reflex had become a little stiff and unpracticed. I could see his smile falter, could see the question in his eyes, before he turned his face away from me and back to the road.

We didn't want to talk about the war; we didn't want to talk about the children. We turned the music up and ate bad food. It was as if we'd shed ten years in the hour we'd spent on the road. All of the road trips we'd taken in the years before we had children came rushing back; stupid jokes and truckstops, late-afternoon sun on asphalt. We passed the Willy Wonka madness of the salt factories on the Dead Sea, candy-striped warehouses and mountains of salt like powdered sugar. The Dead Sea ribboned in and out of sight in the distance, and we descended into the Mediterranean savanna. The air was thicker now. It was late afternoon, and out the window the barrens looked like Africa; burnt-orange sunset and sparse acacia trees, stunted and stately, their flat crowns umbrellaed over narrow trunks. Eilat was spangled in lights.

On the way down to Eilat, we stopped at a desert park named Timna, where the earth was red and the rock striated in bands, like zebra stripes but far more colourful, every shade of beige and orange and crimson and black. There had once been a copper mine there, and a shrine to Hathor, since all this had been Egypt when Egypt was an empire. We walked aimlessly through the deserted park. I could hear Simon beside me, breathing hard as we climbed uphill, but aside from him I sensed no living thing, not even the shadow of a lizard. It was as if we were the last people on earth.

"You wouldn't want to run out of gas here," Simon said. "They would find your bleached bones a month later."

We hadn't brought enough water, and suddenly I felt frightened.

"How much gas do we have?" I said. He looked at me and said, "We're fine. We have plenty."

Still, there was a moment of panic when we came back to the car and he couldn't find the keys. We had run out of water, and I could feel the pressure from dehydration beginning to build in my head.

I said, "Check the other pocket," and he shook his

head and said, "I checked it already."

I narrowed my lips, ready to burst into recriminations, when I realized that I had the keys, zipped in the pocket of my windbreaker. I'd asked to hold them because I didn't trust Simon not to lose them. I fished them out. "I had the keys," I said. "Sorry about that." I stood there meekly. Exasperation flickered quickly across his face.

It would have been good sometimes to know each other a little less well. I was like an antenna that was so sensitive it picked up everything, all the static and the noise. "Do you want to just go back?" Simon said, his voice frustrated, and I shook my head. But the night was ruined.

We drove past the narrow strip of city and to our hotel just south of town, which smelled like fish and floor cleaner. My mother's voice on the phone sounded tired; as always, she seemed slightly offended when I asked her if the children had behaved themselves, as if I was at once calling into question the virtue of her grandchildren and her own dogged competence as a caregiver.

"They're better off with her than they are with us," Simon said as I hung up the phone.

It was true: she would have the children cleaner, tidier, better fed. They didn't sound like they missed us at all, their voices tinny and faraway.

Luckily, in the morning everything felt lighter. We walked over to the beach and rented snorkels, wetsuits, and fins from a beachside stand. The Red Sea was named for the way the water reflected the red sand of the mountains, but really it was more turquoise than red, and purple in the depths, wine-dark like the Homeric epithet. The water was full of lavender jellyfish, pulsing at the core and frilled at the edges, translucent and exquisitely indifferent. The man in the diving shack told us that they didn't sting and I reached out a finger and stroked one; the skin was like wet silk. It was strange to swim through the flutter of jellyfish; they bumped my elbows and hips, and I needed to brush them aside with my hands, a Mediterranean traffic jam.

Near the reef, the water cleared of jellyfish. The coral itself was roped off, but you could swim alongside it. Simon swam beside me, held his breath and plunged under, pointed silently to a frill of coral deep underwater. I liked being beside him without language. I passed a drift of lionfish, fierce and ornate. Later I found the raised welt on my thigh, red and shiny like a burn. My breath was loud and rhythmic in my ears, though occasionally I inhaled seawater and came up sputtering, blowing it back out of the spout. My hands and feet were numb. I didn't care; I wanted to stay underwater forever. There was a whole world under there, glorious and intricate, where all I could hear was the sound of my breathing. The wetsuit kept me buoyant so I felt like I was flying, not swimming.

Without the children, vast expanses of time opened up; we wandered back to our hotel wearing our swimsuits, went back to bed in the middle of the day, walked until our feet were tired. We felt hollow and light from swimming and walking. We avoided central Eilat, with its tacky hotels and crowded boardwalk; instead, we walked as far as we could into the mountains, scrabbling with hands and feet on the red sand. We were raw and eager, sunburnt and sandy, tired and glad. On a day trip to Petra we watched a wild boy, eyes lined in *kohl*, drive a rose charabanc through the gorge that led to the ancient settlement. We wandered around the dead stone city, marveling at how lively it was; in the caves we found bedding, pots, evidence of habitation. Ornate facades were carved onto the sandstone cliffs, and arches framed doorways that would not open.

Petra had been a dream city for so long, rumoured and forbidden. In the 1950s, young Israelis used to sneak over the border to see the city; a dozen were murdered by Jordanian soldiers while making the forbidden trip. The song that immortalized their exploits was banned on the radio for many years in an effort to contain the romance of the expedition. I remembered the tune from when I was a child; the red rock, *"Haselah Ha'adom"*. My mother used to sing it to me at night, though it was no lullaby. Back then I had no idea what the words meant. In the song, the red rock is the impossible place, the place no-one returns from alive. When the travelers arrive at the red rock, they have found death itself.

Looking at Simon now, I realized I couldn't see him except through a kind of film, like old photographic negatives layered over one another. I saw him screaming at me in a yellow room and I saw his tired eyes in the hospital the day my father died and I saw him holding our son all night on the day he was born and I saw him walking away from me and I saw him walking towards me slowly with a cone of purple flowers in his hand as if he was afraid I would throw them in his face. I saw him speckled in light, like a solar system, under the crocheted blanket his grandmother knit him when he went to university. We thought of the same jokes at the same moments, we finished each other's sentences, we knew each other's weaknesses with the intimacy of our own. Every fight we had was a repetition of every fight we had ever had, and every time we kissed there was an echo of all of those prior kisses, so that nothing was new but everything was deep and reached back to all we had been since we had been together.

Sometimes I felt exhausted by all of this weight, and I wished that we could be fresh to each other, people without a history.

On the way back to the hotel we bought pizza to eat on the floor of our hotel room, and then stumbled down the hallway in our bathing suits to the Jacuzzi outdoors. The area near the pool was dark. "I'm not sure we're supposed to be here," I said to Simon, and he said, "Shhhh," and slipped his hand between my legs.

In the distance we could hear a group of people laughing. We were hasty and silly and a little uncomfortable. As we made our way back to our room, holding hands and giggling, I realized I hadn't thought of the children for hours, maybe even all day. It was more than not having thought of them; it was as if I'd forgotten that they existed, just for a little while, or as if they'd never come along.

When we were young we had wandered the world. We had biked around Versailles; we'd hiked the Himalayas; we'd missed our train from Madrid to Granada and sped to catch up with it in a taxi, the sky choked with stars in the black night. We had been accountable only to ourselves, creatures without schedules or obligations, strangers everywhere. It had been so long since we had felt like that.

"We should call the kids," I said as we opened the door to our room, and Simon said, "What kids?" and leapt onto the bed, pulling back the covers so I could join him.

Later on, when we were lying in bed, Simon said, "I forgot to tell you something. I mean, not something important. Just something I thought you would like."

"Yes," I said. I was nestled into the crook of his arm.

"It was in a podcast about a magic trick that nobody could solve. The hosts kept trying out different theories, and hitting dead ends. Finally, near the end of the show, they called up this famous magician and they asked him. He listened to them and started laughing. When he stopped laughing he said, 'Yeah, I can tell you how it works, but are you sure you want to know?' And then he said something else, something I can't stop thinking about. He said, 'There are no beautiful secrets. You want there to be a perfect solution, you know, some particular flick of the wrist. But really, there's gaffer tape over there, where you can't see it, and maybe someone gesturing behind the curtain—it's all messy and patched together and unbeautiful. So I can tell you, but that'll spoil it forever. You choose; do you want the truth or do you want the magic?'"

That whole week we did not listen to the radio. We did not turn on the television. We tried not to speak of the war.

28

The first day back after our vacation, I bumped into Jenna, smoking a cigarette outside the daycare. Outside the car her girls tussled, near the tiled fountain that fronted the YMCA as a symbol of hospitality but that had never, ever worked; the taps were permanently dry. Noor had grabbed Jenna's pack of cigarettes out of her purse, which lay like a flaccid mouth on the ground next to the car. Noor now took out a cigarette. She looked so comical with her plump pierced earlobes and her short tight curls, her round eyes nearly crossed trying to look at the cigarette dangling from her mouth.

"Jenna," I said, "she's got a cigarette."

Aisha cried out and tried to grab the box of cigarettes from Noor. They held onto it together, pulling it between them. Noor couldn't shout because she still held a cigarette in her fat red mouth. Jenna said, "They're always trying to steal my cigarettes. They think it's a joke." She leaned down and swooped a finger into Noor's mouth, breaking the seal of her lips. The cigarette, now paper mush and wet loose strands of tobacco, fell to the floor. Jenna ground it down with her heel as Noor tried to retrieve it.

"No!" she said. "Those are mine!"

Jenna had just returned from her cousin's funeral. He was shot at three in the morning in Zion Square along with another man, a Jew. Nobody knew if the shooting was political. Whenever a shooting happened a little shudder went through the city, and everyone braced themselves for further incidents or news that would link the murder to a new wave of terrorism; then after a few days everything went back to normal—or whatever counted as normal in Jerusalem.

But normal was over for this man's family. Jenna said she was pretty sure he'd been in the square looking for sex. His wife had caught him having sex with a man in their house a few years earlier.

"In their bed," Jenna said. "Can you imagine?"

The family begged her to stay in the marriage and he reformed, she said, and became religious. He started to pray again, five times a day, and they had more children, seemed happy. But now that he was dead, the rumours had begun again, and because the family was afraid that he had been HIV positive they had dispensed with the usual burial rites and put him straight in the ground.

"Why would they think that?" I said. "And what would it matter? There's no risk."

"Nobody wanted to wash the body," she said. "They didn't want to catch it."

The father was angry that his son was buried without the proper rituals. He decided to go straight to his son's widow to ask if they had been having sex, as a way of settling his mind, as if that would foreclose the possibility of infection. And she said, yes, they did, they had sex often. Now he blamed the family for desecrating the burial.

She said, "Can you imagine your father-in-law coming to you and asking how often you had sex with his son? I would have said we did it every day, even if we didn't."

Jenna was wearing a striped pink and grey sweater dress, tights, and tall black boots, and she looked tired because she'd been trying to wean Noor.

"I'm taking medicine to make my milk dry up," she said, "so she won't want it anymore. But when she woke up last night she hit me and then cried and cried because the milk was gone. She just kept sucking, sucking and hitting, as if she just couldn't understand why it wasn't working, like you used to hit the TV to make the picture focus, remember that? Back when televisions had antennas?"

The skin under her eyes looked like someone had placed their thumbs there and pressed, leaving black bruises.

"The war's going to be over by Friday," she said. "Did you hear? The Venezuelans kicked out the Israeli embassy. There's gonna be so much international pressure that Israel is going to have to withdraw."

She took a slow drag on her cigarette.

"Nobody likes Hamas. But Israel is worse. And anyway, it's the end of days. I think he's here already," she said, "the antichrist. Know who he is? That magician, I forget his name. The one who flew over the Grand Canyon. The one who made the Statue of Liberty disappear."

"David Copperfield?" I said.

She nodded emphatically. "David Copperfield. That's right. You know, I saw him perform once. Aden bought us both tickets. And he sawed a woman in half right on stage, and I had to leave. I said to Aden, 'He sold his soul to Satan and Satan gave him power.' You know, that's how magicians get their power, they bargain with Satan. And I really think it might be him. How else could he do that?"

"It's just tricks," I said. I never could tell when she was joking. I mean, as far as I knew, she had never made a joke. "Anyway," I said, "isn't that stuff from the Book of Revelations? Do Muslims even have an end of days?"

"Oh yes," she said solemnly. "I keep trying to read the Koran but I can't because I get scared. There's going to be a long period of peace and then a huge war. Almost everyone will die. That's why the Arabs and the Jews keep fighting," she said, "because they're afraid. They're trying to prevent that long peace, because after that it's going to be the end."

It was a strange day to hear about Jenna's cousin, because I was going to Pride that very afternoon. The streets had been blocked off since the morning. When I walked to the daycare, I had to navigate a cordon of ropes, and men and women in grey uniforms and sunglasses lined the sidewalk. A few years earlier police had increased security at the parade, after a man was stabbed. Ultra-Orthodox Jews and fundamentalist Muslims agreed on the immorality of homosexuality; many factions in the city wanted to shut the parade down. There would be no cheering audience, only the police, unsmiling behind their dark glasses. We would meet at the Liberty Bell Park, would walk through metal detectors, be patted down; we would then, in near-silence, walk the six empty downtown blocks to the park where they held the festival, where eighties cover bands would serenade us with cheesy songs.

These were the last stroller days, and I was enjoying the ability to dictate where Sam went. The movement of the stroller and the heat of the day put him into a stupor. He took a rainbow flag and waved it proudly. A few journalists came and took his picture; there were only a few children at the parade. He smiled at them and sat up straighter. He didn't know what Pride meant. He liked the costumes, liked the flag. The line near the metal detectors was jammed up, and it was very hot. None of the political parties had bothered to show up, except for the Communists. Some of our friends had gone to Tel Aviv for Pride because it was a better party.

Past the metal detectors people sat in desultory groups. I didn't see anyone I knew. There was a group of men and women in their army uniforms, and men wearing *kippot* who wore T-shirts that said "Proud and Orthodox," "*gaeh vedati*"—in Hebrew, the words meant several things at once, "proud to be gay," "proud to be Orthodox," and in a Hebrew/English pun, "Gay and Orthodox." Vendors sold glow sticks and popsicles, and there was a parachute, for no real reason. Once past the bottleneck of the metal detectors, we were a sparse group as we walked down the street. A boy, almost a man, walked alone, wrapped in a rainbow flag. His jaw was set and he seemed very serious. Indeed, there was a seriousness about the entire parade; it felt like a dirge rather than like a celebration, despite the two men in tight white T-shirts and rabbit ears who preened for pictures and held signs that quoted the Israeli poet Leah Goldberg, "And one is allowed, allowed to love." Journalists took photo after photo of them, zooming in, and I realized that if they'd zoomed out the picture wouldn't have depicted much of a story: a few people, not many, had showed up to march down an empty street in an ancient city.

Jenna was right about one thing, at least. The war ended that week. Faster than seemed possible, the media focus turned to national elections. One of the parties poised to take a significant number of seats was called "*Israel Beiteinu*," meaning "Israel is our home," a party whose name announced its ultra-nationalist aspirations. Their leader, Avigdor Lieberman, was notorious for advocating that Palestinians be expelled to Jordan, and for arguing that Israeli Arab citizens must swear allegiance to the Jewish state or be stripped of their citizenship. He was famous for other reasons, too: he was under investigation for money laundering, and had also once been taken to trial for hitting a child who had bullied his son. None of this seemed to have hurt his political fortunes. Meanwhile, Ehud Barak, once the great hope of the left and then its great betrayer, was trying to capitalize on the war by emphasizing his "security credentials." Invoking Vladimir Putin in an attempt to appeal to the increasingly important Russian vote, he said, "We will hit the terrorists while they are sitting on the toilet!" His posters showed a stern, unsmiling face: underneath it said, "*Barak Lo Sachbek*," "Barak is not your friend." I thought it was hilarious, and then tragic, that candidates in Israel ran on their unlikability. But of course it meant he was a tough guy, he'd be unyielding when negotiating with Arabs. Ironically, *sachbek* was one of the many words taken from Arabic that had been absorbed into the Hebrew vernacular.

The daycare had also recently been in the news because one board member had a nephew who was an astronaut. The astronaut had volunteered to take a preschool banner along with him on his next mission to space. A tremendous amount of energy and excitement had gone into the crafting of the banner and the newspaper showed many photographs of lovely children leaning over and helping in its construction. But it was hard not to conclude that there was an irony to his quest; that co-existence worked best in a vacuum.

29

That year Martine was the first of the daycare mothers to leave. I barely knew her; her son was in a different group. Her husband was being transferred to Belgium, which in the embassy world was a promotion, though it seemed to me that after the bright madness of Jerusalem, grey Belgium would be dull.

She invited me to meet the ladies for drinks to see her off. Yumiko was also going away, to Japan for a month, though she would be back. Katie was coming for drinks, and Jenna, and Diane, who was an embassy employee rather than an embassy spouse. I'd never met Diane; the consulate women I knew treated her with a wary respect. They were a little bit disdainful of her husband, for being the one to tag along; they talked about the awkwardness of having him at play dates. And she was to be admired but not to be trusted, or at least that was what I'd picked up from Katie and Yumiko, though I wasn't certain exactly why. Sometimes I suspected that they disliked her because she had kept her career, and they had left theirs behind. She had a son, whose brilliance she talked about all the time. She had a daughter with cerebral palsy, of whom she never spoke.

I walked down to the restaurant after my boys were in bed. It was not quite dark, but the main road was deserted. Parked cars blocked my view of the road, and I walked quickly. That stretch of Hebron Road was a wasteland. Massive apartment buildings fronted the street. Their windows were lit, but their courtyards lurked in shadow.

I could hear footsteps. A young man came up beside me. It was hard to see his face in the dark, but he had a scruffy half-beard and almost-mullet. He held a plastic bag open as if it contained contraband.

"Thirty shekels," he said breathlessly, "only thirty shekels."

I kept my face forward and walked faster. A couple was approaching us, heading in the other direction. In the streetlight their faces were wan and drained of emotion. The boy was almost jogging to keep up with me, and I kept repeating, "No, thanks," in Hebrew.

A young woman I knew had recently been mugged, right in this neighbourhood. A teenage boy pulled a knife on her and took her wallet; it was early evening, and the whole thing happened so fast that nobody had been able to help her. When she told me about the mugging, she said he was an Arab boy, and when I asked her how she knew she looked annoyed and flustered. But the police had found her wallet a few days later, and they'd found the thief. He was one of the Jewish teens who lived in the low-income housing complexes.

Because of the mugging, I was nervous as the boy

reached into his bag.

"Excellent quality!" the boy said. Instead of a knife he pulled out a box. It held a pair of beige nylon underwear, the kind that pulls up over your stomach to hold you in—grandmother underwear, with a young model on the front who looked sullen about being made to wear something so unnecessarily matronly. I wanted to laugh; I'd been mugged by a pair of bad underpants. He pulled the underwear out of the box and they dangled from his hand, limp in that obscene shade called "flesh-colour."

I shook my head, resolute. This time instead of speaking Hebrew I said in Arabic, "La, shukran." His accent had tipped me off. This time his eyes glinted in recognition and he started to babble at me in Arabic as I realized that wasn't the way to get rid of him at all. Where was I from and what was my name and how had I learned Arabic and a hundred other things that I didn't understand because I didn't really know Arabic, I was only just keeping up with the weekly homework and seemed to forget as quickly as I learned. Salem would have been disappointed in me.

The couple in the streetlight passed us, and he bounded after them, interrupting their tense silence in his search for more receptive customers. I could see the man waving his plump hands to get rid of him, but I was glad to have lost him, the persistent boy with the grandma underwear who spoke too quickly and whose enthusiasm had something desperate about it. I was almost through Abu Tor when I heard footsteps behind me again, this time a rapid tattoo on the sidewalk. I was being pursued. I didn't want to look around, didn't want to seem afraid. Around me were closed doors and shuttered windows, and I wasn't exactly frightened but I wondered if I ought to be as I tried to walk faster without breaking into a run, because a run would make me look weak.

He caught me before the corner. With one hand he reached for my elbow. The other hand was holding a paper cone of flowers, carnations and baby's breath. He offered these to me, smiling.

"I can't take those," I said in English, and then, "No thank you," in Arabic again.

He pushed the flowers towards me, and mustering the very limits of my vocabulary I said in Arabic, thinking of Greta Garbo, "I want to be alone!"

He looked wounded and turned back, the flowers head-down towards the sidewalk. I realized two things as I walked the last block to the restaurant. First, for as long as I lived, no one would ever pursue me down the street with flowers again—this was the closest I would ever get to an extravagant romantic gesture, as odd as it had been. And second, I'd completely screwed up my sentence, the sentence I had been working on in my head that entire long walk. I'd meant to say, "I want to be by myself," but I didn't know how to say "to be"; instead I'd said something closer to "do it," "I want to do it alone," "I want to do it by myself" or "to myself." I must have frightened or shocked him.

The Old City lay in a pool of light. The moon was full and swelled with import. The ladies had found a spot on the terrace of the restaurant. They had been drinking for a while when I arrived. Jenna was there, with Yumiko and Katie, but I barely knew Martine, or the other consulate ladies who together formed a strange tribe. Sometimes I saw them coming from the exercise room at the YMCA, in their yoga pants and tank tops; sometimes I saw them picking up their children in the early afternoon, washed and showered and made up. They were talking about possible next postings. Martine had lucked out: Belgium was boring but it was civilized and in Europe. Their husbands needed to rotate through conflict zones in order to advance in their careers; at least there was danger pay, enough to make a down payment on a house in Washington. There was a good American school in Abu Dhabi. There were good embassy parties in Cairo.

It amazed me how little curiosity most of them had about the place where they had landed. Yumiko and Katie were exceptions; Yumiko, because she was already a stranger in America, and had chosen to try to learn the language and immerse herself in the society, and Katie, because she knew the Middle East and loved it in all of its painful contradictions. But most of the women couldn't care less. They had fortified their bubbles; they had narrowed their sights. They lived in a small, self-contained world filled with its own rivalries and desires and ambitions, and Israel wasn't particularly real to them. I wish I could say that their husbands—who were, after all, responsible for implementing and informing American policy in the region—seemed more invested, but in the few conversations we'd had they treated the region like a set of abstract problems that they knew best how to fix. They were frustrated by Israeli bullishness and intransigence; they seemed to honestly believe that all the problems of the Middle East could be solved, if not for the pigheadedness of the Arabs and the Jews.

I told Katie about my encounter, and she laughed at me. "What exactly did you say?" she asked, but I had already forgotten, and kept trying out new possibilities. She told me the right way to say that I wanted to be alone, and I repeated it and then promptly forgot. "Poor boy," she said. "He probably had no idea what was going on."

The food at the restaurant was magnificent: smoked eggplant drizzled with buttermilk sauce and jewelled with pomegranate seeds, sweet potato ravioli in cream sauce, focaccia with honeyed dates and goat cheese. The consulate spouses ate like women eat, with exaggerated ravished faces and exclamations about the deliciousness of the food and with tiny, measured bites. They drank quite a lot.

They were talking about one of their colleagues. He had a mistress, a Palestinian Christian woman. He'd taken her to the embassy for screening four months earlier, which meant they asked her all kinds of questions about her politics and family in order to make sure that the affair was safe for the embassy. "I knew about it first," Katie bragged. Since she had been working at the consulate she liked knowing everybody's secrets. Once she had given Sam and me a lift home, and waved at an Israeli man walking down the street. "He's a spy," she announced, rolling up the windows. He'd seemed like an ordinary man, a family man, walking home with two plastic bags of groceries, a child holding onto his shirt. "How do you know?" I said, and she snorted. "Trust me." Nobody was supposed to know, but everyone knew, of course, everyone knew everything at the consulate. The same was true of the mistress. Everyone knew, except his wife. And it made a certain amount of sense to have the mistress screened, too, from the standpoint of security: it minimized the chances of blackmail, and the odds of betrayal.

Some of the men had even met her, though none of the wives had: Roger mentioned that David brought her out for drinks late one night after work. Katie asked if she was pretty. "Pretty? She was cute enough," Roger said. A few weeks later the wife had come home to her bags packed, and a ticket home. The affair had become serious and now the husband was ready to ship his wife back to the States. And there was nothing she could do about it; no license to work in the country, no right to keep living in the beautiful apartment with its roof terrace and view of the walls of the Old City. She was gone.

"That could happen to any of us," Martine said, picking up her glass of white wine. "None of us have any rights here, and the embassy just wants to keep things quiet. We're disposable."

"Your husband would never do that," Katie said. She did not say anything about her own.

Nobody had liked the wife: they'd all made fun of her, at first behind her back and then, daringly, to her face. She was older than they were, and her husband was higher up in the consulate; she had expected deference. And she was from the Midwest, and didn't curse, and wore pale skirt suits that hit at the knee, and cut her hair to look like Laura Bush. But now that she was gone their loyalty had shifted back; she'd been condescending but kind, they agreed. And she did host a tea party every time a new wife moved in. She would tell them where to buy groceries, and where to buy socks, and where they could send their kids to school. And where they weren't allowed to go, and what they weren't allowed to do. Now someone else would have to take on that role: "Hostess-Initiator."

"Only fourteen couples now," Katie said to Martine. The adulterous husband was being shipped to Cairo; rumour had it that his mistress would follow him. "And half of them are Mormons. They don't even count. And now you're leaving to Belgium, and Yumiko and Hannah are leaving at the end of the year, and I'm going to be here all by myself."

"There's Lisa," Martine said.

"But you know Lisa," Katie said. "First of all, she doesn't have children. And second of all, she seems so busy all the time. What is she doing?"

"Belly dancing lessons," Martine said.

"Arabic class," Yumiko said.

"No," Katie said. "I bet she's having an affair."

An affair! They leaned in, speculating about the young Israeli soldier, or Palestinian shopkeeper, or security guard that Lisa might be fucking. Lisa was younger than all of them by ten years; she didn't have children, so she wasn't domesticated yet. She wore pale linen dresses, said she was writing a novel, and spent hours at the cafe in the American Colony Hotel.

"Why not," Jenna said. "Serves them right. They're all messing around anyway."

I'd recently replaced my wedding ring and I showed it around the table. It had fallen off my finger one winter two years earlier. That wasn't the first time I'd lost it; once, it flew into the sand at the beach, and I scrabbled for it desperately until I saw the telling and unlikely glint of gold. I'd thought it lost forever. Another time I'd believed the ring gone for months before finding it in the crevice between the couch and wall. But that last time it was lost for good; the ring must have slipped off my finger when I was taking off my gloves and buried itself in the snow. I wonder, sometimes, if anybody ever found it. I didn't want to replace it right away. I kept saying that the ring would surely turn up, surely. The price of gold had risen; I said I didn't want to spend the money. But the truth was I was feeling tired of being owned. Already, I was so consumed with the children when I was home; I didn't like walking around the city tagged. I wanted myself to myself.

But my mother's cousin had paid a visit and looked at my finger disapprovingly.

"Your husband doesn't mind?" she asked, in a voice so shrill it was almost a whistle.

"Why should he?" I said. "I don't think so. He never said anything."

"It's a sign of respect, that's all. But if he doesn't mind, then that's fine, and anyway it's none of my business," she said, with the air of someone who never truly believes that anything is none of her business.

That same week I toured the jewelry makers of Ben Yehuda. There was a designer who made rings in beaten, crumpled gold; I walked in, got sized, picked up the ring two weeks later. The saleswoman congratulated me; I didn't bother to correct her. It was as though, without having ever consciously thought of leaving, I had finally decided to stay.

f the year seemed to pass more quickly after the war, it was because Simon and I were no longer strangers to the country. The days went faster because they were more familiar. School, work, home: life.

Raquel's divorce date had finally arrived, and she dressed up for it: white stockings and loafers and a beige A-line skirt embellished with buttons and a big, new, floppy straw hat, an Easter hat, as if she was dressed for a festival or funeral. She didn't seem nervous. She seemed giddy. We were early, and stopped at a cafe. The large glass windows made the shop a stage for the sidewalk. Customers grouped around small tables, framed like a Hopper painting. Despite the windows, it was dark inside, and the space was too large and full of echoes. As we ordered, a Chasidic man walked in.

"I can't believe it. He's here. With his lawyer." Raquel whispered, and grabbed my wrist.

I was watching for our coffee, and hadn't been paying attention—besides, in a way, men like that were invisible.

"Hmmm," I said.

"Here," she hissed more fiercely, and as I wheeled she

said, "For God's sake, don't turn around."

They were right behind us. Two of them: the lawyer, a pretty, dark-haired, powdered woman, large and forceful though also flouncy, and lurking behind her like an awkward teenager a large, bearish man, red-faced, in a long coat and *shtreimel*. Now it was hard not to stare at him through his reflection in the glass. His eyes kept darting between us, but his head was down, so that it seemed like he was looking at us despite himself, and like his eyes could not bear staying on either of us for very long. He had plump cheeks behind his thick beard and seemed the kind of overgrown boy the *yeshivas* specialized in manufacturing, man-children, their *tsitsis* flying behind them, their manner a hot mix of shyness and clumsy ardor. His *peyos* were long and curled; Raquel had told me her oldest son wanted to have his *peyos* permed. I'd never thought of it, how they achieved those vain, perfect curls. Of course.

"Raquel," the woman exclaimed, as if she was a friend and not an enemy. "How are you? You look so cute! I love your hat!"

"Don't," Raquel muttered under her breath. "Don't tell me I'm cute in front of him."

Her almost-ex-husband shuffled his feet. There was something unnerving about the way his eyes darted back and forth, down, a kind of scattered, vicious quality to his attention. He didn't speak, but his breathing was heavy. He seemed like a large animal caught in a trap, inarticulate, suffering, and still dangerous. When they had sex, she said, she cried. Every time.

Though it was morning, in the room it felt like dusk. The cafe tables and chairs were rickety and placed just far enough away from one another for the place to seem bare and empty. The coffee tasted a little bitter, like chicory, and I put one and then two spoonfuls of sugar in my cup. "They're still here," Raquel hissed. My back was to the counter, but I could feel their eyes.

"We'll see you inside," the lawyer called out, jolly, as if we were to meet for cocktails rather than at the divorce proceedings. As they opened the door the noise of the street came rushing in.

On the street Raquel said, "He was trying to figure out who you are and why you're here. It threw him a little bit. That's good, I think." The court was decrepit, a squat building begrimed by the dust and pollution of downtown Jerusalem. I had just dropped off my son at the YMCA and it seemed strange: walk to the daycare, walk to the divorce court, back before lunch. The security guard was cute and wore a nose ring. He smiled at us as he rifled through our bags. Raquel seemed a little giddy. "Did you see him look at me?" she said. "He's adorable." It was as if after all of these years of marriage and confinement, with her legs swathed in tights and her hair tightly covered, she wanted to stretch again, to bask in attention, and become visible. She wanted to take off her layers and walk in the sun, as if she was coming out of a long winter.

As we waited for the elevator, she said, "Your job is to keep me off the second floor. I cannot see the mediators today—my only reason to be here is the *get*. He's going to try to get me renegotiating, but you can't let me do it." As the doors slid shut she said, "No second floor. No more negotiating. This ends today." She gripped my wrist, too hard.

On the third floor, the divorce floor, there was no real waiting room, just a couple of benches cushioned in a cheap green laminate. The carpet was a nubby coarse weave of nondescript colours, beige and black and a pink-ish brown like dried blood, and it was coming up a bit at the edges. The walls were scuffed and yellowing, and only some of the neon lights in the ceiling worked. The doors were painted baby blue with panels in dark blue fake suede, lending a false touch of regality to the shabby bureaucratic space.

Her legal aid lawyer met us there. He was sloppy and seemed already defeated; he spoke with a vague fatalism that boded ill, as if he had long ago given up on making any kind of intervention. Her husband needed to super-vise the inscription of the writ of divorce, he said. Of his own free will. That happened first. Then Raquel would go into the courtroom. She needed to physically accept the document from him. And then she would be pro-nounced "permitted to all men."

She nodded, and I winced at the phrase.

I looked for the table. I had been told that there was a table where the women abandoned their hats after they left the divorce court. Fedoras, wide brimmed hats, headscarves, severe black turbans, even wigs sometimes, left limp and inanimate as if the women had been scalped.

They took off their hats and they walked into the street and felt the sun and wind in their hair. Perhaps for the first time in ten years, twenty, thirty, forty years, their heads breathed in the open air. That feeling of lightness. But I couldn't spot the table, and there wouldn't have been place for it. The narrow hallways were windowless and airless, and aside from their benches, unfurnished.

The halls were full of women and men waiting for their divorces. Some were secular and some were religious, and some joked and others sat silently, and rabbis wandered the narrow halls with file folders and jars of ink. This was the mandated divorce court. There was no other way to sever that relationship in Israel, no marriage or divorce for Jews except through the Rabbinic court. I had read that the word "*Get*" came from "agate," because of the repellent properties of the stone; after the document was handed to the no-longer wife, the rabbis tore it in two as if to rend the relationship.

We were standing on either side of the doorway and Raquel moved across as her husband walked through, on his way to supervise the scribe's inscription.

She said to me, "Did you know? Men aren't allowed to walk between two women or two pigs."

She said, "I'm afraid. He isn't going to do it. I can feel it."

His lawyer had told him if he didn't give her the *get*, this time he would go to jail. There was no way to force a man to give a *get* but there were loopholes, ways to pressure him. Shunning, fines, wage garnishment. Prison.

Underground methods, too: beatings, threats. In the past, rabbis had forced unwilling husbands to spend the night in the graveyard as a warning of what might happen to them if they didn't come around. You had to be sane to grant a divorce, so women married to men who were considered mentally ill had no way out. Raquel had been in a support group for *agunot*, other women denied their freedom: one of the women was married to a man who was both abusive and insane. She called her husband crazy, but a diagnosis was the worst thing that could happen to her; it was tricky, because she needed him mentally unstable enough to deny him custody of their children, but well enough to let her go.

Raquel had a spy, a rabbi from her community who sat with the judges. He had called her the night before.

"Your husband is the devil incarnate," he said. "He told me, 'I'm going to make her wait for her divorce until she's fifty or sixty and then I'll throw her in the garbage.'"

Her friend had followed the husband into the scribe's room, as judge and supervisor. As he passed us he'd glanced at Raquel.

"It's taking too long," Raquel said. "Something's not right."

After about twenty minutes, her husband stormed out. The rabbi followed him, talking to him rapidly, but Samson shook him off and vanished down a hallway.

The rabbi came back, shaking his head.

"What's going on?" Raquel said, and he replied, "He's playing with us—it's not going to happen today. We need the lawyer."

He pulled his cellphone out of the pocket of his long black coat and called her.

"We're lucky," he said as he hung up. "She's down the street. She's going to try to intercept him."

Ten minutes later Samson reappeared, his lawyer beside him. She wasn't touching him—that wasn't allowed. But it was just like she had dragged an unwilling child back by the arm. The door swung open to the court, and I glimpsed a tribunal of men in black hats and black coats before it swung back shut.

I waited and watched a Sephardic couple on the opposite bench. They were both handsome and perhaps in their fifties, and they joked around with the witnesses that they had brought. She sat beside him and checked his file like a dutiful spouse. Their friend, the witness, looked at the stained carpet, the flickering neon lights, and said, "Oh, so this is where you get divorced—how pleasant. What a lovely place to spend a sunny morning."

The husband saw me watching them and said, "After 29 years of marriage we're getting divorced. Maybe," he said, looking at his elegant wife, "we should hold out until the summer to make it to thirty years. We could have a party." He laughed loudly, and she echoed his laugh. They were dressed alike, in crisp white shirts and dark slacks. They resembled each other. They had three children—all grown now—and grandchildren. Their lives had intertwined like tree roots.

He leaned towards me and said, more seriously, "I am giving it to her because I respect her, it's her choice—

we are still friends," and she nodded, her knees tightly pressed together on the bench, her hands firmly clasped on her lap.

The hall was so narrow we were almost knee to knee. Beside me, a woman sat alone. Her back was straight and her hands were shaking. She looked at me and said, "This too shall pass."

This was a place of endings and beginnings. The only room I had ever been in that had felt similarly fraught and transitional was the delivery ward.

Something was going on behind the blue door. It opened and closed and opened again, like a mouth that was uncertain about whether or not to speak, and then it finally swung open all the way. A rabbi poked out his head and called me in. The witness had not shown up and they said I needed to come in. They asked for my passport, but I didn't have it. They spoke among themselves quickly, and then accepted my driver's license. I stood before the tribunal, feeling exposed and sweaty and bare.

The rabbi said, "Do you know this man and his wife?"

"Yes," I said.

Behind me, Samson, loud and angry, said, "She doesn't know me."

"I know his wife," I said.

I realized I didn't know her married name, didn't know the Hebrew name she had taken on, didn't know anything about her anymore. If they had been interested in credible witnesses they would have kicked me off the stand, but they were interested only in closing the case.

"What is the name of the husband," the rabbi said.

"Samson," I said.

Behind me he was muttering loudly. At one point he half stood, and his lawyer put out a hand to restrain him. The threat of her touch was enough to make him sit back down.

The rabbi turned to the tribunal.

"Samson," he said, "listen how she says it. They say Samson in America." He turned back to me. "His name is Shimshon." They chuckled together at the unlikeliness of it. Samson, who brought a temple down on his head rather than surrender.

"And the wife, what is her name?"

"Raquel," I said.

They said, "Also, Rachel," and I said, "Yes, sometimes."

They said, "Also Rochelle," and I didn't say anything, having never known her by that name. They wrote it down.

"And what is the name of her father?"

I couldn't remember. I reached back and nothing came to me. Finally, tentatively, I said "Joseph?" and behind me I heard expostulations of disgust.

"No," I corrected myself, "Joseph is her brother, not her father."

They didn't care. They told me to sign my name and sent me out. Then Raquel and I had to wait. The Sephardic wife was still sitting outside, in her bright white shirt and burnished face. Her husband had gone to supervise the writing of the *get*, and her expression had changed. She leaned towards me and said, "He told you we're friends? We're not friends. I feel like a cancer has been cut out of me." She stared into my eyes intently and said, "Today is like the day of your birth."

"I'm not—" I started, but then I stopped myself. There was no need to tell her.

Then she leaned back on the bench and said, "He's not a bad man, but nobody else exists for him. You have to treat each other with only respect, not put each other down in front of other people." She shut her lips tightly, and I realized he had returned. "All done!" he said cheerfully. He tried to sit beside her and she hissed and feinted, and changed benches so she could not see him.

"I pray to God," she whispered to me, "but after this I believe only in civil marriage."

They called Raquel back in. It felt like they were in the room much too long. I could hear someone shouting and the door swung open again for a moment. I saw Raquel's face, angry and despairing. Samson's lawyer came out and sat heavily onto the bench, her face flushed.

She said to me, "How do you think she's doing?"

I said, "Well, she looks pretty angry to me."

She said, "But why? She's getting what she wants. He is too, but she's doing alright. I'm not going to go home feeling like I screwed her over tonight."

The door swung open again, and I could hear Raquel, angry and atonal, saying loudly, "I have not had relations with anybody else."

It closed again, and about five minutes later she re-emerged.

"It's done," she said.

Samson's lawyer leaned toward Raquel and said, "I tell you, I've never had a client as difficult as this one," and Raquel said, "Tell me about it."

I hadn't realized it until that moment, but Raquel and Jenna were somehow alike. They made reckless decisions, they lied to people they loved, they thought last, they led from the heart. They had made a church of impulsiveness and an altar out of need. They led big and colourful lives, crashed dramatically and learned no lessons. Still, they were braver than I was.

31.

I hadn't seen Jenna for a couple of weeks, and when Yumiko called me to tell me about the accident, I imagined disaster. But Jenna was alright, Yumiko said: scared, but alright. She had been nursing her baby in the front seat. Noor was sandwiched between Jenna's lap and the steering wheel as the truck in front of her suddenly stopped. Jenna's car folded right into the back of the truck, steel crumpling like tissue as the airbags inflated around her. She claimed the doctor said that holding the baby in her lap had protected the child from whiplash. I had a hard time imagining a doctor who would say that, though a lot that Jenna said challenged my imagination. And they were both somehow almost unhurt.

Jenna showed up at the daycare the next day with scratches on her collarbone and on her face, her neck in a grey foam brace.

"Aden hates taking the kids," she explained. "Anyways, he thinks it's important that I get back in the car right away, you know, like getting back on a bike. But I was shaking, a little," she admitted.

She was driving a rental car; the next week Aden

bought her a new one.

"This one has TVs right in the back seats, so they each have their own screen," she explained. "It's much better."

We had been spending less time together, I wasn't sure why. We had decided to get together one last time, because I'd soon be leaving. Jenna picked me up in her new car. It was one of those bullying black SUVs, raised off the ground by tires that claimed the road so that it seemed when you drove you were floating over all of the little tin cans beside you. The car was a shinier, blacker, larger version of her last car, totally impractical for the donkey roads of Jerusalem. We drove with the windows closed, because she liked the new car smell.

I had never been to Ramallah, which was another reason I went along. Jenna's friend Layla was with us to help with Noor and because it was her day off; also, she wanted to buy donuts. "Ramallah has the best donuts," Layla said. "They're just like American ones."

Layla was Jenna's age, but single. "She wants something that doesn't exist," Jenna had confided in me earlier. "An Arab man, who will help equally with the children and the cooking. She doesn't want to do anything—her family spoils her. She doesn't even know how to clean."

Jenna was going to Ramallah to visit the fertility clinic. Her husband wanted another son, and there was something they could do at the clinic to determine the sex of the child. She was a little vague about what they did—spin the sperm or something—but she was clear on the value of going to Ramallah rather than Tel Aviv or Jordan.

"It's just much cheaper," she said. "Everyone who needs a fertility clinic should go to Ramallah. It's a great deal."

As soon as I buckled my seatbelt Jenna said, "You'd better keep a close eye on your children. Someone is stealing children—for their organs."

"Their organs," I said, and she nodded emphatically.

"I'm keeping a close watch, I'll tell you that," she said. "I'm not letting them play outside by themselves anymore."

"How do you know?" I said.

"Know what?" Jenna asked.

"Know about the children."

"My neighbour told me," she said. "She saw it on the internet. You don't have to believe me, all I'm saying is, watch out."

Beth Lechem Road was crowded, and Jenna swung in and out of the lanes. She had just been on a cruise in Turkey with her husband, and she showed me pictures on the back of her digital camera, leaning away from the steering wheel to look. They had gone golfing. They had seen a belly dancer. She said they'd visited too many mosques on the tour, and that the mosques were all boring. She liked the boat. There was a picture of the two of them taken against the backdrop of the water. The light was behind them and their faces were in shadow.

We were driving towards the desert, along the curving highway, the Judean hills stubbled and dry on either side of us, the unfinished security wall rising in and out of the dry landscape, apparitional.

"Watch this," Jenna said, "I never get stopped."

She sped past the checkpoint. Bored faces; eyes barely flickered up.

"Ha," Jenna said.

"You did get stopped with me that once," Layla piped up from the back seat.

Noor was wandering around the back seat, and Layla tried to get her to sit down, but without much conviction. The city gave way to the desert more quickly than seemed possible. In the middle of that tan and arid wasteland, the wall was going up. A bulldozer stood idle beside a grey concrete stretch of wall. It was so brutalist, so unbeautiful; the wall cut into the landscape like a scar.

A few months earlier, a man had commandeered a front loader and had driven into a bus on Jaffa Road, yelling "*Allahu Akbar.*" He was a terrorist or a drug addict or both, depending on whom you believed. Since then there had been several copycat attacks, so that the ubiquitous construction equipment on the Jerusalem roads began to seem threatening—the Caterpillars, bulldozers, front loaders, cranes, the machines that ate up dirt and spat it out in a bulimic frenzy of building.

Ramallah was larger than I expected. Huge white estates fronted the valley, though they seemed strangely uninhabited.

"I love Ramallah," Layla said. "They have the best clubs, the best nightlife. Jerusalem has nothing."

"When's the last time you went to a club, Layla?" Jenna said.

We pulled into the parking lot at the clinic. A boy was walking down the street with an enormous helium balloon in the shape of a fighter jet. My boys would like that, I thought idly, before checking myself. As soon as we stepped outside I felt dusty, just like I did in Jerusalem. At the end of the day, you could rub your skin and the dirt would roll off on your fingers. It reminded me of Freud's first lesson on mortality, learnt in his mother's kitchen, when he was only a child. His mother was rolling dumplings, and she rubbed her hands together briskly and showed him the dark, dead skin. To dust we return.

Recently, Sam had become obsessed with the idea of my death. "You're going to die," he would announce to me. "But not very soon. Only when you are old." Sometimes when we were walking down the street he'd check in with me—"You're going to die, right?" "Right," I would confirm. "Everybody dies. But I won't die for a long time (probably, I added in my head), not until you are all grown up and don't need me anymore."

We'd been in the park with another child, and they'd both been fascinated by a dead beetle in the pathway. "What's that?" I said, coming close to see what their rounded backs were hiding. "Is it dead?" The boy's mother came up behind me and said, "Shhh! Moshe, Moshe, the beetle is only napping." She whispered, "We don't use the 'D' word in our house."

My son was oddly chipper about the prospect of my death. It was just another fact about the world that he was trying to put together in the giant puzzle he had begun to assemble. Except that one day he began to cry, "I don't want you to die, and I don't want to grow up!" Somehow my reassurance—"I won't die for a long time"—had turned into a threat, so he now associated growing older with my death.

The office at the fertility clinic was enormous, clean, and empty. The floors were stone and there were large, uncomfortable leather chairs and glass, hard-edged coffee tables. On the coffee table was a catalogue of jewelry, necklaces of harsh yellow gold and earrings dripping with diamonds. I tried to imagine the calculations: this baby will be equivalent to this many carats of gold, this many diamonds. The fertility clinic had its own logo, a stylized mother and child wrapped up in the Arabic script that spelled out the name of the health centre.

I had never had any trouble getting pregnant. The first time I got pregnant, we had just stopped using birth control; it was in the first month, maybe even the first time. We were playful and vague and theoretical about it; of course, it could take a long time, up to a year or more, we were prepared for that. A few days later the planes hit the towers. I thought I was going insane; I watched the news again and again, as images of the towers collapsing played all day long. "We should wait," I said. "This isn't the time." In my body, the cells had already begun to divide and multiply, to develop a beating heart that would show up a few weeks later on a monitor as a faint blinking point of light, like a star in a distant solar system.

Jenna disappeared with the nurse, and Noor ripped

page after page out of the jewelry brochure. Jenna wasn't in the doctor's office for long; she emerged not ten minutes later. "Not yet," she announced, "which means I have to come back out here tomorrow." She seemed neither relieved nor disappointed. "Donuts?" she said.

When we came out of the building her husband was waiting in the parking lot.

"What's he doing here?" I asked.

She said, "Look at that, he's following me."

Aden stayed in his car. Though he saw me and saw Layla he didn't get out, didn't say hello. He was wearing sunglasses and the windows of his car were only partially rolled down; it was as if he was hiding from someone. Jenna walked towards him, unsteady on her high heels. From the back she still looked like a girl. As she approached him, he revved the car, as if he was about to drive away, then pulled in sharply and turned the motor off. He got out of his car, his back to us. He was like a tight coil, ready to spring.

Layla watched Noor deliberately—it was as if she was averting her eyes from Jenna and Aden. In the end, what did I know about either of them? I suddenly felt very far from home.

Aden was gesticulating, and his gestures were getting broader, as if he was striking the air. But then he seemed to deflate, slumped into his tallness, lowered his head. They exchanged a few more hurried, muttered words and she kissed him quickly on the cheek. He got back into his tall black car without acknowledging me or Layla and rolled up the smoked windows to hide his face as he pulled out of the parking lot.

"What was that about?" I said when Jenna got back.

Jenna was ominously calm. "He doesn't trust me," she said. "You know why? I used to check his cellphone, to see when he was having affairs. And I'd catch him, too, and he'd say they broke up, but he'd find someone else right away, that's how he is. So I got sick of it. I said, 'Do what you want. I'm not checking your phone anymore.' So now he thinks I'm having an affair, because otherwise, why would I back off? But the truth is I'm just waiting for him to get overconfident and then I'm going to catch him again."

Layla walked ahead of us, clicking along, hobbled by her tight jeans and high heels.

In a low voice Jenna said, "Let him have his secrets. I have secrets too. He doesn't know I was married before. To a real jerk, in Jordan. He was ugly and short. A face like a frog. I don't know what my family thought they were doing, letting me marry him. He tricked me into it, some people have that ability. He tried to blackmail me, said he was going to tell Aden about us, but I shut that right down."

She glanced at me, chin up and defiant. The street was loud. It was hard to hear her speaking. "Why couldn't you tell Aden about it?" I said. "You were young. You made a mistake."

"Aden?" Jenna laughed. "Aden doesn't know anything. He doesn't know that I wasn't a virgin when we got married. Layla doesn't know that either, so keep your voice down. What he doesn't know won't hurt him, that's what I always say. Anyway, it's not like he's so pure himself."

We kept walking. Marwan Barghouti's handsome face stared at us from the wall. He was serving a life sentence in prison for his role in the last Intifada, but some people said he might be the next prime minister of Palestine. In prison he had become martyred, heroic, and his image was everywhere. His fist was raised and he wore a *keffiyeh* on his head. When Arafat was alive, people said that he arranged his *keffiyeh* in a triangular shape over his shoulder in order to indicate that he wanted Palestine, all of it. The message was subliminal; back then we were obsessed with subliminal messages, coded signals. I was tired of trying to figure out what was true.

Jenna looked exhausted. "I always feel sad when I come to the clinic, because I had three abortions before we were married. Layla doesn't know that either."

There was a lot of traffic on the street. I wasn't sure I'd heard her right. "Three?" I said, but we'd reached the donut shop and she was heading up the stairs.

When Gabriel was born, I cried for hours every day. I thought that was normal; every mother went through it. I wanted more children but could not think of conceiving again, until one day I woke up to find I had Sam. That was years ago; it was all in the past, only I still couldn't think of it without running out of breath. I didn't understand Jenna, but I admired her fearlessness. Nothing would slow her down: not Aden's suspicions, not her secret history, not her crazy family.

The donut shop looked like a Tim Hortons, only even a little seedier and with servers in headscarves. As we drove back to Jerusalem, Jenna said, "It's a good thing you weren't kidnapped or nothing, with my family they'd think I was in on it for sure. They're—not Hamas, but something like Hamas, you know?"

"Are you kidding me?" I said, but she didn't answer me. Once again, we flew right through the checkpoint. We were past the wall, and back in Jerusalem.

If you look at a map of the separation wall, it runs for hundreds of miles around a section in the middle of the country, more or less along the Green Line, except that squiggles allow for the inclusion or exclusion of territory. The area around Jerusalem looks like someone has taken a big bite out of its bottom third. From North to South the wall runs parallel with the Mediterranean, and in some places the ocean is only ten miles away as the crow flies, or twenty by the roads. When the wall was built, it cut the territories off from the ocean, except of course for the toenail sliver of Gaza, between the devil and the deep blue sea. You can even see the ocean from some of the hilltops if the day is clear. On a hot day in summertime, when the air is so thick and choked that walking is like moving through quicksand and breathing is like sipping air through a straw, it must feel like you are Tantalus with his vanishing pool of water when you look over the wall at that ribbon of blue. It must feel like being robbed of the very horizon.

32

Simon's sabbatical was almost over, and we had only a few weeks left to our year. I couldn't walk past a corner without wondering if I would ever walk that way again. Our days were full of hectic final meetings, and furiously crammed with the things we loved.

I had never been to the Dome of the Rock, and I wanted to go at least once before I left the country. The mosque was a forbidden fruit; I had always been told never to go, because you could accidentally wander into the spot where the Holy of Holies, the sacred crucible of the Temple, was once located. The shrine capped the Old City like a golden peach. I was no longer worried about the exact location of the Holy of Holies, though I would skirt the centre of the site, just in case. Belief was a residue; it had degraded into superstition.

I'd dressed for the mosque but also for the heat—it was nearly forty degrees. I stopped at a jewelry stall I had frequented to say goodbye to the owner, but this time it felt strange.

He said, "I will have to hug you for one half hour!"

I must have looked a little confused, so he added, "Because you are my friend."

He seemed different, more distant and more lewd at once. He kept glancing at my chest. I would not realize until the end of the day that my T-shirt was translucent in certain lights. He hung a collar of silver pomegranates around my neck and said, "Everything looks beautiful on you because you are beautiful."

I said, "And your wife must be very beautiful."

He said, "But you are *achla*," which was a superlative.

I said, "Not really," and he looked embarrassed and said, "That is an expression. If someone gives you a compliment you say that."

His father disapprovingly folded scarves at the entrance to the stall, his back turned away from us.

Further in were the rank butcher shops of the market, the smells coppery and thick. I passed rows of chessmen and walls of tiles and every so often the green and red graffitied entrances that marked the houses of the *hajji*. Vendors called out, "Come into my shop! Only look! I have everything!"

One of the stall owners asked me where I was going and I said, "I'm going to the mosque."

He said, "Wait, you can't go like that. They won't let you in like that."

He reached for something on an open shelf and came towards me, his arms filled with russet fabric. "You can put it on in here," he said, gesturing towards a nook in the shop, and he faced away from me to give me privacy.

He'd handed me a long tunic, a floor-length skirt and a scarf; I could see myself in pieces in the copper mirrors on the walls. Crowns of thorns hung on a rope over my head. The clothes smelled metallic and new.

As I stepped out he nodded, and said, "Just bring it back when you're done."

There was a checkpoint, and then a rickety walkway that led up to the Dome of the Rock. I had seen the walkway from the platform at the bottom a hundred times. It was walled in because people had once used it as a launching point for throwing stones. The scaffolding looked sloppy and poorly constructed, cagelike and undignified. Two security guards lounged by the metal detector, their long guns strapped to their hips. There was no line.

The first security guard was Ethiopian, and looked no more than fifteen years old. Each year that passed, the soldiers looked younger to me, and it seemed stranger and stranger to be surrounded by teenagers with guns.

He leaned towards me and said, "Are you Muslim?"

I thought of saying yes. I said, "No."

"Then why are you dressed like that?" he asked. I had wrapped the scarf from the market around my head, and was beginning to feel very hot.

"Out of respect," I said.

His friend, who was still leaning against the wall, said, "*Kvod hamakom, nu, hi mechabedet hamakom*," "Respect of the place, come on, she's respecting the place." I couldn't tell if he was being ironic—with Israeli men it was impossible to tell.

The guard who was questioning me paused, and I thought he was going to turn me away. "Do you drink coffee?" he said. "Would you like to have a coffee with me?"

The platform was immense. It was splendid at the centre, but desolate at the edges. A guide approached me and said, "Are you Muslim?"

I said "No," and he said, "Well, you can't go inside but let me show you around this place, you know, by the side windows you can see into the mosque."

I waved him off but went over to the windows anyway. They were latticed with iron diamonds. Through the glass panes I saw a woman sitting quietly in an expanse of red carpet as two children played around the pillars. She seemed peaceful and at ease, kneeling in a sea of space. I was beginning to get worried about the old taboos and holy tabernacles, so I walked to the edge of the stairs by the Golden Dome but went no further. Some children were begging, and as I gave one child a few coins the others pressed around me. They reminded me of children that I had seen in Morocco; they had the same aggressive, ragged insistence. A woman was with them; she sat on the ground a few feet away in a small triangle of shade, in a puddle of dark fabric. A tall man came up to me and waved the children off. He wore mirrored sunglasses, a pink short-sleeved polo shirt, pressed dark jeans, a belt, and a fanny pack.

"Don't have anything to do with those children," he said. "They should be in school. Look at them, they are not poor, they are well dressed. If you saw that woman in the afternoon, she would be better dressed than you are now."

He ran a travel agency.

"They become used to begging, and the Israeli police won't kick them out because they like the tourists to think we're all beggars. Everything is politics up here, all very complicated."

He wasn't interested in my business; he was just bored. I asked to take a picture of the dome mirrored and doubled in his sunglasses, so he tilted his head back for the photo. He drew a business card out of the fanny pack and handed it to me, but the gesture was dutiful rather than in earnest.

The platform surrounding the Dome of the Rock was mostly empty that day. There was a Japanese tour group bunched together like flowers and holding colourful umbrellas to protect them from the sun. A few clusters of tourists wandered the platform aimlessly. The heat was like weight, and everyone seemed to be moving slowly through the thick air. The dome shimmered in the sun, hallucinatory; under the thin soles of my sandals the marble burned my feet.

A Chasidic man was skirting the edges of the site. Despite his black hat and long white beard, he reminded me of Professor Calculus from the Tintin comics: he had the same backwards-leaning walk, the same air of deep distraction. He walked back and forth, pacing nervously, but never coming closer. I kept glancing at him, wondering what he was doing there. Perhaps he belonged to one of the Jewish groups trying to reclaim the site; but he seemed too anxious and alone. His long black coat flapped against his calves as he walked, turned on his heel, and walked back in the opposite direction, compulsively tracing a border between himself and the shrine.

I passed the Western Wall and walked back into the market to return the dress. The storekeeper was gone but his son—teenaged, heavy, with soft wide hips—offered to bring me coffee and I waited. I expected a hard sell when he returned, but he didn't try to sell me anything, only said meaningfully—"We are Bedouin"—and saw me off.

I thought I would complete the trifecta of holy places, so I walked over to the Church of the Holy Sepulchre and drifted between tour groups speaking Hebrew, English, and Russian. I could hear fragments of presentations as I walked through the church. One guide said, "Here, they say, at the time of the crucifixion, the earth shook and cracked." Another said, "And then they passed the keys and the knowledge of this place, father to son, father to son." An old monk saw me trying to listen and said, in a British accent, "Excuse me, do you speak English? She is saying that in this place, St. Helen was lifted up to heaven."

The Church of the Holy Sepulchre was not one church, but many. Its sovereignty had been carved out among a number of different religious groups; most of them refused to recognize one another. On the roof were

the mound-like huts of the Ethiopian Church. In the basement was a small chapel that was claimed by the Greek
Orthodox Church and the Armenian Church alike. A
bulb had burned out in the chapel and it was left in darkness for months because changing the light would have
been an acknowledgment of jurisdiction; neither faction
would let the other do it. The darkness down there was
truly, appropriately sepulchral and the chapel was closed
for months. Finally, the Minister for Religious Affairs
had acquired the key from the Nusseibehs, the Palestinian
family who had served as doorkeepers for centuries. He
went by himself in the middle of the night and changed
the light. The chapel opened the next day, illuminated;
nobody acknowledged the long squabbling that had re-
sulted in months of darkness, nor even that there ever had
been a darkness.

When I was younger, I had explored those lower
chambers. Back then it was not only my first time in the
Holy Sepulchre, it was my first time in a church, and the
expedition felt daring and confusing. I was struck by that
chiaroscuro combination of glitter and shadow, sump-
tuousness and must. The marble floors had worn into
grooves over the centuries from all of those feet and the
portentous weight of pilgrimage. It was unclear which
parts of the church were open to the public; velvet ropes
barred niches blazing with candles, and dark staircases lay
unguarded. I walked down one of those staircases. The
steps were narrow and uneven, so I needed to brace myself against the wall while climbing down. At the bottom

was a low-ceilinged room. Monks milled in a corner near an icon of a saint I didn't recognize. But what struck me the most about the room, what stayed with me even years later—and stayed with me not as a memory but as an object, in its dimensional and disquieting integrity—was the turd that lay, whole and undisturbed, on the chapel floor. Years later I realized it must have been left by a goat or even a dog—a decade ago animals roamed the church, especially on the lower levels—but at the time it shocked me. I turned and fled up the uneven staircase.

It's possible that the person I once was could have stayed in Jerusalem. Not this time, but back when I was eighteen. Or perhaps I could have never been that woman; I was too cautious. I liked risk, but I liked being able to walk away from it, like a book that you close when it gets too frightening. I am the kind of person who could never see a precipice without thinking about jumping off. But I think I would never jump; I just like looking down. Part of me knew we had always been leaving.

On the stone where they washed Christ's body people were laying down their trinkets to be blessed. My bag was heavy with last-minute souvenirs. It was time to go home.

33.

was never able to ask Jenna more about our conversation. After Ramallah, I felt like she was avoiding
me. It was as if she knew she'd said too much.

I thought often about what Shayna had said, that I was
being an anthropological friend, a perpetual voyeur. I had
always gotten in trouble for that. When I was a kid in
camp, sitting at the picnic table, one of my bunkmates
had said, "Why are you always doing that?" "What?" I
said, and she said, "You're always looking at people." The
trouble was, I didn't know any other way to be. How did
people not look—I mean, what were you supposed to do
with your eyes?

But I did see Jenna one last time.

She invited me over to her house so that the children
could say goodbye. Jenna looked tired again, the two
bruised half-moons under her eyes, her hair falling out of
the ponytail at the base of her neck. She saw me looking
at her, and pulled self-consciously at her striped sweater.

"God. I've been so tired. I'm getting up to pee all
night."

She put the children in front of the television set, tore

open a family pack of potato chips, and scooped *labne* into a bowl. Now they were sitting in a row on the couch, dipping their hands in and out of the bag of chips as their eyes stayed glued to the screen, and my heart sunk as I thought of the supper I had not yet made, that they would no longer eat.

Still, I walked over to the bowl of chips and took a barbecue one, curved and corrugated like a shell, and slipped it into the bowl of *labne* that the children had left untouched, the smooth cheese so creamy and stiff that the chip could have stood upright. I put it in my mouth and the combination of tart and cold and salty and sweet was so good that it was as if my tongue had started humming. It was a revelation.

I took another bite and said, "This may be the best thing I've ever eaten in my life."

Jenna said, "I always eat my chips this way, it's the only way to do it. I buy the American Lays even though they're more expensive, because they're the best, and this is the best *labne*, I can show you where to get it."

Then she grabbed a handful of chips.

"You know," she said. "I used to think about doing what you do."

"What do you mean?" I said.

"You know," Jenna said, "being a writer. A journalist or something. When I was a kid, I used to love to write. I had a notebook, and I wrote little stories all the time. Crazy things happen to me. I could write a whole book about it, believe me."

I didn't do much writing anymore. In fact, I had decided, after that inertial year, to give up on my poor and neglected dissertation, the shrunken child of my distracted mind. I didn't know what I would do next, but the decision had made me feel lighter. I didn't have to drag it around anymore, like a school bag that was stuffed with old papers and notes, or like the ghost of my father. I could do—I didn't know what I would do, but I could do anything else, anything.

Jenna looked wistful, and then she shrugged.

"But who has time for that, anyway? Come into the kitchen and talk to me while I cook," she said. I followed her, looking back at the bowl of chips, floating a hopeful, "Boys, don't take too many," at my children, who nodded without looking up and kept on chewing.

Noor followed Jenna into the kitchen, clambered to the counter like a rock climber, hoisting her body with her chubby arms. Jenna looked over, reaching out a practiced and steadying hand.

"Yeah, she just learned to do that," Jenna said. "As if life isn't difficult enough. Now that's all she wants to do is to be on the counter."

Keeping one hand on Noor, Jenna reached under the sink for a jug of vegetable oil, and poured freely into a battered and enormous pot. Noor reached for the spitting oil, and Jenna swatted her back, reached over, and placed her firmly on the floor. Noor stood stock-still and reached her arms up. She began to emit a whine that lived somewhere in her upper palate, and Jenna reached back down and swept her back up to the counter, an arm's length away from the boiling oil. From the next room I could hear the pat-a-pat-pat of a machine gun from the television. They must have changed the channel. I said, "Should I go check what they're watching?"

Jenna said, "It's just a cartoon, don't worry about it."

I stood suspended between the boiling oil, the baby and the machine gun fire, and I thought, Why Jenna, why does this always happen with Jenna. Then the sound of the gun was replaced by a cartoon cackle and the sound of the children laughing and Noor decided to wander back into the living room and it was as if the room had exhaled, had turned from the theatre of impending accident and horror to just an ordinary kitchen and ordinary children having a good time.

Jenna sniffed hard. "I can still smell that damn cat," she said.

"What cat?" I said, my attention shifting back from the living room.

Jenna said, "Well, let me start at the beginning. My sister-in-law has this housekeeper, and she's terrified of her. She says she can see the future. But I don't believe in that. So I said, 'Let me come over and talk to her. Only, don't tell her anything about me. We'll see if she's faking it.' So I came over and the housekeeper said, 'Something is going to make you very happy.' I said, 'Yeah, like what?' Anyone could say that. That could mean anything. So she said, 'Maybe furniture.' It's true that our new couch was coming. Still, it didn't convince me. Everybody buys furniture. Then she said, 'I see a weight on you. Something heavy.' 'What is it?' I said. She said, 'I can't see.' Anyway, then she said, 'There's an animal—is there an animal that bothers you?' And there is, this black cat that I hit once with my car. 'Well, he has something against you,' she said. And I thought of this other cat that used to come to my window and open the screen by himself. It drove me crazy, but anyway, I hadn't seen the cat for a few days. 'He's going to come back,' she said, and I said, 'When?' She said, 'More than three days, less than three months.' And three weeks—three weeks exactly—the cat came back again. That made me think. The housekeeper said, 'It's a spirit, that cat, it's an angry spirit. Like a lost child.' And that was when I got really scared. Though, I guess everyone knows that about me, they just have to have read the paper. So I don't think she can really read minds, though I don't really want to see her again."

"Knows what?" I said, suddenly alert.

"Oh god," she said. She turned off the stove and the room was filled with silence. "It doesn't matter now."

I waited.

She said. "Everybody talks all the time at that daycare. I thought everyone knew. I guess it was a while before you came."

She leaned back against the counter, and crossed her arms tightly against her chest. Her extraordinary river-green eyes. She looked older than I'd ever seen her look.

"Before Noor. There was another boy. His name was—well, never mind his name, that's bad luck. It was one of those things at five months, crib death. SIDS. Nobody knows what happened. That's why I'm having this one, to replace him."

Her hand drew a half circle on her stomach. I suppose I'd known without knowing why she looked tired and a little heavier, but my eyes still widened and I drew in a breath.

"Anyway, it was the worst thing that ever happened to me. It's the worst thing that can ever happen to anyone. And Aden's family, you know what they're like, they said it was my fault, they were talking about me behind my back, telling stories. Some people don't have a life, so they have to spend all their time making bullshit up about other people."

I moved towards her, but she shuddered as if to shake me off. She turned off the stove and then turned her back on me, towards the sink, and started washing dishes.

"I'm going to finish these, and take you home," she said.

From the back you couldn't see the way her stomach was starting to pull at her sweater. She was herself as narrow as a child, with her brown and bowed neck, all knobs and hollows, and the clipped and vulnerable wings of her delicate shoulderblades.

34.

On our last day in Jerusalem, Simon and I took the kids to the park. We were packed, and at loose ends. We had said our goodbyes. That day the sky had the quality of a bowl of water filled to its rim; it seemed on the verge of spilling over, to be barely containing itself, mirthful, irrepressible, and filled with light.

I sat beside Simon, and he reached for my hand. We looked at the boys on the swings. I could see that over the year they had changed. They were stronger, less soft. Their faces were a little thinner and more mature. They were more confident, too—they owned the park now. They were pumping the swings as hard as they could, until they rose almost parallel to the ground, and when they jumped it seemed like they hung in the air for just a moment before plummeting to the sand.

Gabe paused on the bench beside me to rest.

"How do you feel?" I said. "How do you feel about leaving? Are you sad?"

"A bit sad," he said, "I'm also excited to go home."

Simon squeezed my hand.

300

And we went home, to our cold and quiet country. I thought that we would feel at home right away, but sometimes when you travel you become a stranger everywhere. I missed the intensity of Israel, the liveliness and loveliness, missed even things I thought I would never miss, like the strangers who accosted you in line at the supermarket and told you what to buy.

Then habit took over, and we became ourselves again.

Simon settled into work, and the boys settled into school. I started working in the library part-time, and that leaves me time to pick up the children and to volunteer at the school. We are pretty happy. There isn't much of a story in that.

It's been years now that we've been back. The boys have grown even longer and thinner, and they don't remember much about our year in Israel. To me, too, it seems more like a dream than a memory. I've mostly lost touch with Jenna, and that makes sense. It was a friendship of convenience, after all. Every so often I click on her Facebook page to see the changed faces of her children, which like mine have grown narrower, less babyish. There was a baby boy born that winter, and since then there have been another two children. They look like Noor to me since Noor was still a baby when I left.

I rarely leave a message for Jenna, but the strange thing is, I think about her all the time. Sometimes in the winter when the ground is covered in snow and the sky is the colour of an oyster shell, all luminous layers of grey and silver and smoke, and the sun goes down at four o'clock,

and I'm waiting for my children to come home with all
the mothers waiting for all the children to come home,
and nothing could be farther away than that desert city
nestled like a pearl in the seven hills under the relentless
blue sky, I sit at the window for just a little longer looking at the disappearing light and I think of Jenna, I think
of the baby that died and of the babies that I never met. I
think of Jenna.

ACKNOWLEDGEMENTS

Many thanks to the Quebec Writers' Federation's mentorship program, and to Elise Moser for her guidance and support.

To the friends and family who read this book in various stages and incarnations—Sandie, Jeremy, Imma, Menachem, Elana, Julie, Emily, Bill, Anne Mette, Sivan, Zara, Katharine, Ivana, Alyssa, David, Norm—I am so lucky to have your support and encouragement.

My thanks and love to Orit, Avidan, to friends and family, too many to list, and to my students and colleagues at the Liberal Arts College. My father introduced me to the world of books, and I wish he could read this one.

My deep thanks to Linda Leith and to the editorial, publicity, and production staff at Linda Leith Publishing.

Jer, Ben, Lev, this book and all my love is yours.

Printed by Gauvin Press
Gatineau, Québec